THE RISE OF ZENOBIA

OVERLORD   I

THE RISE OF ZENOBIA

JD SMITH

TRISKELE BOOKS

Cover design and formatting www.jdsmith-design.com

Published by Quinn Publications

All enquiries to editor@quinnpublications.co.uk

First published, 2014

ISBN Paperback: 978-0-9576164-3-1
ISBN Ebook: 978-0-9576164-4-8

For William and Alexander,
who have impeded the publication of this book by repeatedly
requesting 'more breakfast' and 'need wee, you come'.

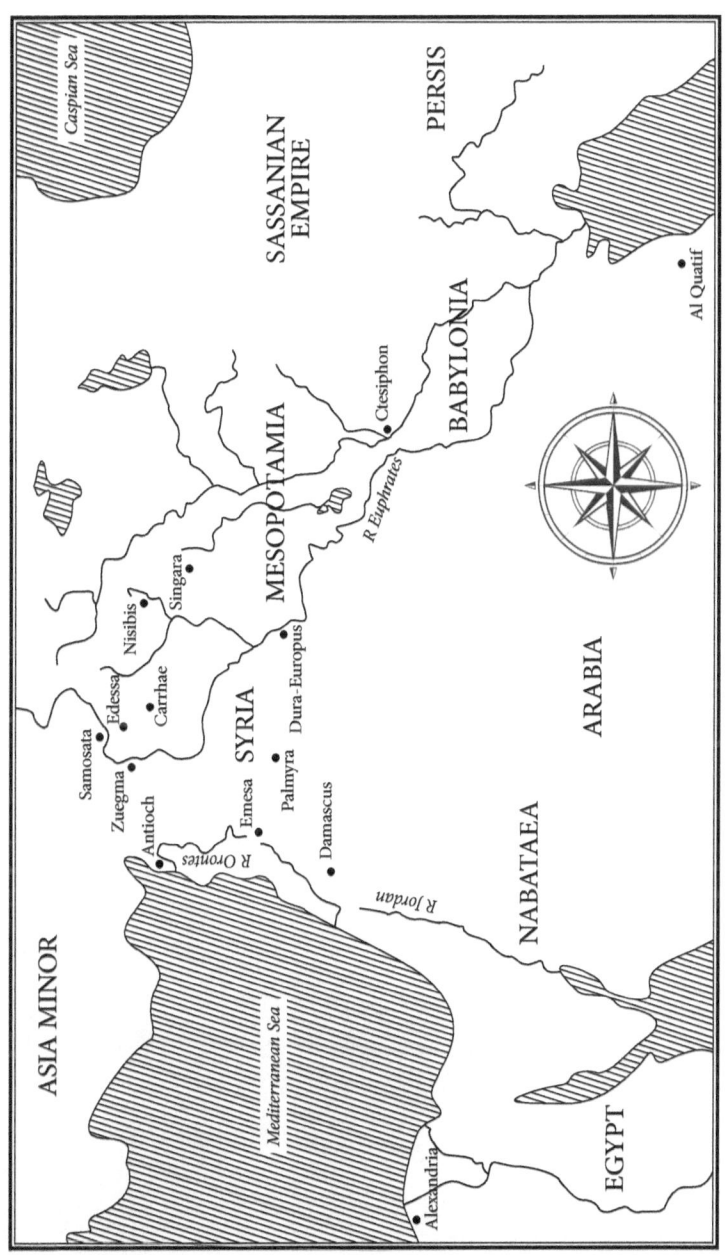

Roman East, 3rd Century AD

PROLOGUE

Zabdas - 290 AD (Present day)

CLOUDS OF SAND BILLOW across the road into Palmyra. I sit upon my horse, back to the city; the rubble and dirt and deadly silence of a place that once chimed with life. Walls that scraped the sky now stand two men high and cast us in shadow: five men beaten by time. Two of us defy death, restless for one last clash of iron before we make peace with our gods.

Behind the walls near five hundred of my men hold the remnants of the broken city. Beyond, thousands of citizens who spent years rebuilding with dust shelter in their homes, afraid of our common enemy. I sense their fear, the panic rising in those who cannot muster their own defence in the uncertainty of what may come. And who would not feel fear, alone in a desert oasis, with only crumbling walls and two carts to block the city gate?

I rub the pommel of my sword with my thumb, the grip worn smooth from a lifetime of killing. Killing, or defending? Suddenly I am unsure of the difference. Which am I, a soldier or murderer, a keeper of peace or a warrior who would have men under his command? Bent on revenge or broken man, or both? I shake the thoughts and watch the road with keen eyes. The Tanukh tribe bring their army north, raping and raiding, pillaging the cities of Syria; plaguing the sands. Scouts tell me they are close, and my breath quickens as I await first sight.

'The Tanukh march two thousand men along this road,'

Vaballathus says. He is mounted on my right, and I hear the man beside him, a priest of Palmyra, suck in a sharp breath and begin to chant.

'A thousand, two, a hundred thousand,' I say, 'it does not matter.'

'You told me they numbered a thousand.'

Vaballathus speaks to annoy the priest, a jest we do not share. He knows the numbers I told the city leaders: the city commander and the priest who stand with us now.

'I told the people they numbered a thousand. A lie to stave fear. What would you have? The streets swarming with citizens attempting to leave, only to find themselves in more danger still?'

'You could have told *me*,' he says more quietly.

I breathe deep, close my eyes, and open them again, my gaze resting on Vaballathus. He sits as tall as his father once did, a full head above an average man. He holds my eye a moment, then looks away. There is much guilt and regret and promise resting on our standing before the Tanukh army. Most of it mine, not his.

'I did not think you would come,' the commander says, forced calm in his honest voice. Appointed by the people of Palmyra, he has their respect and mine.

'I swore to protect the people of this city and bring aid if ever it was required,' I say.

'And it is most welcome. But you lead the largest force in Syria. Why not station it here, in Palmyra? The people are afraid. They would welcome your continuing protection.'

I shake my head. He does not understand.

'The Romans have not forgotten the threat of Syria commanding large forces. My men lurk in the shadows of what this country has been. We must remain so.'

'The Romans would not know,' the commander protests, glancing at Vaballathus.

'If the Romans knew my warriors lined these walls, that we

still lived, they would strip the city bare until they found us. They would not rest. You are not old enough to remember.'

The commander shades his eyes against the sun. He has seen perhaps thirty-five years. I have known fifty. He cannot comprehend the hatred of the Romans and the power Palmyra once held – the threat we were.

'So be it, General Zabdas.'

Perhaps he uses the rank I once held to flatter, to remind me of the oaths that tied me to this country, that tie me still, but I cannot be sure.

'I am no longer a general,' I murmur. 'I am but a warlord.'

'And yet this country still looks to you for leadership, to keep the peace and provide our defences.'

'I live to serve.'

'And I live to bed whores,' Bamdad says, my oldest companion and a leader of our men. 'And drink and eat.'

I laugh. 'And gamble.'

'That too. Is there anything more I should do that you disagree with?' he says, a proud, playful grin upon his face.

'I will think of something before this day is done.'

I shift from one foot to another, my joints stiff despite the heat. I have spent a lifetime riding the sands, hunting those who would strip Syria bare, keeping order where I can and bringing a certain peace to a country that has known too much war. We are invisible to all but the people my silent warriors protect. It is not the dream I once had, and I cannot call it greatness, for it is barely freedom. But it is what *I* have chosen for these lands.

'The last of the scouts have not yet returned.' Bamdad speaks. He shifts in his saddle, leather armour creaking and his horse snorting complaint beneath the weight of the huge man. Skin thin and loose over seasoned muscle; sweat collects beneath a red bandana.

'I will ride out,' Vaballathus says.

'No,' I reply. 'We wait.'

'For how long?'

'Until they come,' Bamdad says.

'You are old and cautious,' Vaballathus snaps.

Bamdad grins.

'I am alive.'

'Only just,' I reply, returning his grin.

'That is true, but I have ten years on you and half the scars,' Bamdad says.

I glance down at my arms and the hatched lines which cover them. They are my warrior bands, proof of the man I have been and the life I have led.

'I have more scars because I saw more battle.'

Bamdad snorts. His horse paws the ground.

'They are coming,' the commander says.

I urge my horse forward, listening for the sound of men on the road. A faint hum. I glance to Bamdad and Vaballathus and nod.

We wait in silence. I hate the waiting. Behind us my archers line the walls at a signal from Bamdad, and heavy cavalry flank the outer perimeter of the city, hidden from sight.

The Tanukh emerge from the haze of sweeping dust and sand. Two hundred men in all. No more than my own force. They stop a few hundred paces away, enough for me to see they are a ragged band of warriors with no banners and few horses. A grey mass behind grows darker, a firmer image, becoming steadily larger as the bulk of the army forms.

I turn my horse and say to the commander: 'Invite the King of the Tanukh to join you in the city this evening, and for drink and food and provision to be sent beyond the walls for his men.'

'Are you sure, General?'

'I am.'

He nods agreement as the priest beside him chants louder still.

I signal for the archers to stand down and the gateway to be cleared. Vaballathus rides into the city ahead of us. Bamdad gives an imperceptible nod. I take a look at the road and the

Tanukh army growing ever larger and my stomach tightens. Then I urge my horse to follow Vaballathus inside the walls.

Tonight we dine with an old enemy.

The palace has long been stripped of marble and statues and stone. First by the Empire and then by the citizens and merchants, sold off or used to build new homes and repair crumbling fortifications.

Instead of receiving the king of the Tanukh in royal chambers, I sit in the commander's house, drinking his wine and waiting.

'Will he enter the city?' Vaballathus asks.

'We will see,' I say.

'He will come. He cannot resist sacking another city, and he has longed to sack Palmyra. He thinks they have no defence,' Bamdad adds, and laughs. 'He is a greedy fool.'

'He takes advantage of the imbalance in Persia. He is not as stupid as you think, Bamdad.'

The commander enters, sits down on a low couch opposite me, worry lining his face. He is anxious, afraid of what will become of the city, what the king of the Tanukh is capable of.

'Does he come?' Vaballathus asks.

'I ... I am not sure.' The commander shrugs first to himself, then looks at each of us in turn and shrugs again. 'I do not know.'

'You sent a messenger?' I ask.

'I did, yes. Of course ...'

'Did the king reply?'

'Apologies ... no, no he did not. We have heard nothing. Provision waits to be sent to his army beyond the walls. As soon as we hear ...'

Vaballathus pulls off his boots and reclines on another couch, his hands behind his head, a smile playing upon his lips.

'What amuses you?' Bamdad asks, his voice clipped.

'This,' Vaballathus says, gesturing our company with a sweep of his arm.

'I do not understand,' the commander says.

I glance to Vaballathus. He is my son-in-law and I am his guardian, trainer, warlord and father. In him is a fiery youth I once knew. He has a passion for tomorrow I no longer know and a thirst for vengeance that in me has faded after every oath. And in Bamdad I see my friend, my companion, a man who has watched my back. But he is old and tired and worn, and in him I see myself. We have not moved on. We cling to our past. That is the cause of Vaballathus' amusement.

A slave enters, her head downturned, and I feel the itch of my own slave mark upon my forearm. A reminder of my childhood.

'What is it?' the commander says.

I see the girl is shaking. Her mouth moves but she utters nothing.

'The Tanukh king is in the city?' I ask.

She gives a rapid nod.

'Then let the feasting begin!' Bamdad cheers.

'Where is he?' I say.

'Approaching the house, General.'

'See to the kitchens.' Then turning to the commander: 'You would do well to find other slaves to greet your guests. You betray a great deal of fear with this one.'

'Apologies.'

'No need, merely the suggestion of an old man.'

We walk through the house and into the atrium where more slaves clutch shadowed walls. We linger too, out of sight, a pause to gain the element of surprise and to steady the rush of blood in my veins.

'You must greet him,' I say.

The commander nods, but his complexion is grey and his eyes show nervousness.

'He will betray our presence,' Vaballathus says.

'It does not matter. It will be too late when he does,' Bamdad replies.

The sky is smoky-blue and the air so still I could push it

aside with a wave of my hand. I can hear the breathing of the slaves, fast and fearful. The king of the Tanukh is introduced as he passes through the gate and into the courtyard. I watch the commander's feet as he walks down the steps to greet the man who would sack his city.

His city.

Is it now the commander's city? I had not intended that. *Their* city, I correct myself. A city of the people, or what is left of it. A place neither ruled by Rome nor, I ensure, plundered by neighbouring tribes or Persians.

The king of the Tanukh moves into view, twenty men in his company. He has not aged. The scars of old still line his face and a dirty cloak hangs from his shoulders. Armour is strapped tight to his chest and shins and his sword hangs ready at his thigh.

The gates swing shut behind him. A locking bar clunks into place.

And a rain of men and steel descends from the gods.

I beg with an outstretched arm for Vaballathus to stay back, to remain in the shadows as we have always done, but he cries a war cry, a shriek louder than any I have heard before, and forces his way into the dim light of the courtyard. Bamdad draws his sword and follows. I go too, dragging my blade from its scabbard and jumping from the top of the steps of the villa and into the fray.

My sword strikes home before my feet hit dry earth. A dozen dead already and more fall as I slice and cry and my blade cuts through flesh and bone. Aches fade and limbs fill with renewed energy, coursing with the youth of my past.

Man after man falls to my sword, more to Bamdad's, and within moments I find myself facing the enemy I have not seen in thirty years.

'You are an old man, Jadhima,' I hiss at the king of the Tanukh.

He is puzzled a moment, furrowed brow and darting eyes. Then his face relaxes in recognition.

'And you will always be a boy. I remember you stood on the

banks of the Euphrates hiding in the skirts of a woman. You are not a man. Look at your beloved city! Look at what it has become. Full of ragged whores and men who pray not to hold a sword. Stubborn fools.'

Jadhima's words do not touch me. His tongue has formed worse. Behind him, Vaballathus kneels in the dirt, head bowed, hair slick with sweat, as he bleeds on the sands.

'Bind him,' I order of Jadhima.

I walk past him to Vaballathus. I sheath my sword, blood and all, and kneel. I know this dusty ground, these walls, as home. I know them still.

Vaballathus groans.

'You should have listened,' I say. I do not think his wound too serious until I pull his hands away from where he grips his stomach and I see, between the folds of leather armour, his guts urging their way through, following the blood already leaking out.

He grunts and falls back. I press my hands on his wound to stem the escape.

'Bamdad! BAMDAD!'

He is already at my side.

'Damn him,' I say. 'Gods' strength, what have you done, Vaballathus?'

His eyes roll, flickering lids, lips pale.

'I cannot die yet,' he murmurs.

'Commander, where is your physician?' Bamdad yells.

'On his way.'

Vaballathus' body weakens beneath my palms, still and quieter than in sleep.

'Do not go. Not yet,' I say. I have loved him since he was a boy, bound by promise to keep him safe, but in truth I am afraid of his death. Of my failing.

Behind me, wrists bound behind his back, tied to single post, Jadhima laughs, wild and wicked.

'There is no end. You and I, Zabdas, we will always have a

revenge to exact. Fortune's wheel. There will always be a life owed between us; the gods are laughing.'

His words do not touch me. I am lost, memories skipping the years, skimming history, reliving the moments I have known. I cannot bear the moment, but I live it still.

'He is gone,' I murmur.

Bamdad grips my shoulder, leans down and closes Vaballathus' half-open eyes.

'And he joins many a great warrior in the otherworld.'

I nod. Bamdad is right. He joins his father, my daughter, and many other souls who would know him.

I stand. Beyond the walls I hear screams and shouts, the roar of my army massacring Jadhima's men who are drunk on Palmyra's wine and mead. For a moment I listen to the sound, relishing the knowledge that the city will not be sacked; that Palmyra still stands, albeit a shadow of what it once was. But it stands all the same, guarding the people within, keeping safe the heart of Syria.

'The gods have long laughed,' I say, turning to Jadhima. 'But now they laugh with me. Today it is you who causes them amusement.'

'I believe in no gods,' he says.

His dirty, matted beard clings to his chest. Blood trickles from his brow, through sweat and grime and lines of defiance.

'You have long plagued this city,' I say. 'Enough. It is time to put an end to this.'

I unsheathe my sword. Jadhima bares his yellow teeth and breathes a hiss of hatred. And with a brief cut of my sword, I open his neck and his blood runs through his beard and onto the ground. Hiss turns to choking gurgle.

My last enemy is dead.

CHAPTER 1

Samira - 290 AD (Present day)

I HAVE BEEN TWO days in Palmyra. The bustle of the city is much louder and busier than my home in Tripolis. The city is in disrepair, as I had been led to believe, with walls missing stone and defences crumbling; homes in some parts hastily rebuilt and in others little more than footprints of what must have been.

I travelled by camel with Bamdad, my grandfather's man, across the desert, plodding ever inland. Now I sit in the commander's house, waiting to speak with my grandfather. I glance at the commander's wife, her hair piled high, eyes black with kohl, jewellery hanging from wrist and neck and hair and ear. And I think then how drab I must be. No jewellery of any kind, my travelling clothes filthy, my hair limp and unkempt, hanging about my shoulders just like all the other girls in Tripolis. But not here. Here the women show fierce dignity, a lift of chin and a hardened eye, caused by a history I cannot remember. Or perhaps secretly they think they are still greater than those beyond their broken city walls …

Bamdad sits with me, his face grave. He is old, very old, and I think the lines on his face make him always grave, always grumpy, but then I have known him forever and I have seen him smile.

I nudge Bamdad with my toe.

'How much longer must we wait?' I whisper.

'Three full moons,' he says.

'Very amusing,' I say, rolling my eyes.

'I could fetch you a puzzle. Or a doll?' His voice is dry. He does not smile, but his eyes are bright and dancing with humour.

'I hear you have a doll of your own, that you take to bed with you each night,' I say, leaning closer on my couch, eyebrows raised. 'Is it true?'

'Who let slip my secret?'

'I have seen you combing its hair,' I tease.

'I will cut yours off if you open your mouth again.'

'Will not,' I laugh.

'Such long hair would fetch a fine sum,' he grins.

Ah, there it is, the familiar grin of my grandfather's most beloved warrior.

'Where is my father?' I ask.

The grin falls from his face.

'Your grandfather will explain,' he says.

I know it is grave. He is injured or dead or disgraced. I wonder which is worse, to lose a limb and never walk again, to be dead and gone from this world never to embrace me again, or to have committed a deed so atrocious as to have disgraced himself beyond redemption. I know my father, and I know that all are possible.

My grandfather enters the room, face heavy with grief, and his eyes lock on mine and I know.

'Your father is dead,' he says, no preamble or pause. He delivers the message as swiftly as he would deliver a sword blow.

Tears threaten and I look down at my hands. Grandfather sits down on a couch opposite me, but it is Bamdad who sits beside me and rests a comforting arm around my shoulders.

'Why did you not tell me when you first arrived in Tripolis?' I ask him.

'Ah, Rubetta,' he says. 'It was not my place to tell you. Zabdas needed to tell you himself.'

Through tears I smile fondly at his nickname for me.

My grandfather leans forward and places his hands over mine, awkward. He is not used to closeness. I think it has been a long time since he was truly close to anyone save those warriors he calls brother: Bamdad, my father …

'How?' I ask, and I can say little more for my voice is breaking.

'Killed by the Tanukh as they tried to take the city …' my grandfather says. He looks as if to say more, but his words fade.

I swallow hard. 'You do not tell the whole truth.' My grandfather is old, and with a creased brow and tiredness and guilt troubling his features, he is older still. 'What is it you do not tell me?'

He glances at Bamdad and I see his hesitation. I long for him to be open with me, to be honest. My father was never that. He masked his feelings, never talked of the past or his childhood. And I feel the same frustration now, as my grandfather struggles with himself and whether or not to speak.

'Apologies,' he says, 'I should have done more to protect Vaballathus. It was not his time.'

I do not know if the tears running down my face are anger and frustration at my grandfather keeping something from me, or because my father is dead and I will not see him again. He was kind and he was energetic. He loved openly and embraced me whenever he returned to our home in Tripolis. I knew when I left home with Bamdad that I would not feel his protection again, and I will never know it again, because my grandfather cannot be close. I have run to him and leapt into his arms as a child, and always he wraps his arms about me, but he is stiff and unsure and does not feel at ease in such moments.

Bamdad looks at me. He is thinking. His face is as old as the wise women of our village. He is like a second grandfather, for I know no other. He must see my pain written plainly upon my face.

'They sought revenge,' he says flatly. 'Zabdas swore an oath to take Jadhima's life.'

'And my father, he swore that same oath?'

'No, your father was just a child at the time. But the revenge was his to share.'

'But why? What revenge?' I am confused by this, and also curious. They were always a puzzle to me, the men of my family, and now, suddenly, with the death of my father, I think I might discover what in life he would not utter.

Bamdad creases his brow, looks away. Regretting perhaps his words, his revealing what my grandfather would not.

'Tell me,' I say.

'It is not my place, Rubetta.'

Honeysuckle and jasmine breathe the summer air. The late afternoon sun glows deep yellow and the skies are pale. I have wandered the gardens of the commander's house all day, weaving the paths, thinking of my father. I have not cried fully. I feel the tears prickle but in my chest I feel the ache of a heartbeat that will not come, of a breath I cannot take. Silent tears at night have not left me exhausted of emotion. I can feel it all around me, suffocating and dark.

My grandfather is sat writing in the shade of the colonnade, surrounded by parchment. He sets down his stylus and yawns, stretching back in his chair and rubbing his eyes. Curious, I walk across, trying to catch a glimpse of the secrets he scribbles as he surreptitiously moves a blank parchment over the others, obscuring them from view.

'What do you write?'

He looks about to lie then sighs and half laughs to himself. He rubs his face, looks up at me and says: 'You know that Rome sacked Palmyra? You know of the history of this place and this country?'

'Of course, it is known by all.'

'I attempt to document it before it fades from memory entirely.'

I am intrigued. What secrets will he divulge on the page that are not common knowledge? He was a general; what more did he know that others did not? Palmyra fell almost thirty years ago, destroyed by the Romans and rebuilt in a fog of fear by the people. They do not bother us now, the Romans. To them we are defeated and destroyed. We are no longer a threat and the Persians quiver and quail under new rule. But what story, I wonder, will my grandfather tell? What truly happened in the end?

'Can I read it?' I ask.

He frowns. 'It has been a long time since I spoke of the years before the fall. I had not thought to let you read it until I was gone.'

'Does it tell of my father?' I ask, wanting to know more, to explore the man lost to me. He has no life to lead now, gone from this world, but there is a whole life I feel I do not know.

He nods. 'It will. I have only just begun …'

CHAPTER 2

Zabdas - 253 AD

AFTERNOON SUN HAMMERED DOWN and the interminable heat caused the ink on my hands to run with sweat as I scribbled a calculation. Firouz, the dockside chief, loomed over me.

'How much?' he boomed.

'One moment.' Forgetting the addition, I quickly attempted to recalculate the value of the shipment.

'The captain is waiting. Filth and scum, you are useless. Hurry. Be quick. This day would be good.'

Firouz spat each word. I worked faster, the figures and sums muddled in my mind, refusing to gel and merge and form the total which my master desired.

He stalked to where I perched on a crate of spice. I kept my head down as he kicked the crate from under me. My tablet fell from my grasp, clattered on stones and I sprawled on the floor, scrabbling and shamed as I tried to retrieve it, shrinking from the laughter of men whose shoulders were burdened with barrels of Chinese spice.

Firouz crushed the fingers of my left hand beneath his heavy boot and I whimpered. Tears filled my eyes as I nursed my hand, and Firouz retrieved my notes.

'The final figure,' he said, prodding the tablet. 'What is it?'

I could move my fingers and through the subsiding pain I managed to mutter the total.

Firouz lumbered back to where the captain of the ship waited with his companion, noting down the calculation on the tablet. The captain looked at me, his leather-tanned face impassive. Beside him, the merchant he moved goods for surveyed my master.

'You have the figures?' the merchant asked Firouz. He was much taller than me with a long, strong nose. Rich silks hung from a tall frame and fragrant oil smoothed black hair down his back. In a year of service to Firouz I had seen many merchants transport exotic wares. They travelled north from Yemen to Nabataea, and from there across land, either trading on route or moving directly to Rome to sell at a higher price.

Firouz surveyed my notes and quoted a price twice that on the tablet.

My expression dropped and the captain saw it.

'Preposterous,' he snorted.

'This is correct?' Firouz asked me, gesturing the tablet, and I knew I should agree. 'You are sure?'

'I am sure.'

Firouz shrugged, unabashed.

'I know your ways, Firouz. The price is outrageous, and you know it. You cannot possibly think …'

'Youness,' the merchant cut across the captain, his tone soft, 'I am happy with the price. I will pay the man.'

I could not understand why he accepted the ridiculous figure, but he was calm as he flicked a hand behind him and two men scurried off the boat carrying a small chest.

The captain walked back to his boat, muttering of robbery as coins were counted. I knelt down and double-checked them, and confirmed them to be of adequate value. Firouz would check them himself and, if he found them short, would beat me and accuse me of stealing. It had happened before. I remember the first time he inflated the worth of grain from Ethiopia. Firouz had charged much more than its value, and I, thinking he had made an honest mistake, corrected him. His boot had hammered into my face. Again and again he kicked me. And when he had finished, my ribs were cracked and my nose broken and my body bloodied.

The merchant said, 'I will pay the coin you have counted for the shipment on the condition you include the boy in the sale.'

'What?' Firouz said.

'I wish to purchase the boy.'

At first I did not realise it, did not believe it, that it was about me he spoke.

'Have you an objection?' he asked.

Firouz contemplated for a moment, then shook his head and slurred, 'He's not f'r sale.'

I glanced at the slave mark upon my arm, frustration burning in my chest, and wondered if it were possible to have a better life. But I was not for sale, and it did not matter. Yet there was something in the merchant's face I could not dismiss, a hope I had not felt for many months, a belief that my fate might change as the wheel of fortune spins.

'Then I must reconsider the price I pay for the goods,' the merchant said.

I knew Firouz enough to know him stubborn.

'The boy was never included in the price.'

'And yet you yourself have shown me that he holds little value, unable to work to your satisfaction ...'

'Not for sale,' Firouz grunted.

Firouz was not interested in why the merchant wanted to purchase me. I knew the merchant was right, that I was a disappointment to Firouz, was not as productive as he would like. I was good with figures, but never quick enough. I could spin numbers and make them dance for me. I wondered what the merchant saw, what thoughts crossed his mind and urged him to secure my sale.

'Youness,' the merchant called, 'have your men unload the cargo. There is no purchase to be made here.'

I stood motionless. What made me think my life would

be better with the merchant, I could not be sure, but his soft expression, the tone of his voice and the manner in which he conducted himself led me to believe that he might possibly provide the means of my escape. I willed him to argue further with Firouz, to claim me for himself.

The merchant gave me a look of resolution and a curt nod of the head.

'As you will,' Firouz said. 'This load will sell to the next ship in port and you will find no better at any dock in Syria.'

'I have purchased from other tradesmen in this port,' the merchant said. 'Your wares are of little consequence.'

Firouz glared a moment, then grabbed the shoulder of my tunic and shoved me forward. 'I have enough work to last you a lifetime, boy,' he spat. 'No merchant dictates to me.'

Stars shone and the moon cast shadow as I sat cross-legged in the courtyard at the back of Firouz' house and shivered. I ate the remains of his meal: a little fruit and a few lentils. I ate using my right hand, my left numbly clutching the bowl.

What did the merchant want with me? The question plagued, the desire to know burning constantly, and the faint promise of a master more gracious than Firouz lingered. Many trading in Yemen were regulars, returning every now and then, always wanting a better price or a higher volume, looking for the luxurious and the rare, the popular and the staple. Firouz provided everything that held a profit. Yet the merchant buying spice and silk I did not know. His face had not passed through our port before and he was unknown to any man save the captain.

Darkness swallowed the sky as I trudged back to the dockside, my duty to ensure everything was in order. The cargo sold that day would have been loaded by now; the ships ready to leave at first light. I hurried through the dark, silent streets until I heard the gentle lapping of water and the sound of voices.

Twenty or more men relayed barrels and crates up a gangplank and onto the ship commissioned by the merchant who had offered to purchase me. I watched, lurking in the shadows as moments passed and the warehouse was emptied of contents destined for the southern coast of Syria. Bellows of 'Faster' and 'Pull your weight, we need this done before morning' echoed across the dockside. A figure approached. My stomach lurched. I pulled back, pressed myself against the sun-warmed stone wall, and wished that it would conceal me from sight. A man strode by, tall frame and face shrouded in a thick cloak.

Fear should not have gripped me, I had done nothing wrong. Too many beatings and the heavy hand of many men who ranked above slave gave me pause.

'Are you hiding, boy?'

The man paused, his back to me.

Words escaped my mouth, but I could not control them.

'Apologies, I will say nothing of what you do here.'

He turned, lifted the hood from a face deep with furrows of age, growing more prominent as he smiled warmly.

'You are the merchant,' I said.

'*The* merchant? You have met many today I suspect. Not only me.'

'You were the one who wanted to buy me.'

'Indeed, I did. It would appear you are more valuable to your master than he would care to admit. Please, let us not stand here in the shadows. I was in fact on my way to seek you out.'

With a hand on my back he guided me onto the moonlit dock.

'Teymour,' he shouted.

A moment, then a man leant over the side of the vessel.

'Julius?'

'Have you a moment? There is someone I wish you to meet.'

Teymour disappeared from view.

'Ah,' breathed the merchant, 'I have not yet introduced myself. My name is Julius Aurelius Zabdilas.'

'Mine is Zabdas.'

'I had hoped as much,' he said, nodding.

Teymour joined us on the dockside. He did not have the kind and gentle features that I saw in Julius. I trusted Julius on appearance alone, yet I felt uncomfortable in Teymour's presence. Both men wore short clipped beards and loosely bound hair. Julius' black curls softened his face further, yet Teymour's straight hair served to harden his jaw and deepen his brow. They appeared as brothers, the opposites of one another.

I looked from one man to the other. Julius smiled. In the darkness Teymour scowled as if looking up into the sun.

'You know my name?'

Julius placed a hand upon my shoulder, his mouth twitching and his eyes searching the ground, looking for words, waiting for the dust to yield. What question lingered that he could not utter?

'How old are you now, Zabdas?'

'Thirteen, almost fourteen.'

'Are you sure he is the one?' Teymour asked. 'What if he is not?'

'Which *one*?' I asked. 'Who do you think I am?'

'Do you remember your parents, Zabdas?'

'Khenut and Nepherites. To me they were Mother and Father, but those were their given names.'

'How long have you been here, in Yemen?' Julius asked.

'Eight years.' Fire burned in my eyes, tears hot and thick pushing forth at the thought of the years of slavery I had known. 'I turned five a month before I was taken.'

Teymour's scowl lifted and he said to Julius: 'You told me he was taken a slave five years ago, not eight.'

Julius shook his head. 'That is when I discovered him gone, not when it happened.'

Two bellows echoed across the dockside and Julius startled.

'I must go,' Teymour said. 'I need to ensure everything is loaded if we are to leave before dawn.'

Julius nodded and Teymour strode away.

Julius' arm still rested upon my shoulders as he said, 'I came to take you back with me. My apologies that it took so long to find you.'

'Take me with you?'

Julius chuckled. I frowned back and he returned an apologetic expression. 'It is not my place to take what belongs to another man, but you were not born to slavery and no man's slave to sell.'

'What am I to you?' I asked. What made him come here in search of me? To take me where, another house, another business, where I might be of use?

He closed his eyes for a moment and when he opened them again said, 'We must continue loading. We leave at dawn. Does the man who would call himself your master expect you to return this night?'

'He will. I am to report back that nothing is amiss at the dockside before he retires.'

'Then you must go, I cannot risk him noticing your absence and report theft to the town's commander, it would raise too many complications that we could well do without. I will take you with me, I promise, and I will explain everything to you on our journey.'

My stomach plunged at the prospect of returning to Firouz' house, and more so at the knowledge I must later attempt escape.

'I beg you, take me now.'

'You are of great value to him, it seems, and he knows of my desire to purchase you. He will not let our ship sail if he suspects you are on board. No, we must wait until the last moment before you board.'

I knew him to be right. I turned to go then paused.

'You would have bought me, if you could?'

'I would have paid a high price to take you away from here. Instead we must resort to other measures. I will not leave you here, I give you my word.'

He turned and walked back to the ship. Darkness swamped their work and torches choked in the night.

I trudged back to Firouz' house, my limbs trembling and the thought of never returning here spurring me forward. For years I had thought of my past, not my future. Now my mind skidded and slipped over visions of a life as a citizen, no longer a slave.

CHAPTER 3

Zabdas - 253 AD

FIROUZ LEANT BACK ON a couch, his eyes closed, an occasional grunt escaping his lips, and his arm resting over his belly. Hundreds of gold coins lay scattered across a low table beside him. I thought to take one, a handful, perhaps more, to repay Julius for his troubles and to give me worth. With a sickening realisation I acknowledged the thought of theft had presented itself.

I am a better man, I told myself; I will not take what does not belong to me.

I did not sleep nor feel the cold bite, but felt the warmth of hope as I listened for any sign of Firouz' awakening. I thought of my father, a cool man, who could not share his feelings nor console my bruised knees. 'Come now, lad,' he would say, 'it is not as bad as that. Pick yourself up.' Fond memories of my running to greet him, of his abrupt ruffle of my black hair, and of my mother kissing his cheek in greeting. My mother's face flitted into view and I witnessed her gentle smile, reliving my short childhood. She was kind, a farmer's wife, following my father as he tended his flock and making the food we ate herself. We were a carefree family, with no home save the hills in which we took shelter and the insides of our tents.

She once told me that fortune did not offer itself to those who lived simply but contentedly, those for whom it was enough to be happy. Fortune's wheel had a cruel edge, and rotated and sometimes paused, but would never cease turning. I do not remember stepping on fortune's wheel, but it found me and it turned.

Firouz did not wake. He slept still as I ventured out into the early morning, or the late night, I could not be sure at first. Then I saw the sky, blue-black, broken by a smattering of stars and a crescent moon. Excitement, not fear, stole over me as I raced along the deserted streets, the soft slap of my sandals disturbing hunting cats.

I felt elation as I neared the dockside, punctured briefly by the thought that the merchant's ship might have already departed, a fear allayed as I heard the voices of sailors and the last of the cargo being loaded. The merchant stood on board the ship.

'Zabdilas!' I called.

He turned, smile broad upon his face, and raised a hand. But his smile evaporated and his hand fell as he looked beyond me.

My senses yelped. I sank to my knees behind crates and fishing nets and barrels and sacks, my mouth turning dry and my heart beating in my throat.

I heard Firouz bellow my name, saw Julius begin to walk down from the ship. I could not see Firouz, but I knew his face well, and would bet my life the expression it would have. He must know I had left and did not intend returning to his house.

Heated words distorted on the breeze. I must move, to hide or to run I did not know. My back to a wall I recalled a doorway to one of the warehouses, and with a small movement, I slid the latch and slipped inside.

Shafts of moonlight fell through the open doorway between clusters of barrels, crates and sacks. I pulled the door closed and waited, unsure whether to pick a path through them, knowing that if I did there would be no leaving should Firouz enter. No other escape beyond the wares.

I heard a sound, a clatter, outside. Resolved myself to hiding deeper, concealed better, and squeezed my way to where I knew empty barrels stood. I found them with ease, rolled one to join those heavy with goods, slipped inside, and lowered the lid. My limbs complained as I crouched in the dark, breathing like a dead man.

Moments passed. My actions had freed me because I had gone from Firouz without his bidding. Caught, I would be known a disobedient slave and whipped until my blood coated the hot and dusty dock. I thought of that as I crouched, knew that it mattered not if I died then. My resolve was found, I would die liberated.

'I will find the boy,' I heard Firouz slur. 'No man takes what is mine. Thievery. I will have you before the city commander!'

'Apologies, but we are only taking what we have been instructed to,' said another. 'It is a misunderstanding.'

Firouz muttered inaudible words. Silence fell. I tried to think, the scent of ingrained spice intoxicating me, my head swimming until blackness followed. I lost myself in hard images of beatings endured, mines I had worked in, the whippings received, raw flesh and the sting of many a tongue. My heart thumped but my eyes refused to open, my mind could not be stirred. Limbs slackened and trembled.

At Firouz' voice I wrenched myself back.

'No ship will leave this dock until I find him.'

'I am happy for you to search the ship, if you wish, I have nothing to hide. Your slave boy is not there.'

'And here? You guarantee that too? Your word is nothing. My man saw someone come in here.'

'My men are in and out. Look, you see them now?'

'You mock me?'

'I state a fact, Firouz. I bought goods from many merchants in this dock. That my purchase with yourself was not successful does not trouble me, and should not you.'

I heard Firouz grunt. My legs were numb. I shuffled, restoring flow of blood, and found a tiny crack between the strips of wood. Pressing my eye to it, I saw my master.

'Open them,' he said.

'This is not your cargo, and you have no right to delay my departure. By all means you can search my ship and you can check my inventory, but you cannot open crates of precious spice and risk spoilage. They do not belong to you. And if you persist, I will call the dock commander myself.'

Firouz moved aside and revealed the second person. Teymour.

'The commander is in my pay. Open them,' Firouz demanded again.

In the darkness of the store, Teymour's features were harsher than before. He turned his back on Firouz, shouted a command. More footsteps sounded and two men entered.

Julius sighed, as if tiring of the game. He gestured with his hand to proceed.

The two men moved forward. Panic rose and my bladder contracted. I pulled back from the crack in the barrel, breathing rapidly, afraid of what would come, of Firouz finding me. I did not want to be discovered. More than that, I did not want to lose the hope I had found since the merchant's arrival, I wanted to pursue it, to be more than a free man. I wanted to know what the future might hold.

Splintering wood ricocheted. Splitting, cracking, tendons snapping.

I pressed my eye to the crack once more. Firouz looked on, arms folded across his chest, drooping eyelids betraying the effects of mead. Fresh scratches rose in welts on his left cheek, laced with crusted blood.

More crates ripped and wood torn. Julius looked on, calm, no intimidation showing. My own heart hammered.

'Enough,' Teymour said. 'You have seen enough. Or are we to stand here all night whilst you check every last piece of cargo? It is imperative we catch the morning tide. We need to load. I insist you leave us be.'

'My men will stay. I will kill him when I find him.'

Heavy footsteps moved away.

'Move the rest of this cargo,' Teymour snapped. Then, more quietly, 'Where is he, Julius?'

'I wish I knew, Teymour.'

I wanted to shout that I hid feet from them, that I was safe and would join them, but Firouz' men remained, and I could not risk it.

The two men lifted barrels onto their shoulders and carried them out of the warehouse. Teymour and Julius' footsteps did not follow. Had they gone? I thought they had, then a heartbeat later Julius' voice sounded so close I suspect he breathed on the barrel.

'Stay where you are.'

Sick with fear I waited for another murmured word. Nothing. Goods were loaded onto the ship and the passage of feet lulled me. My eyes became accustomed to the dark, and the sound of my breathing gave me comfort. Firouz had not found me, and as time passed I grew confident that he would not.

I tired. My eyes closed and I passed into fitful slumber.

I woke with a start as the barrel jolted, my bearing gone. I drew deep breaths as the air changed from humid and warm to cool and fresh. A thud as the barrel hit the floor, then another next to mine, and another, and another, all the while I wondered what had happened, where I was, whether Firouz had found me.

Senses alert, I crouched, darkness swaying, contemplating what I could do with freedom if it became mine. I could be a merchant, a seaman, a scribe or a philosopher, perhaps farm and raise my own livestock. I was excited by the choices, but I was also scared. I did not know what a freeman could do, how he should act, what choices he could make, and wondered if a man could go from slavery to freedom and find happiness, whether it was possible to have a life of my own.

I dared not lift the barrel lid. Exhausted, I slipped once again into uneasy slumber, dreaming of a land where buildings were tall and made of gold, and people wore vivid colours which pinched your eyes.

I woke once more, not knowing whether it was day or night or where I was. I listened. Silence. Clothes clung hot and damp. I rubbed my face, sniffed the scent of sweat and piss.

The silence did not break. Time ran by, it could be morning but I was not sure. I lifted the barrel lid just enough to survey the space around me. Compact cargo. The ship's hold? Netting secured barrels and the smell of rancid saltwater overpowered. Alone, I levered myself out, took a knife from my pocket and scored the wooden lid with two parallel lines, then replaced the knife. I clambered over crates and barrels until I found a set of steps and a hatch in the ceiling.

It opened with ease and I glanced around, saw nothing, and climbed out. The corridors swayed and I used the walls to steady myself. A lean man dressed in rags appeared, his jittery body full of haste. I leapt back as he dashed past, his movement in time with the rocking ship. He did not acknowledge me and I collected myself and continued on.

Whose ship was I on? The merchant's? Another?

Clunking footsteps sounded above and below. Salt air filled my lungs, the sound of water sloshing against the ship constant. A lantern swayed ahead of me, the only light in the passage, and water ran along the planks beneath my feet. The conditions became rough, as if we had moved further out to sea, and I struggled to keep my footing. Somewhere, voices cried out.

'I wondered when you would appear.'

I turned to face Teymour.

'Julius waits for you in the captain's cabin.'

He moved ahead of me, a lantern in his hand. Without a

word, I followed. We emerged onto the deck to find it was no longer night. The sun broke above the hills to our left; a golden glow on a black sea. A mild breeze promised a warm day inland.

And in that moment I felt safe, far out from the shore, the dock no longer in sight. I took my first breath of air as a truly free man. Tears sprang. I could not beat them, could not keep them at bay. The ship had not been called back to port, we had left, and Firouz would never find me. I took a breath of the warm air and tasted only freedom.

Gods, but that sun looked different, the paleness of it, the slight yellow tint, the fresh lemon colour. Wisps of cloud breathed and the sea reached up to meet them. Why had I not seen this before?

I hurried to keep up with Teymour's giant stride. Watched with keen eyes as men carried sacks, hauled ropes or peered out on the horizon. Teymour came to an abrupt halt before a cabin door and knocked. A muffled voice spoke and Teymour opened the door and we entered.

Dozens of candles contributed to a warm enticing glow and a voice said: 'Come, sit with me.'

Julius reclined on a couch and gestured me to take up an embroidered cushion opposite. The man Julius had been talking to bade him goodnight and left.

'There will be nothing else, Teymour,' Julius said.

Teymour gave a curt nod and he too left the cabin.

Julius took a grape from a bowl in front of him.

'Help yourself.'

'Gratitude.'

'It is I who owe you gratitude, Zabdas. And my sincere apologies. Your presence eases my conscience greatly. There have been many times I have thought of you and what became of you. I should never have let this happen, never allowed you to be taken as a slave. We thought you were safe.'

Did he mean Teymour? I understood Julius' guilt as little as I understood what had become of me, of the night that had just passed and the future I would see.

'How do you know who I am?'

'I knew your mother and father well.'

I stared at Julius, attempted to take in the words that seemed to roll with the deck.

Julius steepled his fingers and gave a short nod.

'As I said, Zabdas, you were not born a slave, and when your parents died …' He shook his head. 'I should have come for you sooner. Your mother and father always moved, farming and living the lands. You must have felt a great sadness when they died.'

A sharp stab of pain at their loss punctured. I had not felt it for a long time because I had not allowed myself to think of them.

'They were murdered,' I spat. I thought to feel and appear angry, but I felt only empty.

'I know,' Julius said, nodding.

I found myself unable to form words. Julius appeared to be waiting for me to say more.

'How did Teymour know I hid in the warehouse?' I asked.

'Our cargo was marked. The barrel in which you hid was not. And because Teymour saw you enter the warehouse.'

Julius rose from his seat and from a tankard filled two cups with wine. I surveyed the cabin. Small and furnished, with rich swathes of fabrics and inlaid wooden chests.

Julius returned to his seat, swaying with the roll of the ship.

'When I first heard of your parents' death, I came immediately to Egypt. It was already too late. Years had passed and trace of your fate had grown colder than a desert night. I stayed two months before I had to return to Syria. I spoke to everyone who could possibly know of your whereabouts, and when I heard nothing, I feared you were dead.'

'You searched?'

'Of course. You are beloved of the house of Zabdilas. I searched five long years for you, my boy, and I would have gladly searched eight had I known of your fate sooner.'

He looked down at the cup in his hands, lost in thought. A tide of confusion swam around me but I could not find the question to ask, my mind blank, the need to know my past evaporating with the prospect of a future. I too looked into my cup, wondering what Julius saw in the liquid. I took a sip of the wine, rich and sweet; most unlike the watered-wine Firouz kept.

'Who am I to you?' I asked.

Julius studied me, smiled. I wondered what thought lurked in the pleasure I sensed, the turn of his mouth and satisfaction in his eye. This man had found me after years of searching, and suddenly that realisation warmed me. For a moment I looked at him and saw my father. Could it be him, returned to me? I tried to recall his face, his expression, the lie of hair and build of muscle, the image hazy and changing, I could not fix it and dared not ask.

'You are my nephew by marriage, Zabdas. Your mother and my wife are sisters.'

My heart sank a little.

'Then I am not related to you by blood?'

Julius' brow creased, his look concerned.

'As good as. You are family. We are your guardians now. It is our responsibility to care for you.' His words were careful, as if realising that my escape from slavery was not the end of my troubles, and that my mind would still be haunted and the brand upon my arm unchanged.

We sat in easy silence a time. I drank more than the wine. I soaked the rich surroundings, the strangeness of sitting upon a cushioned couch, eating foods that were not scattered remains. I ate as a free man ate, as Julius ate, and knew the pleasure of it in the sigh of my muscles and the contrast of the rich room against the rags hanging from me.

'Are you a merchant?' I asked.

'I am. My trade dealings have become vast these last years. The king of Palmyra has made my occupation very profitable.

Syria does well from the tax revenue, as does Rome, of course. But you will know this, will you not? You have seen the goods passing through Yemen.'

'The dockside was a busy place,' I confirmed.

'You were a good mathematician, it would seem,' he said.

'I was … I am.'

'And Firouz valued you for it.'

'He …' I tried to find the phrase. 'He collected: slaves, obscure items that passed through the dock.'

Julius raised an eyebrow.

'Busts of aristocracy, precious stones, rare spices. He could not bring himself to sell them on and so kept them, secreted away, with no purpose, for no reason.'

'I see. Come, Zabdas, I must tend to my men. I will see you in the morning. I will have someone find you a cabin.'

And with that he left.

In his absence I walked out onto the deck, to a rising sun illuminating the sea a deep blue-green, flecked with white like stars. I breathed fresh sea air, thought of my new life in Palmyra, a city renowned for its prosperous men. What could I make of myself when I arrived? What could I become? The horizon blurred. It was not a sad blur, but one of promise.

CHAPTER 4

Zabdas - 253 AD

WINDS WHIPPED AND THE sea writhed as we travelled north. We brushed the shore east and west, land never far away, stopping only for fresh water and supplies, Julius intent on reaching Syria soon. Days vanished in a salt spray and rich food and the crew's banter was our rhythm. I should have craved Egypt, yet I yearned for Julius' home. To see it, hear it, smell it. To experience the life he knew. I wanted to know Palmyra.

The crew told me of her beauty. They described her coliseums and temples, the vast trade she saw each year. Each word heightened my excitement.

'Palmyra has made many a man rich,' Teymour told me one night, 'but none so much as Julius Zabdilas.'

We sat in Julius' cabin, drinking and eating. Many of the crew retired to their beds, others keeping watch above deck.

Julius sat, his eyes resting closed, listening to us talk.

'We have both profited, Teymour. You share my wealth, you always have,' he said mildly.

'Indeed, but you made it,' Teymour replied.

'I made it, of course. No man gained anything without a little work. But the gold Palmyra holds comes from King Odenathus' rule. He makes trading with Rome possible; he exploited the opportunity, keeping trade routes open and safe. We are fortunate. He is a man of practicality and vision.'

Teymour lifted his cup to his lips and drained it, thumped it down onto the table. 'You rarely speak of the king so well, Julius. You left Palmyra because you could never agree, yet you accept gold from his rule and thank him for it?'

Julius opened his eyes and set down his cup beside Teymour's. I sat in silence, my presence suddenly unwelcome, the thoughts unsaid between these two men hanging in the space between them.

'The king and I have our differences, my friend. Indeed, I have *earned* much gold, but there is no denying that trade through Palmyra has prospered under Odenathus and his father before him. The country was not always so wealthy.'

'Ha! You should not speak of him so well. People may think that you were friends once.'

Julius looked a little taken aback, hurt, but said nothing. Finally, he sighed as if the argument were an old one.

'I go to my bed,' Teymour slurred.

He pushed himself from the table, stumbled out of the cabin door and slammed it behind him.

'He does not think the king a good one?'

'No, it is not that. I am unsure myself what Teymour thinks. He does not speak his mind, but judges others. Sometimes I believe he is jealous of the power Odenathus holds, that the people love him for the opportunity he provides and the peace in which they live. Teymour also holds my beliefs which are not the same as the king's. I sometimes think he would prefer me to turn my back on Odenathus and Palmyra, but I would not. I may disagree with Odenathus on some counts, but I cannot deny that he rules better than most.

'Come now, enough talk for tonight. We have a long day ahead.'

I bade Julius goodnight and left. Outside, Teymour looked out at the moving water. I joined him, both standing with our backs to the sea, our faces and expressions unlit and unreadable.

From a skin he took a slug of wine, a dribble down his chin, slurred words on a careless tongue.

'He holds Odenathus in too high a regard,' he said of Julius.

'Julius has become rich from trade?'

'He is a shrewd man, calculating, and knows how to handle business.' Teymour gave a short laugh. 'He knows people, the right people.'

'How long have you been in his service?'

Teymour stood up straight and turned to face me, swaying, unsteady, wine slopping on the dry deck.

'I am not in his service. We are equals in trade.'

Railing at my back, I willed it to be further away, troubled by the anger in Teymour's face.

He grunted. 'You are afraid, boy. I see it, I smell it. You should not show it. Take warning from me, there are many who would take advantage of you.'

'No more than they have before,' I said, tone curt, hostile.

'Then you should know better than to let your fear show.'

With no retort and his words heavy on my mind, I turned to look out at the water.

'A couple more days and we reach the mouth of Aqaba and head up to the port at Al'Aqabah. From there we travel by land across Nabataea and north into Syria. And there, my little friend, we cross into the Empire of Rome,' Teymour said. And under his breath: 'Robbing bastards.'

I knew of Rome, the city whose lands stretched across half the world. I had lived once under the influence of Roman law, the same laws that had done nothing when my parents were killed and I was taken a slave. One day, I thought, I would like to go there and see the splendours spoken of by admirers, the greatness I did not know. For now we sailed on, the sea still and black beneath us. But despite the calmness of the water, my excitement of reaching Palmyra burned.

I felt her drawing nearer. I could smell her on the breeze.

Days passed and the port of Al'Aqabah emerged from the horizon. The sour mood of a crew confined aboard ship lifted at the sight. Teymour appeared more jovial, though his sour mood could not be fully erased. Julius and I were light of heart, as if we both felt a return to home.

The port differed to Yemen. More buildings cluttered the water's edge, the place smelled of warm, welcoming land, not of sea or stale cargo. Teymour waited aboard ship, impatient for permission to unload cargo.

'Would you like to join me?' Julius said, gesturing towards the town.

'Where are we going?'

'I have camels stabled here. I am hoping they have not been sold for a night with a whore and a cup of ale. Come, they are on the outskirts of town. We need to move quickly. I do not wish to stay here longer than required. Not with this volume of cargo.'

He beckoned two of the crew join us.

Julius leaned on a staff as we walked, a limp in his stride I had not noticed in our time aboard ship.

'This way,' he said.

Streets narrowed, darker and cluttered, opening onto market squares or leading to what seemed like nowhere before joining another, larger street. I became lost in the maze of passages and alleyways and my own curiosity. I saw places, lots of places, wandering as if I should not have a care; as a boy — a man — who did not have a mark upon his arm. I became aware that I was not truly free. My master had not freed me, Julius had not purchased me. What right did I have to call myself a freedman? I should not have been a slave, I told myself over and again.

The port was large, but the houses and buildings soon grew thin, the smell of shit and dirt subsided. I spotted a small farm ahead. Looking back, I saw the vast spread of buildings, ship masts teetering above, blue water beyond.

The farm comprised a small house and a few outbuildings, a high wall, and beyond an expanse of cropfields.

A dog barked. Julius' pace slowed.

Just feet from the farmhouse and the door swung open. A man lumbered down stone steps.

'What is it, boy? Who is out there?'

He paused and appeared to stare straight at us. We walked nearer and he shouted no question of who we were or acknowledged our approach. Sunlight illuminated his large physique and straggling grey hair.

'It is I, Julius.'

'Julius? I should have known. I can smell your sweet perfume. Has no one told you it is a woman's scent? I despair of you. Too worldly now, my boy. Seen too many things and taken a fancy to others' way of living. You have taken your time. Been gone a while, you have.' He stopped, thumped a nearby wall with a fisted hand, and cursed. 'There are others with you.' He pointed a finger. 'You should have said.'

'There are only three others. Two of my men and a boy.'

'A boy?' He took a step forward as he spoke, as if closer proximity would assist his sight.

'Indeed. Egyptian.'

'His name?'

'Zabdas,' Julius replied.

'Light!' the man replied. 'Yes, I thought I could see light. That is how I knew you were coming; that there were more of you.'

Julius walked up to him, clasped both shoulders and kissed his cheek. 'A hope growing in the darkness.'

'I met the other two before?'

'You did indeed.'

The expressions of the two men beside me remained impassive.

The old man grimaced. 'I wish you had come sooner.'

'What is it?' Julius asked.

'Come inside.'

I took a pace forward, but the man's eyes fixed on me. I stopped.

'Wait here, Zabdas,' Julius said. 'I will not be long.'

Julius' men and I stood in silence. After a time my legs began to ache and I sat on a bench in the courtyard of the farm. The two men followed my lead and sat too. I knew both by sight.

They were equal in height, build and facial structure, so similar that I supposed them brothers.

'I am Shahin and this is Ramtin. My cousin.'

'Zabdas,' I replied.

'We know,' Shahin said.

'Who is he?' I asked, referring to the blind man.

'Navid,' Ramtin said.

'How does he know Julius?'

'Julius always leaves camels here. They have known one another for many years. Rumour has it they fought together, though Julius does not speak of those times.'

'Fought?' I could not imagine Julius, eloquent and gentlemanlike, brawling. Then I realised they meant he was a man of the army.

'Julius was a stratego, a general of the Palmyrene army. Navid fought with him in Egypt before he was taken captive by a Persian warband. They tortured him and took his eyes.'

The two cousins complained that the night chill would soon be upon us. I sat, silent and thoughtful, contemplating Julius' past. He had been a stratego. Not once in our weeks aboard ship had he mentioned this position. Neither Shahin nor Ramtin knew anything more. Teymour had not talked of it either and I wondered why it had not passed his lips, why he kept quiet. I felt betrayal, as if he should have told me, and wondered at the connection of Egypt ... how many years had it been since he fought there? Was his connection more than a military position, or could he conceal a secret? That perhaps his tie to me was closer than that of a nephew ...

'We will end up having to stay here,' Shahin said.

'He cannot be much longer,' Ramtin replied. 'He wanted to make haste and reach home.'

'Should we ensure all is well?' I said, but as the words parted the door of the farmhouse opened. Julius stepped out into the weak light.

'Shahin. Ramtin. Go back to the ship. Come back and fetch the camels in the morning.'

'Where will you be?' Shahin asked.

'No questions,' Julius snapped. 'Teymour is to command the transport of goods into Palmyra. You will take orders from him. Tell him I have already paid the captain for his services, so not to yield more should he claim otherwise. You need to bring another two men to fetch the camels. Navid has no one to spare and I am taking two. Split the goods a little heavier amongst the rest.

'Zabdas,' he said. 'We will spend the night here. Tomorrow you come with me.' His words a command, not a request.

'Do we still head for Palmyra?'

'We do, but I wish to see my family first. *Your* family, Zabdas. They live in a town no more than two days' ride from Palmyra. Once I have —'

'You were asked to head straight for the city,' Navid said, voice loud, authoritative. I would not have dared speak to Julius so, but he did not raise his voice nor curse the man he had once fought beside.

'My family come first,' Julius replied softly.

Navid's head twitched, his eyes gaping holes, face riddled with concern. 'So be it. Ensure it is known I passed the message on.'

Julius nodded. 'We leave with the sun.'

He dismissed the cousins and we followed Navid into the house. Would the captain attempt to double charge for his services? I wondered, and imagined Teymour's face if he tried.

Sleep evaded me that night. Julius turned every so often, restless and troubled, sighing every now and then. Eventually he left his bed and stood outside. I watched him through the window, quite still, gazing out at the farmlands. I wanted to join him, to know why he had never mentioned his being a general, the reason he no longer served the army; he was in his middle years, not old enough for retirement, still a friend of the king, no disgrace I could summon thought of.

He paced, over and over, the ground dark and footsteps quiet. Lost in thought.

It was almost morning when he returned to our room, took a small comb from his pack and drew it through his dark, glossy hair, then replaced the comb together with other belongings and turned to me.

'We must go now.'

I had seen many a camel on the dockside, the better specimens fetching huge sums of denariis. These camels had cost a prince's fortune.

I mounted. Never having ridden before I found the sway alarming, but the plodding soon settled into an easy rhythm.

Blankets of golden sand climbed and dropped across the horizon. Blue sky met the hard edge of the plain and wispy trails of white cloud hinted a rare promise of rain. I had seen landscapes to rival these many times, but hidden beneath years of slavery they refused to form in my mind. Caravans lined and blocked roads heading north. Camels and carts moving painstakingly slow, yet with Julius at my side I did not worry about hostile nomads I knew thronged these roads.

Julius barely spoke, but still he smiled and gestured for me to take a sip from a skin each time he caught my eye. Time passed and I saw the deep lines of worry soften as his urgency to see his family grew into excitement. And with this gradual change my courage, too, heightened. I dared to ask the question long harboured.

We stopped in the desert, with darkness for company and a fire of camel dung to keep us warm. We had food enough to last, though without adequate means of cooking it was limited and fresh fruit scarce.

'Julius?'

'What is it, my friend?' His excitement no longer hid his weariness. He adjusted himself and rubbed his knee. Nearby, the camels mewed.

'Navid said to travel straight to Palmyra. What did he mean?'

Julius' eyes flickered orange in the firelight.

'I thought you might ask. You took your time. I fear you lay trust too easily in people, Zabdas.'

'You have never given me a reason not to trust,' I countered.

'It was not criticism. It is an endearing quality, and one that often comes with youth.'

I looked back at the fire.

Julius laughed. 'I am honoured by your trust. And hope that I have earned it.'

I continued to stare at the flames, unsure if it was the fire's heat I felt on my face.

'So, you wish to know more of Navid's words? He told me that Odenathus, king of Palmyra, sent men to track and hasten my return. They left word with Navid that, as soon as my feet touched these shores, I was to head straight for the city. You look worried, Zabdas?'

'You see your family first. Will that not anger the king?'

'Undoubtedly. I owe Odenathus nothing. My family comes before anything he wishes of me.'

'But why does he need to see you so urgently?'

'My reason for travelling to south Arabia was not to fetch goods. I correct myself. It was not my *main* reason. That was to find you, of course. But I have also been in search of the Black Stone of Elagabal. Have you heard of it?'

No worshipper, but I had heard of the Sun God Elagabal, as I had heard of many gods associated with black stones. Elagabal was most dominant of the gods in Syria at that time. And the Black Stone of Elagabal the most powerful.

'I have heard. The priests of Yemen claim the Black Stone is in Emesa.'

Julius looked into his lap and said, 'That does not surprise me. They say we merchants strive only for gold, yet they use the gods' presence to take it from others. But you are right, most believe the stone to be in Emesa; a secret long harboured by the rulers and priests of Syria alike. Julia Mamaea was the young mother of Emperor Severus Alexander of Rome. It is believed she ruled through her child, unyielding to any but her own desires. With more influence on the dynamics of the Empire than her son, she had the Sun God banished from Rome more than thirty years ago. And the stone returned to Emesa.'

'It is not there?'

'The Black Stone never reached the city. The priests awaited its return but it never came.'

Julius adjusted his position again and eased his limbs against the fire's heat.

'But why? Why claim they had it when they did not?'

'The Syrian people placed such faith in the Stone that I believe the priests felt masking its disappearance their only option. They produced another in its place and claimed it to be that of the great Elagabal.'

'What happened to the true Stone?'

'There are rumours. Odenathus believes that if we have the true stone we will be protected from any threat to these lands; the Persians, Tanukh, other tribes. He thinks peace can be found in holding once more the Stone of the Sun God.'

I wondered how true that could be, how peace might be found in a stone you could hold in your hands.

'And you do not?'

He shook his head, looked out across the dark plain.

'Odenathus is influenced by his mother, much the same as Julia Mamaea influenced her son. Only Odenathus' mother has worshipped Elagabal for many years, with no desire to banish him. It is she who desires the stone, playing to her son's weakness: his passion and need to rid Syria of the Persian threat forever.' Julius sighed and stared into the fire. 'I fear he is driven for the wrong reasons. I doubt even his mother believes the stone will actually defeat the Persians. She influences Odenathus for her own ends. Its only real value is in the peoples' belief that it is here.'

'And they already believe that,' I said.

'Indeed.'

'And still you looked for it? Surely the king listens to others?'

'He used to. But after his wife's death he became more reserved in accepting counsel. Now he prefers the whispers of his mother and her associate, the city commander. I left court over eight years ago because Odenathus' decisions and motives became very different from my own. I fear I would be too old to stand as general now. I enjoyed those years, the frontier and responsibility that came with leading arms. Now Odenathus requests my presence in Rome and to follow whispers of the Black Stone's location.'

'And you do not decline.'

'I do not object to serving Syria. And Odenathus and I, we may not be as close as we once were, and we may not share the same opinions, but I respect him a great deal. The pressure he is under from Rome increases daily. There was a time when they would listen and send aid, secure and protect our frontier. Now they do nothing. Odenathus struggles to maintain the borderlands from invasion, and each day more slip into Persian control. As such Odenathus has become increasingly paranoid, and I cannot blame him. He does his best by his country, but he will not listen to advice, even from me.'

Julius' face hung with grief. Kind eyes sparkled, heavy with regret.

'If he does not want your opinion, why does he ask to see you?'

Ebony swamped the sky. Cool winds brushed warm sands, and whistled across our fire. Behind us shadows danced wild. I stifled a yawn and pretended to scratch my nose. Sleeping camels, the rustling of nature and our low voices were the only sounds on the plain.

'I have been wondering that myself.'

CHAPTER 5

Samira - 290 AD (Present day)

I PUT DOWN THE parchments my grandfather allowed me to read. I am almost afraid of the secrets they might reveal, and his past I do not know. No mention yet of my father. I long and fear his name written in my grandfather's hand, of finding more than I wish to, and stepping through memories in life he would never share.

Tempted to flick forward, I lay down history upon a table and sit back. Grandfather has already written twice what I have read. A writer, I think. How strange. He writes still, on the other side of the room, hunched large and cumbersome over a desk, calloused, dry hands holding a stylus. I try to remember if I have seen him sit and write before. I have, I think, but when? Some time ago, this I know.

'How far are you now?' I ask.

He looks up, as if I speak another tongue, then seems to understand the question.

'I am not writing Zenobia's tale now,' he replies. 'A letter only.'

'Did you go to Palmyra, with Julius?'

'I did,' he mutters.

'And meet the king of Palmyra?'

'You will have to keep reading if you wish to know.'

I look down at his words and know my tired eyes cannot read more.

'Or you could go to the market, fetch food for the commander's wife. She would appreciate that.'

'When do we leave for home?' I say instead. I am eager to return, to be away from the city my grandfather loves so much, back to the sea and salt air. Here I am surrounded by my father's death, citizens apologising as if it is their fault, so that I no longer step outside.

I cannot bear sorrow, the sadness in the eyes of my grandfather, the sickness I feel when I imagine my father laughing and jesting, their arguments and hot words.

'Do you miss him?' I ask.

'Who?'

'My father.'

My grandfather continues writing for a time, deliberate concentration, avoiding my question. I think he might not answer, until finally he pauses and turns to face me.

'Samira, I am sorry, but I cannot bring him back. He is gone from us now. Gods know I would gladly exchange places with him, and he might return to you, but he would never listen. He was just like his mother. He thought he was right, that his way, the path he chose, could not be wrong. And now he is dead. Of course I miss him, little one. Of course.'

His eyes shine and he rubs his face with his hands and his scars are deeper than ever and I feel my own brow crease with concern.

'You look tired,' I say.

He smiles.

'We will not return home.'

Fear runs through me, the thought of staying here, the place my father died, a sudden dread.

'You cannot consider staying in Palmyra. You said yourself, if you stayed, Rome would know, that they would sack the city. It is why we live in Tripolis! Ever since I was a child, it has been my home. Please, grandfather, I do not wish to stay here.'

I go to him and kneel beside him and place my hands upon

his own. I am thinking of the memories I have, of my father and I racing the tide, of grandfather frowning at my attempt to fish, because it is taboo. Of him and my father returning home, their armour dirty and marked; my cleaning it.

'No, Samira, we will not stay here.'

His large, rough hands turn and he grips my own.

'Then where?'

He lets go my hands and turns back to his writing.

'To Emesa,' he mumbles.

The city of pretenders, I think.

It is a chill morning as we wait inside the city gates, white blanket sky and the taste of rain. Citizens fill the streets to bid farewell to the man who killed the king of the Tanukh. I cannot help but smile at his embarrassment and his incapability to accept, despite his being a general.

A general no more.

I see in his eyes and his expression as he looks out at the city of Palmyra that he does not intend returning here. He is pining for it already, these crumbling walls, the memories he only now begins to share.

I scuff my sandals on the cobbles and wait. Bamdad has yet to arrive and grandfather wishes to bid him, above all, farewell.

'Stay,' the city's commander begs.

He is afraid of the enemies he might face without my grandfather's presence, of a force as great as the Tanukh, who now lie defeated in mass graves a few miles south.

Grandfather shakes his head.

'I leave my men with you for now. They will protect your city.'

'Where do you go?'

'West.'

Slipping and sliding our way toward Emesa. West. What for and what then?

Bamdad pushes his way through the crowds. He wears his

sword and his armour beneath a cloak.

'You are needed here, Bamdad,' Grandfather says.

'And you cannot travel across Syria alone,' he replies. 'And I fancy too well the trip. Stretch my legs. Bit of an adventure, don't you think, *Rubetta*?'

Grandfather scowls at that. He does not like it when Bamdad uses me to change his mind. Then he nods. I am surprised, that he changed his mind without hesitation.

Bamdad says, 'Very well then,' but looks unsure.

A day and a night and I walk along the remains of Emesa's outer walls: stone no higher than my knee. I think of my lessons and of the city's past, giving birth to some of Rome's most influential leaders: Marcus Aurelius Antoninus; Julia Domna ... But it is no longer a large, empowered city, not even a shade of what Palmyra is now.

'Was it never as wealthy as Palmyra?' I ask Bamdad.

'Palymra worshipped trade, Emesa worshipped the gods. Here, the priest kings ruled.' He smirked. 'They hailed the sun god, Elagabal.'

'Grandfather wrote of Elegabal,' I say.

'He wrote?'

'Indeed, he is documenting the fall of Palmyra.'

Bamdad laughs, his teeth shining bright in the sun.

'What tickles you?' I ask, already unable to help but smile with him.

'I never thought Zabdas would relive the past. This is Vaballathus' doing. His death brings change in Zabdas.'

'Do you know the story he tells?'

'I lived it, just as he did. We made Rome tremble.' He stands on the rocky stones and wobbles to demonstrate. 'Bel's fucking balls, they didn't know what to do with us.'

'Bamdad!' my grandfather calls. 'Samira does not need to hear a soldier's tongue.'

'Samira is thirteen. She would have heard a lot worse in our day.'

I look out at the hills and try to picture the buildings that once stood amongst the rocks and envisage how much marble and stone has disappeared, how much has been taken in the years since this city fell, since the days my grandfather walked these sands as young as I?

'Almost twenty-two years have passed since I last entered this city,' Grandfather says. 'I thought I would remember it better, but it has changed too much.'

'Just rocks and dust and emptiness now,' Bamdad replies.

'Julius was a kind man,' I say, thinking back to the story, wondering, secretly, what Bamdad knows that my grandfather has not written down, what I do not yet know. I catch him rolling his eyes, and he winks.

'He was a generous man.'

'Did you know him?' I ask Bamdad.

'No, but I heard Zabdas profess his greatness plenty.'

Grandfather stops walking.

'What is wrong?' I ask.

'The remains of Elagabal's temple. I sought refuge here more than once. This way.'

We climb steps onto a terrace. From here the entire city is mapped out and unkempt. Grass protrudes through wall cavities and disintegrating colonnades. We skirt round and down into the centre of the temple, all lifeless gloom bar the fading footprints of habitation here and there. Grandfather walks across what I think to be a main hall, where feast, prayer and gifts might once have been offered to the gods. No statues, but pedestals upon which they have sat here and there. I feel a flutter inside me, but I am unsure what it is. It is this city, I think, and wonder at its greatness, what it would have been to belong to a place of such splendour. I did not feel it in Palmyra, the palaces, temples, baths taken over, remoulded, re-used. But I feel it here. She echoes with the sounds of a bustling market, dozens of priest-kings, nobility born and a life my grandfather once knew.

He removes his pack, bends down behind a great pedestal. Where Elagabal himself sat? And scratches at the earth with his bare hands.

'Here,' Bamdad says, 'use this.' He offers him a knife and together they dig down, almost four hands deep, and stop.

'What is it? What have you found?'

'This is one of many promises I have sworn over the years. One I intend to keep.'

He pulls from the ground a pouch. He opens it and tips the contents out into his hand.

'Let me see it,' I say, and move closer. A gold ring with a clasp the shape of a hand holding a stone nestles in his palm.

'Here.' He turns the ring to reveal marks on the inner band.

'Are they Egyptian? I cannot read them.'

'It says: "*God of the People, Protector of the East*".'

'Why is it here?'

'Because many years ago I dug this very earth and buried it.'

'Who does it belong to?'

Grandfather smiles, a fond smile, full of warm memories.

'To the person who fought, above all others, to defend this ground, this country, from her enemies.'

'But *who* does it belong to?' I say.

Bamdad sighs.

'To a woman.'

CHAPTER 6

Zabdas - 253 AD

JULIUS AND I RODE hard, no sign of Teymour, the cumbersome cargo miles behind. Julius talked of his family, each detail a little piece of his longing for home.

'One of my daughters looks a little like me, but the other is the image of her mother. She is turning into a great beauty,' he said. 'Both, however, have my wife's spirit.'

'How did you meet her?' I asked.

'In Egypt. I have told you much of my family and little of myself.' He sighed and closed his eyes briefly, swaying with the camel's rhythm. 'I have been many things in my life. I do well, I think, as a merchant, but there is much of me that cannot forget being a soldier.

'I began life here, in Syria. My father was also a merchant, a prosperous man, and he drove trade hard, fulfilling Rome's need for grain, silk and spice. But I saw no excitement, no challenge; no thrill. I was too young to know trade as anything more than the passing of goods across land. I had no desire for it. And so I went where I felt honour lay: I joined Palmyra's army, serving Rome and the Empire.

'I trained each day, from before the sun rose until it set again. I did not feel satisfied until I was the best I could be, I suppose. And I became a stratego, a general, of the Palmyrene army.'

Julius the General. I could scarce understand why he was no

longer the proud soldier he had once been.

'Before I earned the title of stratego, I travelled on campaign into Egypt. We had been ordered there by Rome to man the transport of grain in and out of the country. I fell for a girl so sumptuous in her gold paints and jewels that I could not resist her. She was a temptress, put before me by the gods. I have done many things in my life with a clear head, knowing fully the decisions I have made and why I have made them, but like many, I became love's servant when I met her, and when I think back on that time I do not believe I was fully in control of myself. She listened to me in a way I had not experienced before. I had mentors, of course, but mentors do not listen, they teach, you are there to learn from them, not to express yourself. But Meskenit, she listened in a way that made me want to tell her every thought, every idea, every belief. I became fired by our similarities.

'Where most of our army bedded the women and left them with child, returning home to Syria and their wives or lovers, I did not. I could not leave Meskenit, but nor could I stay in Egypt. I had to return to Syria, to show her the splendour of what we had, that it was a match for the buildings of Egypt, and dared hope she would love the sands of my home as I did.' Julius' face creased. 'She in turn fell for my military bearing and my high rank, and left her life of finery to return with me.

'I made her a vow, though, Zabdas. I promised I would one day bring her luxury to rival that of Egypt. And I never did.'

'But as a general you must have been wealthy.' Julius' clothes, the cargo he had purchased, his command over men, all proved this. 'And you have shown me a great kindness. In what way did you fail her?'

'You, Zabdas, are the one who is too kind.' He shook his head, as if I did not understand. 'Indeed, I have given her much — much more than you have ever known — but nothing compares to the riches she knew in Egypt. She was of the blood; of royal descent. Meskenit lived in palaces larger than you or I can ever dream; bigger, even, than those of Palmyra and Rome. I was forever afraid that she would one day return to Egypt, and I would be faced with the choice of staying in Syria, or going with her ...'

I wanted ask him which he would have done, but thought better of it. I did not think he knew himself. A strange determination rested in his eyes, the set of his mouth, the care with which he chose words.

'I care for Meskenit in ways I believe many husbands and wives do not,' he went on. 'And yet we were punished for our happiness. I fathered three boys and none survive.'

With watery eyes, Julius turned his head and twitched the camel's reins. I felt my throat constrict. Ahead of us, rolling sands showed no sign of life, and still I felt the presence of our destination on warm winds.

The day dragged. We barely slept the night before and every click of his tongue indicated Julius was impatient to reach home. My head lolled once, twice ... Jolted awake I opened my eyes. A blurred dark mass hung on the horizon ahead.

'What is it?'

'Home.'

Town gates opened and the keeper bowed deep. People stopped to lower their heads in acknowledgment of our arrival, and Julius mirrored them. I had never seen anything like it; for a single man to hold such a place in hearts. Firouz held authority, but not this, not *respect*. Here were smiling faces, not cowed and frightened people bowing in fear of retribution. We sailed and rode many miles together as equals, and now I was cast in shadow, unnoticed.

We pushed our way through streets full of gossip and transactions. Ahead, Julius turned to speak. 'It is a small place, Zabdas. Everyone knows everyone,' he explained, as if embarrassed by the attention we had received.

'Have you always lived here?' I asked.

'Ever since I returned from Egypt. It is a good place to watch children grow.'

The buildings thinned and the houses became larger and more ornate, the air free of market noise and the streets uncluttered by people, stalls and animals. We walked through gardens, past fountains, the tinkling noise rhythmic. Olive trees stood tall on marble paved streets, offering fruit. Is this what Palmyra looks like? I wondered.

We came to a house that was as perfect in its form as Julius himself: symmetrical in frontage, each column standing proud and strong. Flowers clung to the walls, breathing life into the stone. Outside, children ran, screeching playfully, chasing, pausing, watching. Up a half dozen steps and between columns, I discovered a handsome garden. Pedestals with busts of men and women and more with plants of deepest green dotted the courtyard, and in the centre water flowed down layers of stone, pooling at the bottom, a mirror to reflect sun and stone, to capture and multiply the effect, and in turn carry it down to troughs either side of the walled oasis.

Julius leant toward me and whispered with a pride I could never claim to have experienced, 'Welcome to my home, Zabdas.'

A tumultuous squeal of excitement and the moment was disrupted as two girls ran to greet Julius. The girls kissed him, then parted and immediately I knew the woman standing before us to be Meskenit. I shrank back, an intruder upon a private moment.

'My love,' he said, 'the gods know I have missed you.'

'And I you.' She kissed him, brief but sure.

Julius urged me forward. 'Meskenit, I have found him. At long last, I have found him, this is Zabdas.'

My aunt, I thought. How alike might we be? But I could not see myself in her ageing features, the high, prominent bones in her face. She regarded me, her expression stern, hard, even, her eyes glowing black. Then she glanced to Julius and I noticed her uncertainty. She let out an audible breath, and moved forward to embrace me.

'I am glad Julius found you, that you are safe with us now. We cannot imagine the troubles you have known.' Then to one of her daughters: 'Hebony, take young Zabdas inside and find him a room in which to sleep.'

The shorter of the two girls took my hand. The elder followed.

Cool air filled the house. Rich tapestries lined every wall; a backdrop for numerous sculptures and statues. Hebony led me through to another room and I was awed. Dim light shrouded the fineries on this side of the house. I looked about me, amazed. Padded couches formed obstacles, neat rows of vases ran the length of the room, and a single golden figure posed atop a wooden pedestal.

Hebony flopped onto one of the silk covered couches. Dark hair tumbled to her waist. She had a gentle face, more Julius than Meskenit.

'You are our cousin, then,' she said. 'We did not think to ever meet you. Where did father find you? Tell us, please ...'

I felt awkward, wondering whether to sit.

'Yemen,' I answered.

Hebony's sister sank down beside her and gestured for me to take a seat opposite. She looked down at my arm, and the slave mark upon it seared.

'You were taken as a slave,' she said, a statement, not a question.

I looked from Hebony to her sister, feeling uncomfortable, not quite knowing what to say, wishing I had Julius beside me. The elder sister's strong nose and her eyes, black, reflective, unreadable, were identical to her mother's. I looked at her a heartbeat longer than I ought to, and her face broke into a smile and I saw Julius in every contour of her expression.

'I am not ashamed,' I said, feeling suddenly that I should defend myself.

Hebony said, 'There is no shame. We are each born to what we are, and you were not born a slave.'

'Untrue, sister,' the elder said. 'We are born in one place and we die in another, and the distance between is of our own design.'

Hebony indulged her sister with a small nod. 'Of course, Zenobia is right.'

'You must be thirsty after your travels,' Zenobia said. 'Let us fetch something for you.'

She leapt from the couch and pulled a silk tassel. Somewhere in the house a bell sounded and shortly afterwards a servant appeared.

'Refreshments,' she said simply and with a smile, and the servant left.

Zenobia took my arm and ran her finger over my slave mark. 'A brutal branding,' she murmured. 'Something my sister may well be able to remedy.'

Hebony leaned forward for a closer look. 'Perhaps. There is a poultice I know that could help fade the mark.'

I looked down at the crude F, the puckered skin, purple and red, and knew a great moment of gratitude, that they had not recoiled from me, or thought me diseased.

The servant returned with a tray of cups and a jug.

'A drink for the young traveller,' Zenobia said.

She lifted the jug, poured and handed me a cup filled to the brim. I accepted and drank as she watched curiously. The wine was satisfying, delicious, and I half wondered if the girl had bewitched it. Her every movement and word appeared surreal, graceful, as though energy shone from her dark skin. She shadowed Hebony without effort. You could have told me particles of the sun danced in the waves of her black hair and at that moment I would have believed no different.

She smiled at me with an unworldly charm.

'Too many years without family,' she said. 'We must make up for that.'

I nodded, incapable of speech. Her confidence commanded respect. Like her mother, like me, she too was descended from Egyptian royalty, and in turn, the gods themselves.

Our day of reunion came to a close. Unable to sleep, overwhelmed by the kindness of Julius and the sincerity of Zenobia's words, I walked through the house and gardens breathing my new life. Julius I knew well, and my cousins I would in time, I was sure.

I heard voices and froze.

'I had no choice but to bring the boy here. Have you seen the marks upon his arm, or known the life he has experienced these past years? He has been a slave, and not to a family like ours. The gods know what he suffered that he has not yet spoken.'

Julius' voice checked me, his words shook me. I thought of the beatings I had received, the favours forced to perform, and demeaning tasks undertaken. There were no secrets kept from Julius, he was too astute for that.

'I agreed you could look for him, ensure his safety,' Meskenit replied, 'but I never agreed to him coming here, to our home.'

'What would you have had me do?' Julius asked. 'Leave him with a family I did not know, find him and abandon him on the same day? Do not be cruel.'

'Cruel? You call me cruel,' she shrieked.

'Hush or he will hear you.'

'How dare you,' she hissed. 'It is you who is cruel, bringing the boy here to torment me, and for what purpose? Because I cannot bear you a son and you wish to ease your own longing? He looks just like them after all. Or do you wish to simply punish me?'

'Punish you?' Julius' voice caught with hurt. 'Why in Bel's name would I want to punish you?'

'Why do you think?'

'It was not your fault, my love. I would not punish you for anything.'

I could barely catch my breath when I heard the words; that I looked just like her sons. Of course I would, I was her nephew, son of her sister, my royal blood tainted by slavery. Did Julius bring me here only to fill his emptiness? I tried to recall if my mother had ever spoken of Meskenit. She must have, but I was too young then, and it was too long ago to remember.

I peered beyond the leaves and I saw them standing together. Julius held his wife and tears trickled down her face as she clung to him.

'I have missed you,' he said. 'I have missed you so very much.'

Plants rustled in the light breeze. Insects clicked and buzzed. Meskenit pulled away from Julius, wiped her wet cheeks with her hand, and her hard, dignified expression was once again in place.

'He cannot stay here, Julius, please understand that. It is too much to bear.'

'He is just a boy. He has no family. He has nothing.'

'Do not make things difficult.'

My heart thumped, my head span. I did not want to leave. To be sent away.

'I do not wish to make anything difficult. When I go to Palmyra to see the king, I will take Zabdas with me, and we can both think of what will be best for him.'

Meskenit said, 'Then it shall not be long. King Odenathus has sent soldiers requesting your attendance every week since you were last home. He grows impatient.'

'I have heard as much.'

Meskenit nodded. 'The boy must go, Julius. I could never wish him ill, but I cannot have him here, each day. The reminder is too great.'

Despite the king's demand, we stayed in the villa for weeks. Time slipped by in a medley of assorted bliss as Julius demonstrated how life ought to be lived.

I rode out hunting with Julius, a day's ride beyond the city. Sometimes Zenobia came too, joyful as she rode the horses hard and the servants struggled to keep up. We ate well and bathed daily. Every morning I woke with renewed appreciation of the simple, elegant house and the contrast with the life I had known. But I lived in fear of Meskenit's disapproval, of offending or upsetting her, and willed constantly for her to change her mind and request I stay. She would watch me when she did not think I noticed, or she would not look me in the eye at all. That and my fear of going to Palmyra, of Julius leaving me there, marred the otherwise peaceful weeks.

No word came from King Odenathus in that time. Julius refused to speak of it as he enjoyed the company of his household. Rumours of disturbances in the east reached us, of Persian warriors raiding Syrian lands, but Julius brushed them aside.

'I am no longer a general of Palmyra; it is not for me to become involved. But I assure you, it is a typical occurrence, nothing to concern ourselves with.'

Hebony and Zenobia proved to be very different from each other in spirit. Hebony was serious, disapproving of her sister's directness, perhaps even a little jealous of Zenobia and Julius' relationship, and of Zenobia's thirst for politics. But Hebony knew so much of the fruits and herbs and spices in the marketplace, the history of the town, that it was wonderful to explore together.

One evening, as the whole family gathered, Zenobia said to me, 'Father says you have great mathematical skills. Will you teach me what you know?'

'You know far more than I do already,' I replied.

Zenobia had received an education only the aristocracy could buy. I knew mathematics, but I had learned my skills as a slave, not from scholars and philosophers.

'Leave him be. You have hounded him since his arrival,'

Meskenit said, careful not to speak my name. She glanced at me, impatient for my departure and reluctant for the time with her husband to come to an end.

Uncomfortable, I said to Zenobia: 'Would you recite for us this evening?'

'Of course,' she replied with a coy smile and narrowed eyes. 'Come, we can choose a verse together from father's library.'

Father's library. I pondered her words as we walked, spoken as if he were both her father and mine. Could I be equal, as she saw me? Julius appeared to think of me so, and my stomach leapt as I thought again of leaving.

Whilst Zenobia picked through scrolls in the library, I amused myself looking at unfamiliar Greek, Latin, Arabic and Egyptian texts. I could read none, but the words, the markings on the papyrus, intrigued.

'You would do well not to take my mother's coldness to heart.'

'She does not want me here.'

'Perhaps that is true, Zabdas, but …'

Julius entered the room.

'Father,' Zenobia said, as if expecting him.

'Have you found what you were looking for?' He took a seat and held out a hand for the scroll Zenobia clutched. 'Ah, Latin.'

The scroll prompted desire. 'Will you tell me of Rome, Julius?'

He laughed. 'You wish to know of the Empire's capital?'

'I have always wondered what it is like.'

'Sit down and I shall tell you a little.'

I crouched on the floor at his feet, Zenobia beside me. Julius was the first man I had known to have visited Rome. I could scarcely imagine the distance travelled, the greatness of the city, the way of life.

'I travelled bearing demands for aid many times before I retired,' Julius began. 'The Persians have ever pressed hard on Syria, and a force from the capital could have put an end to it. But Rome has its own problems to the north and Odenathus holding the frontier was considered sufficient. Indeed, I have seen the wonders of Rome, and they are little more than politics and finery. Their outposts are weakening further each year and they are plagued by inner conflict; emperors raised and quashed every year. Rome conquers and leaves and we must fend for ourselves.'

He spoke with a bitterness I did not understand, shrouded with discontent.

'The Empire is unstable,' Zenobia added.

'And no longer my concern,' Julius replied.

'Do you miss being a stratego?' I asked.

'In part. I do not miss travelling to Rome to request troops from the senate. They sit at the centre of their empire, far from reality, leaving generals to fight on their behalf. It is little wonder the army raises emperors now and not the senate. They do not know what the brink of the Empire consists of, the look and smell. They hail their heroes of war when they have crushed another enemy, but if the troops lose, they are seen as failures. In reality they are just men who did not have enough resources or help, whose critical position was misjudged. I no longer care for the destruction or the appetite for killing a man needs to lead men to war. I do not even miss the rank.'

I thought of the citizens as we entered the city, how they bowed their heads to him. He still held respect, general or no.

'I wish I could continue to make a difference,' he said. 'I thought that by the end of my military career I would have carved an impression of good, yet I have not come close to my hopes.' He paused, his expression calm, proud, if not a little resigned. 'This is all the peace I can hope for now, my family and my home.'

He cupped Zenobia's chin in his hand, smiled. I sensed that his dreams were not over, that he still hoped for more. Zenobia's expression showed understanding of this. His words of pushing Palmyra forward and making a difference were more than just echoes of a past life; they were dreams of the future.

Three weeks after our arrival I woke to the sound of voices. I pulled on my tunic, splashed cool water on my face and rushed through the house. Servants ran back and forth. Whispers relaying. I stepped into Julius' beloved gardens, and there stood Teymour and Julius' men.

Julius greeted them. I watched. Teymour pulled away from Meskenit and gripped Hebony affectionately, as old friends might, no preamble, pause or awkwardness. Yet he caught Zenobia in an uncomfortable embrace. For him, not her. She kissed him as she pulled him close. He blushed, but appeared to enjoy her proximity. Meskenit scowled; her daughter's behaviour flamboyant, her attitude carefree. She glanced at me and turned away. I wanted to say something to Meskenit, to reconcile her attitude, to fix what had been broken, but I could not. She was hostile, and yet I wanted to comfort her; I could sense the pain my presence brought. Should I leave as Julius suggested?

When Teymour and Zenobia parted, I heard him say to Julius: 'Were you not headed straight for Palmyra?'

'I have worked long enough to earn a short rest with my family,' Julius replied, a note of irritation. His tone suggested he resented the king's expectations.

Teymour raised an eyebrow. 'You would make him wait?'

'A little longer.'

'My father is no longer in the army,' Zenobia said. 'Perhaps our king is too well acquainted with Rome's expectations. We are in Syria now.'

Teymour caught my eye. 'How do you like the country?'

'I have seen little beyond this town, but if the rest is as welcoming, I could like it very much.'

A girl of Julius' household wove amongst the men, catching more than one eye. She had hair sun-burned brown, flecked with the colour of sand, and carried a tray bearing water and wine. She neared and offered me the tray, eyes downturned, a sweet hint of lavender emanating. I had thought her servant before, but now I saw then the mark upon her hand.

'You are a slave.'

She inclined her head further still in answer.

I poured myself a cup of wine and returned the jug.

'What is your name?'

She looked up, calm eyes.

'Farva.'

'You enjoy the house of Julius Zabdilas?'

She glanced to Julius, bowed her head once more, and said, 'He is a generous master.'

I was tempted reveal my own mark upon my arm, to prove myself equal to her. But I had been a slave for so long I felt unsure how to think differently, to accept I had no master save myself.

'And tomorrow,' Julius said, loud enough for everyone to hear, 'we shall hunt.'

A cheer erupted, reverberating around the courtyard garden.

'To the hunt!' Teymour said, lifting his cup.

But there would be no hunt. The following morning, soldiers arrived.

Dirt clung to their skin, dusty and pale. Armour covered torsos and swords hung at waists. Their faces were blank and their eyes roved above the heads of the people. Julius, Teymour and a number of other men walked out to the courtyard to greet them.

Zenobia and I followed, hanging back against the house wall, shaded by colonnade.

'What do they want?' I asked her.

'Soldiers have come and gone for weeks. They never state their business, insistent upon seeing my father. Mother sends them away before father knows of their arrival. She is afraid he will go back to war.' She gripped my arm. 'They fight now, Zabdas, in the east. Father has told me of it and I have heard talk in the town also. Some say we are weakening, that Rome ignores us, and the Persians will invade the whole of Syria. You, I think, would not see Syria under Persian rule?'

'Of course not,' I said, easily enough.

'I pray to Selene each day that we should see an end to the Persians,' she continued. 'And Rome.'

I started, not understanding what she meant, why she would want an end to the Empire.

'An end to Rome?'

'They do Syria no favours. We are responsible for our own frontier. My father is a merchant, and the taxes he pays … line the pockets of Romans.'

The soldiers drew up before Julius and his men. One stepped forward, hard face scanning the group.

'I ask Stratego Julius Aurelius Zabdilas to step forward and present himself.'

Julius did not move. The soldier pulled his height. Eventually, Julius stepped forth.

'I am Julius Zabdilas. Who asks for me, gentlemen?'

'The Illustrious Consul our Lord, King Odenathus, sends his greetings. You are to accompany us immediately.'

Julius inclined his head. 'As the king requests,' then to Teymour and his men, 'Come, gentlemen. It is time we returned to Palmyra.'

That night, Farva came to my room.

Pigments exuded a feminine charm and her slight face was marked with much kohl. A smile hovering on rich lips. She wore the fine silks of the Orient. Her body, barely concealed, bore no marks of unkindness save the mark upon her hand. A slight jealously found me, that she might have found a better master than my own in Julius, and reminded myself I was no longer a slave, I was the nephew of a Palmyrene general. But if I was left in Palmyra, what then; a slave once more?

She dropped her silks to the floor, revealing a naked body.

'It is customary to please guests,' she said.

I wanted her. My body wanted her. But there was something about her, the eagerness to come to my rooms and reveal herself to me, that left me uneasy.

'Julius did not send you.'

'He did not need to.'

'I too am a slave,' I said.

'No longer.'

'Why are you here?'

Her smile faltered.

'There are usually rewards for such service.'

For a fleeting moment I imagined her visiting Teymour's room next, and how he might return a favour in exchange for her service and silence beneath Julius' roof.

'Gratitude, but I must decline.'

She scowled, a less appealing expression.

'You like boys?'

'No.

'Then why?'

'Should there be a reason?' I paused, trying to find words to express the unease I felt. Perhaps it was that I did not know whether Julius would sanction this, or it might have been my own nervousness, but I realised finally it was neither. I had once been a slave, and I could not take one now, knowing they offered themselves to me because of their position, and the acts they were expected to perform. I had seen much of that myself, I could take no pleasure in it now.

'You do not like what you see?' she said.

Scooping up her clothes, I pressed them to her nakedness and pushed her back through the door of my room, offering thanks once more, hoping not to offend but at the same time wanting the confrontation at an end, my embarrassment to subside, and the rage I felt of having once been a slave to be pushed back down inside me once more.

We rode at first light, on cool sands and a full stomach. I had slept fitfully; Meskenit, the soldiers, the slave girl Farva, all playing on my mind. As we departed, Meskenit looked me in the eye, an expression of scorn, and wondered had I upset her enough to inspire hatred.

Julius kissed her, swore to be home soon, that we would ride safely. His words brought a jolt of sadness that I may not return with him. He idolised Meskenit. I had seen him watch her walk in solitude, content simply to look. She pulled away from him, eyes down-turned, face hard and unreadable.

And I broke her expression as I walked up to her and said with boyish ignorance, 'It has been a pleasure to spend time with you, aunt. I hope we shall meet again soon.'

Shock erupted on her face. Composure returned followed by a discreet nod of her head. So long without a mother, I realised I was desperate to be liked, and loved, and to live once more.

We left through the gardens I had paced often in my weeks here, taking a last draw of its precious scents. Outside, citizens lined streets, murmured thanks and prayers. Julius touched their bowed heads with his hand, persuading them there was no need to bow for him. They refused, chanted louder and bellowed gratitude.

'Why do they offer thanks?' I asked.

Zenobia said, 'My father's men protect the city.'

'I simply protect my family, whilst bringing the citizens a little peace,' Julius replied.

'Father cannot help himself. He will always be a protector of people. He brought you back to us.'

Her hair tied back, Zenobia had exchanged fine silks for a travelling cloak, but her expression was still beautiful and her mischievous grin bright.

'You know,' she said, pushing through narrow streets, 'I have never been to Palmyra, even though we live so close.'

'You have,' Julius interrupted.

An old woman pushed her way to Julius, and he stopped, took her hands in his for a moment. Then he continued walking.

'When you were very small.'

'You did not tell me this.'

'You were perhaps two or three years of age. Your mother had just given birth to Hebony, and you stayed there whilst I campaigned that year. Your mother loved Palmyra.' I saw it, a flicker of desire. A longing he could not mask. He might have hated aspects of his old life, but his excitement of returning to Palmyra, being a part of the society he once held, was evident.

A strange look lingered on Zenobia's face, unnerving, longing for something that perhaps Palmyra could yield.

'Why do you go?' I asked. 'Because you wish to see the city?'

'Of course. I have been destined to visit.'

'And Hebony, does she not wish to visit Palmyra also?'

'My sister does not wish to explore the world as I would, Zabdas. She is content to marry a merchant of our town. A rich man. She loves him dearly, as does my mother. My father sees that she is happy to accept him as a husband, so he is happy for her.'

'And do you have suitors?'

A look of acknowledgement, a shrug.

'Teymour asked my father twice though he thinks I do not know. Both times father refused him.' Bangles on Zenobia's wrist rattled down her arm as she swept a hand through her hair, brushing dark curls from her eyes.

'Why did Julius refuse? They are friends.'

'It is not meant to be. I am not destined for Teymour. Do you have a woman?'

'None.' I slipped into silence, feeling that she knew more than I about life and husbands and wives, worried that she might mock my own experience or lack of it.

The road east provided too much time to ponder. I was excited to visit Palmyra and see the greatness of a vast city, but equally afraid Julius would leave me there. Could I persuade him to speak again with Meskenit? I thought of my own mother, my father telling of my glossy curls being the same as hers, of the brothers and sisters I could not remember. Were there any? I tried to think back, to remember what had become of my family and the sparse years of childhood I had known. The memories blurred. Had my mother died in childbirth, or did I remember wrongly? Had her laugh been identical to my own? Or had they both died the day I was taken slave?

My subconscious prickled.

I cried out into a night of cloud and no stars, my father's finger to his lips. I cannot remember his voice, but in my dreams I hear his words: 'Be quiet now, they will be gone soon enough.' And then I see the movement of his lips in shadow.

Midday became far cooler. Teymour assured me the weather would be much the same as Yemen, that we moved into colder months. Men who had travelled aboard ship now journeyed with us east. Some had fought under Julius when he was a general. They were *his* men. Loyal men.

Our camels lumbered across the plains, a reminder of the journey north with Julius. They were marvellous beasts of burden, their long, methodical stride lulling me to sleep more than once, so that I would jolt awake. Zenobia sat proud as she swayed with the rhythm, scanning the horizon for the first glimpse of Palmyra.

'We cannot be far,' Teymour grumbled.

'We are almost there,' Julius agreed.

No more than three strides and we had our first sighting of the desert oasis. Sun blinded me. Shielding my eyes, I saw a city sprawled across the plain as Zenobia gasped. Our group halted as the king's men moved to the fore. We continued on and one soldier turned and said, 'You are expected before the sun begins to fall.'

Zenobia stared, her eyes wide and desire obvious. I nudged my camel onward. The walls and distinguishing features became clearer. My concerns dulled, placed now at the back of my mind, thoughts only for this city and what glory might be contained within the walls.

Julius came to my side. 'You are impressed, Zabdas?'

'I can scarce believe the size of it.'

'Palmyra is the richest city in the east; a vital link on the eastern trade route. She profits well enough.'

'Julius ...' I began.

'What troubles you, my son?'

I started. *Son*. He called me his son. A word, I thought. A phrase. But to me it was not. I longed for a father, for the man I had once known and could barely remember. Gods could be cruel, taking and giving at their pleasure, watching men suffer as we entertained them. And now the moment to speak had come, the words had gone, forming deep inside me but not on my tongue.

'When we were in your house, I heard you talking with Meskenit.'

'Go on ...'

'Will I be left in Palmyra?'

Julius took a deep breath and cool breeze caught his hair and he squinted.

'Meskenit was upset, that is all. You look a lot like our sons. She knows not how to order her feelings. Give her time, Zabdas, and she will soften, I promise you.'

'Then you will not leave me?' My muscles relaxed, the sickness I felt subsiding.

'Not now we have found you.'

'And when you return home?'

'You will come with me. Meskenit and I know one another well. She will accept you. Our trip to Palmyra should give her time enough.'

'Do I really look like your sons?'

'A little. They were young when they died, too young to compare. Meskenit believes all boys resemble our children.' Julius paused for a moment. 'You are not a replacement, Zabdas. That is not why I searched for you. I understand how you must feel. Your aunt and I, we owe your mother and father a great debt for not finding you sooner. I went in search of your because you are our family and our blood. And I am in no danger of wanting you here because you remind me of my sons, when you remind me so much of myself.'

Zenobia edged closer and I blinked back tears.

'Have the king's soldiers told you why you have been summoned?' she asked her father.

'They have not.'

'It could be about the Black Stone?' she said. 'If Shapur presses with greater force, Odenathus will seek the true stone more than ever.'

Julius hesitated. Had he thought this since the port in Al'Aqabah, or suspected another motive? He continued to search for an answer and after a while he said, 'Possibly.'

'And what if he wants your men to fight in his war? He has asked you before.'

'That is another possibility. But I do not know, Zenobia.'

'You know I am right,' she retorted.

Julius' face grew stern. 'My men are few compared to those Odenathus already has under his service. I find it unlikely.' An undercurrent of command to a soft voice. 'We should not continue to tire our ears and minds with speculation. What Odenathus wants will become clear when we reach the city.'

CHAPTER 7

Zabdas - 253 AD

BUILDINGS SPARKLED, TOWERING AND elegant, marble paved the streets and fountains threw up streams of water. Locals bustled about their business. Gowns draped women, embroidered and woven with threads of gold and silver, sewn with rare stones, and men wore colourful robes or leather armour, carrying shields and spears and swords. Deep scars marked olive skin, and on their arms warrior bands were found. The raucous noise of the busy city deafened. Not unpleasant, but an exciting, pounding rhythm of a prosperous city. I stepped cautiously, for everywhere seemed so fresh and clean and delicate.

Market traders pulled their wares from the path of elephants, camels and horses. Stalls packed every space. I thought many things a rarity, but found them now in abundance. Silks hung from racks: blues, greens, yellows, reds, golds; every colour in between. Bottles of coloured oils and potions swung from wooden pegs, clinking, swaying, jostling to the city rhythm. Ginger, poppy seeds, aniseed, coriander, cumin, fennel, pulse, cloves, bay leaf, Indian spikenard, costly saffron shouted as being for sale, their names spoken for all to hear, yet I smelled them, rich aromas and head-dulling scents of the east.

Walking, looking, gazing, experiencing this city, a giant place beating with trade, I saw it all. Then we were at the bottom of steps. I looked up. Tall, magnificent marble and stone, a place fit for kings and gods.

'The palace,' Julius murmured.

Calm and cool, I welcomed our retreat from the baking sun. But as the chill settled I felt the urge to return to bustling streets, to experience everything the city offered once more and over again.

'Follow me,' a man of our escort said.

I blinked, eyes adjusting to dim light. Guards lined walls, motionless. Through room and hall we walked, each one richer than the last, every stone polished to reflection. We stopped in a room of low benches, where great tapestries of battles hung upon the walls and three statues of men stood in the centre.

'Wait here,' the soldier said.

We sat down. Time dragged. Teymour breathed deep in annoyance and Julius tapped fingertips on his knee as Zenobia stared down at the floor, expression glum, seemingly unimpressed with our surroundings and without a care for the guards. I closed my eyes, wondered what the king would be like: young, handsome, a great warrior in battle and heroic leader of men, or a rhetoric, philosopher, learned man? He and Julius had once been close, perhaps they were similar. Julius and Teymour were friends, yet I found them different.

Sleep took me and I was awoken by a nudge from Teymour. 'Get up.'

I shuffled to sit up. Two soldiers had returned. Without a note of apology, one said to Julius, 'He will see you now.'

Zenobia raised an eyebrow. What man keeps a friend waiting? I wondered. An ignorant man, with no care for others.

We followed the soldiers into an adjacent room where heavy drapes hung at every source of light; the room cast in impenetrable darkness. Guards lined every wall. A figure sat at the end of a long, pillar-lined space, hidden in shadow. Julius approached ahead of our party and I felt fearful, but he betrayed nothing.

'You come at last,' the figure said. 'I have sent many messengers requesting your attendance.'

Julius did not reply. Beside me, Zenobia stood motionless.

'Have you made any progress in our quest for the Black Stone?'

Julius shook his head. 'None.'

Silence ensued, uncomfortable, deliberate.

The king spoke again, his voice no longer authoritative, but gentle, almost pleading.

'Must we continue to hate one another, Julius?'

Julius sighed and the tension of the room lessened.

'I do not hate you, Odenathus, but I do wonder at your demanding my presence. I do not think it is to discover my progress on the quest for the Black Stone.'

The king shifted on his throne. 'Times have changed. Many things have changed since you were last in these parts; since you were a general in my army. Were we not friends once? Can we now put feelings aside and embrace one another again as brothers?'

Julius regarded him. 'I design to make nothing hard, but ever easy, Odenathus. We were friends, and still are. No bitterness lies in my heart, no ill-feelings. I merely pity your position, as I always have. You lay guilt at my door, Odenathus,' Julius said, flicking his hand. 'You know why I left your court. We could never agree how best to secure Palmyra. You want freedom for your people, but you are too afraid to take it. You persuade yourself that you need Rome, and yet they still have not sent reinforcements requested and required. Have they? The Persian threat in the east is far greater than the Goths in the north, yet you are content to fight alone. To accept Rome's decision.'

Julius breathed deeply. His fiery words echoed long after he had finished.

The king swept a hand through his hair. Perhaps he thought time would quell that which had driven them apart.

'It is not as simple as that, Julius,' Odenathus said, his voice small. 'You know this.'

'No, it is not simple. Kingship can be everything but simple. I do not wish to tell you how to rule, Odenathus. I cannot criticize your efforts, because they have kept your people safe and your city prosperous. But if you want more, if you want all of Syria to be safe, not just Palmyra, if you want to ensure that safety and push the Persians so far back into their own land that you might pause to breathe once again, then you cannot continue like this.'

'My allegiance is to the Empire,' Odenathus replied. 'Syria has been in Roman hands for almost three hundred years. Have there not been enough generations born in that time that we might consider ourselves part of that empire? You are a Roman citizen yourself, Julius, bearing a Roman name.'

'A name, not blood. Not safety or future. We will never be part of the Empire. Remember, I have been to Rome. I looked into the faces of the men under whom you serve and saw how little they cared for our troubles. I watched as they argued amongst themselves. I heard the city whispers that if the worst came, Syria would be sacrificed to the invaders.

'We have talked of this before; so many times before. I am tired of arguing, of debate. Rome rules Syria, taxes us, and yet refuses to send troops enough to defend our frontier. Sever yourself from Rome, form an alliance with the Persians if it is possible. Rome's policies would never allow it whilst we are a part of the Empire. Rome is on the brink of disintegration. You *need* to secure your position.'

Odenathus rose from his seat. 'I am a king, Julius,' he said, stepping down from the dais, 'I do what I need to do. The result of turning our backs on Rome could see us fall at their hands. They would not see us stand independent.'

'If Rome falls, we all fall.'

I saw the king's jaw tremble as the words hit. Julius stood up straight and tall. Two men who must once have been great friends, I thought, for Julius to speak thus to his king, with no restraint or thought to choose his words more tactfully.

Odenathus took a deep breath.

'My family has lived in these lands for centuries, witnessed

Palmyra grow from a village on a caravan route to a city of marble. We prosper. I cannot risk losing all we have achieved. Rome sees fit to grant me reign in the east. I *must* abide by their laws, if only to protect this city.'

'And here we must agree as ever to disagree. You cannot continue fighting the Persians without aid. Your armies were exhausted under my command. Are they any less diminished now?'

The king must see Julius' argument, I thought. How can he not? What blinded him? And yet it was me who was blinded. I could see only Julius' argument, and not the king's. Odenathus stood feet from us now, face flushed with frustration. He was as old as Julius, dressed in Roman garb. But I saw first his battered face, gashes to both arms and legs. He clutched his side, a patch of deep red seeping through his toga. Was this the reason he had not sought Julius, but requested Julius come to Palmyra? Shadowed eyes pleaded with Julius for compassion and understanding. Put our disagreement aside, they begged, and let us address other matters.

Julius' face dropped. Teymour lifted an eyebrow. He knew Julius well, but I think his friendship was somewhat more distant than the connection between these two men. Zenobia smiled ruefully. I felt overwhelmed by the way in which the king of Palmyra and the merchant I had come to know spoke to one another.

'What happened?' Julius asked, in a voice weaker than I had heard before.

Odenathus looked down at his own blood. 'It is nothing. The physician dressed my wounds as you arrived. Please, Julius, I must speak with you.'

We sat in the feasting rooms. Julius contributed to conversation willingly, despite words exchanged, as Odenathus pressed upon us wine and food and hospitality.

'I have been at the frontier for some months,' Odenathus said. 'The Persians still desire command of our lucrative trade route. They thought I was dead.' He patted his injured side and gave a hollow laugh.

It had not occurred to me how close we were to the enemy, how near to soldiers fighting. Seeing the king injured, I tasted war. He appeared a modest man. Yet tales of leadership, honour, justice, war and victories were pulled like silk from a worm, spinning into vivid scenes of heroic deeds. We listened, curious and enthusiastic, as he described the moments he came close to death; of battles fought and won. Only Zenobia and Teymour sat back, mild disinterest betrayed. I was impressed by Odenathus, believed his talk of responsibilities, that he put first his people, second Rome.

But I loved Julius. My judgement grew reserved as he spoke. I was not Syrian, and he was not my king. My loyalty was open to the highest bidder, and the price of that loyalty was love.

Odenathus asked of Julius' family.

'Meskenit is well, and Hebony is to be married.'

'Married? It seems like only a moment ago she was a babe in Meskenit's arms.'

'I think the same all the time,' Julius replied. 'I also have with me Meskenit's nephew. I have been trying to locate his whereabouts in Egypt for some time. Eventually I discovered him in Yemen, of all places. I will not bore you with the tale, but suffice as to say I am pleased to have him with us now. And Zenobia you know.'

Zenobia smiled, warm, inviting, an expression of confidence beyond her years. She placed gentle fingers on her father's shoulder and stood. I noted the king's expression, curious, pleased; perhaps even a little distracted. I burned with a sense of protection. She was young, he an old man of her father's age. I sensed his desire. I thought of his harem, described by Julius' men, thought of him taking her, assigning her a life amongst his women, called upon at his bidding. I hushed my thoughts, knowing Julius would never allow it.

'I remember you better,' Odenathus said, tilting a cup to his lips. 'You were but a few years old when your father left Palmyra.'

'My Lord,' she replied, bowing her head. An amused, quizzical look upon her face.

'You have your mother's extraordinary looks.'

'I believe so,' Julius said.

Zenobia appeared to weigh the king's sincerity.

'Does Herodes thrive?' Julius asked.

'My son is a senator now, and serving in the army,' Odenathus said with pride.

'He follows in his father's footsteps?' Julius replied.

'He does, but he is not yet married, of course.' As Odenathus spoke, he glanced to Zenobia, a flicker in his eyes. 'We have been too occupied with the Persians to discuss the matter. He is on our eastern frontier.'

They fell into silence. Perhaps due to talk of the king's son where Odenathus had none.

'I have missed this,' Odenathus said.

Julius drew a blank expression. 'I am afraid I do not follow.'

'This. Speaking with you. Sitting and drinking and eating together. I remember those times well.'

Julius lowered his eyes. 'I have missed our friendship too, Odenathus. I have missed it greatly.' He looked up. 'But you have yet to tell me why I am here. Was your summons simply to ask after the Stone? A messenger could have carried news. Or to restore our friendship?' Though gravely spoken, Julius' voice quavered.

Silence a moment, heavy and still, as though the king expected Julius to say something more, to reconcile their differences.

Odenathus said, 'I have news from Rome. Emperor Trebonianus is dead, killed by his own troops whilst fighting Goths in the north. Valerian has succeeded him.'

'What of Trebonianus' son?' Julius asked.

Odenathus shook his head. 'Also dead. Aemilianus tried to

usurp, but Valerian somehow managed to seize power.'

'I remember him. He was always an ambitious fool,' Julius replied.

'I believe he continues to be. Something we agree on at last.'

Julius did not respond to the barb, but instead said, 'Then Syria will need you more than ever.'

'Indeed.'

'And you still have no reinforcements?'

Odenathus hesitated.

'No.'

'Then what is it you want from me?'

The king's expression lightened. An instant and he appeared younger by five or ten years or more.

'I respect your companions a great deal, but might we speak a moment alone? There is much we need to discuss.'

'Of course,' Julius said.

Zenobia bent down, kissed her father's cheek and bowed to Odenathus. Teymour nodded and bowed too, and we left the room.

'I must see to the men,' Teymour said, and left us to walk the corridors.

'Do you remember the king? I asked Zenobia.

'A little, perhaps. I was very young when we left and I remember father being always at war.'

We walked the long corridors and great halls, our conversation subdued.

'This palace is full of listening ears,' Zenobia said.

'Who are you?' a crisp voice rang out.

Torchlight fell on a woman. Her lips thin and pursed, mouth lined. White cloth clung to a fragile frame.

'I am Zenobia. I accompany my father.'

'Your father? What business might he have in my halls?'

'His business is with Odenathus.'

The older woman scowled at Zenobia's scant reply. But Zenobia did not move or offer further reply. She simply looked at the woman, waiting for her to respond.

'I am Mina, Queen of Palmyra.'

Queen, I pondered. No mention before of the king's wife. She appeared mature, too old for the man we had a moment before sat with, talked with. I envisaged him with a woman younger than the one before us.

Zenobia bowed her head. 'It is an honour to meet you. I am the daughter of Julius Aurelius Zabdilas, retired stratego of Palmyra.'

Acknowledgment flickered in the queen's eyes and they softened and warmed.

'Zabdilas is here?'

'He is,' Zenobia said.

'In Palmyra?'

'In this very palace.'

'I did not expect to see him here again. It has been a long time since he last walked our halls. And who are you?' she said me.

'My name is Zabdas, nephew to Julius.'

'Julius has no nephew,' the queen said, eyes narrow.

'Nephew by marriage.'

'Meskenit's family,' Mina replied. 'Ah, yes, I see that now.'

'What words are spoken?' Odenathus said behind us.

'I was not aware we had guests,' the queen said, her voice light and pleasant. She looked around us, around Odenathus. 'Julius! How long it has been?' She held out her arms, beckoning him to her.

Julius took her hands without enthusiasm.

'A good many years. You look well, Mina, very well. I am glad to see you so.'

'You flatter as ever, Julius. I am well. Times are hard, of course, with the Persian invasion and southern tribes harassing the borders. I am sure Odenathus will bore you with the details.'

Rome has its problems too. Last month I received correspondence from a Greek I would have had at court, to say he was unwilling to travel because of the nature of the roads. But you know us, Julius. We do as required.'

'Indeed we must.' Julius bowed and kissed her hands.

Mina said to Odenathus, 'I will leave you to entertain your guests. Have your dressings seen to before you retire. They are stained.'

'I shall, mother. Goodnight. Come, Julius, there are other things I would discuss before we see our beds.'

'I shall join you in a moment,' Julius replied. Then to Zenobia: 'Mina is a forceful woman. Tread carefully. Her son may be strong in battle and decisive in the senate hall, but where women are concerned, Odenathus can be quite the fool. And his mother holds much authority here.'

'I shall, father. You know her well?'

'A little. She promoted my friendship with Odenathus many years ago. Until she discovered I did not wholly agree with her opinions.' His eyes were tired. 'I must return to the king. I shall see you both in the morning.'

I found little sleep and morning came seemed a long time coming. Eventually I woke in a bed more luxurious than that of Julius' house to a lingering unhappiness.

Zenobia entered my rooms before the servants and slaves stirred. She sat on the edge of my bed, expression alert.

'Father is not in his room.'

'You think he is still with the king?'

'Possibly. Teymour is not in his room either. I think they have gone to talk.'

I rubbed my eyes, a full night's sleep a long way off.

We found Julius strolling in the palace gardens, brushing the scent of home with his hands, teasing the plants with his breath. Teymour beside him, his hands fierce gestures. Julius nodding absently as Teymour spoke.

He greeted his daughter with open arms and kissed her forehead. 'I trust you and Zabdas have managed to stay out of mischief. How are you liking the palace?'

Zenobia glanced around the gardens as though affirming her opinion. 'It is a place of sorrow. I expected it to be livelier, like the streets outside.'

I looked about me too, realising she was right. Everything seemed gloomier and more lifeless than the city we had seen the day before, as if the whole place mourned.

'I hear you met the king's mother,' Teymour said.

'I do not remember her from my childhood,' Zenobia replied.

'She is reclusive,' Julius said. 'She attempts to gain some say in the kingdom through Odenathus alone, as she did when her husband ruled. She pressed upon her son his first wife. Not a happy marriage for either party, but a successful one. Syria has an heir.'

Teymour said, 'Odenathus' wife once took a knife to him. Told everyone it was an accident.'

'She did?' I said. 'And he did nothing?'

'Some think Odenathus brought about her death,' Teymour replied. 'That she did not die of disease.'

Julius glanced to Teymour. 'An unlikely rumour.'

'What does Odenathus want of you?' Zenobia asked.

Julius looked thoughtful and said nothing. He walked to a bench, behind which water trickled, the only noise in the garden except our conversation. Beyond the palace walls, the city hummed.

'Sit next to me, Zenobia.'

I moved aside, Teymour too, to allow a little privacy. Julius gestured we should stay and listen. I felt nervous, unsure I wanted to hear his next words. His face grave, he took Zenobia's hand in his own and looked down at their joined palms on his lap.

'You know that I have travelled to Rome to request reinforcements on behalf of Odenathus in the past?'

'I do.'

'Since I retired, he has sent others, to plead with each new emperor and various senators. Alas, to no avail. Shapur's force hits the east harder than we have known. We will crumble at any moment, this Odenathus accepts. I had thought we could buy a peace with the Persians, but it seems Odenathus has ventured that route with little result. He holds them for a time, but concern falls to other threats. Syria is under invasion in the south. Do you remember me telling you of the Tanukh?'

Zenobia nodded.

'The Tanukh are a people of plunder, a splinter of Persian descent, taking mercilessly. They have no real homes, no farms, and no trade. They rape lands and move on. I have fought them before when they tried to break north and take control of the Euphrates. We beat them back. Few were killed on either side, and the Tanukh resolved to stay in Ardashir.

'The threat of them taking the river was great. It would have caused endless problems trafficking goods, not to mention their insatiable ambition to move further north, plundering as they went. Soon the Tanukh would have been on our doorstep; the likelihood that they would forge an alliance with the Persians growing stronger with each passing day. The Euphrates would be an ideal base to take every settlement on the river and control traffic.'

Zenobia's face hardened. 'And they are back?'

'They are. Yet to reach the Euphrates but they have taken Al Quatif. They are led by a new king, someone I have come across in the past, many years ago. His name is Jadhima. Supported by a strong family of warriors, which is why Odenathus asks this of me, why I have once again been granted the title of stratego, and why I must go south and purge the Tanukh from these lands. Any disagreement between me and the king no longer matters. I believe Syria will fall if I refuse.'

'When will you go?' Zenobia asked.

She showed no sadness, only acceptance. I felt numb, the

unknown more present, my fate less certain than before.

'A few days at most. I am sorry to leave you, Zenobia. Odena-thus and I have spoken of it much. Provision has been made for you to stay here, in the palace.'

'Of course, father.'

'You must speak to the men,' Teymour said.

'And what of me?' I asked. 'Am I to come with you?'

Teymour laughed. 'You, little one?'

'Then what?' My heart hammered. I would stay in Palmyra, but not without him. What place could I have? A slave once more? No, I could not be that, I could not go back. My arm burned. He had said he would not leave me alone in Palmyra. He gave me his word. I thought of my love for Julius, of his being my father. Could it be true? Was I his son? Is that why Meskenit could not bear the sight of me?

'You know nothing of combat, Zabdas,' Julius said. 'Great dangers face us, and you are young and inexperienced in war. I could not bear your life on my conscience. You have become like a son to me. I need to know that you are safe and no harm will come to you. Do you understand?'

I nodded sullen acceptance.

'Do you understand?' he asked again.

'I do.'

'I will make provision for you also. You can train here in Palmyra with the army, if that is what you want.'

Tears stung my eyes, but I refused to let them fall. I walked away. I knew Julius had no choice. He was right; I had no experi-ence of combat, never held a spear or sword or shield to protect myself. He cared for me like a son, he said so himself. I had just met him, and he was being taken. The Tanukh tribe were the cause, but Odenathus the reason. He commanded Julius to Palmyra, ordered him south. I had detested Firouz, but only now did I know how to truly hate.

Almost at our rooms, Zenobia caught my arm. She clutched her side, breathless from running.

'My father is right, you cannot go.'

I turned from her, not wanting her to see my face.

'Listen to me, Zabdas, I understand your hurt, I feel it myself. If you train in Palmyra's army you will be based here, I think, in the city. With me.'

Her words were hard, sure, but rang soft with promise. I looked into her face, so young, no line or crease marking her smooth complexion. Her long, strong nose almost touched my own. Her eyes checked me, hard with resolution, glistening without tears, almond shaped in an oval face.

'If you want to be with my father, Zabdas, then you must first become a warrior. He has made that provision. Take it and thank him.'

I let her take my hands in her soft fingers, but as she turned my palm in hers, I saw the calluses of a slave, not a soldier.

'Your father said himself, I know nothing of war. I have not held a sword or spear before.'

'Gods, Zabdas, do not mourn this chance for something greater than you ever imagined. You have your freedom, now you have a chance to walk a soldier, your guardian a stratego.' Black eyes bore into my own, fiery hot but barren of sympathy. 'Take it, because you will not be offered twice.'

I sniffed then wished I had not. She was right. My mind played back and forth the possibilities of being a soldier, a career before me, holding a sword and fighting for Julius' beliefs. Apart, but at his side.

Was it possible? Could a slave-boy become a soldier?

'And what of you?' I asked.

'I will do what I have always done, Zabdas. Believe in my father.'

CHAPTER 8

Zabdas - 290 AD (Present day)

I CANNOT STAY IN Emesa, the events of the past reeling, swimming, sliding their way into my mind. My past becomes real once more. The heat of battle and the screams of the fleeing ring in my ears. This place ... I cannot bear it, being back, reliving, retelling, reviving.

Sweat breaks.

'We need to leave,' I say.

Bamdad nods. He knows the time to jest, and this is not it. I am drowning in this city, in past blood spilled and oaths broken.

Samira found food in a local town and now kneels down next to me as Bamdad looks for a ship travelling upriver.

'You became a soldier?' she asks. 'Under Odenathus' command?'

'We were all under Odenathus' command. Julius, Teymour, myself. Perhaps not Zenobia. I am unsure she could be under the command of any man. But we all served Palmyra.'

Samira falls silent, easy and without expectation. She looks at the vessels on the river, squints against the sun. Her dirty face and dirty clothes stab my conscience. What have I taken her from? A simple life but a good one, a life like the one I would have known in Egypt before slavery. Where to now? I have thought of little else.

'Could Zenobia truly speak so many languages?'

'She spoke more. She was incredibly accomplished. Julius bought her an education, and she did not rally against it. She devoured anything that would broaden her knowledge.'

'What of Teymour?'

'What of him?'

'He asked Julius for her hand in marriage. Did they marry?'

I feel weary. Exhaustion took me as I held the ring that once belonged to Zenobia. Now it sits against my breast, next to a heart that still beats, that has not quite finished with this life.

'You ask many questions.'

'And you explain little of what you tell me!' She stares up at me, cheeky, challenging, everything my granddaughter could be.

I sigh and look across at the dock. No sign of Bamdad.

'No, they never married.'

Samira's shoulders slump.

Bamdad appears.

'I have a boat. Be ready to wade! Oh, and the captain says Samira will suffice as payment. I did not think you would mind, Rubetta.'

He grins at her, and she laughs at him. I wonder why he thinks his humour entertaining, for it has been a while since I thought as much. But Samira laughs, encourages. She understands him, and I try to remember if I once did. When I was young, did he humour me?

A man comes in a rowing boat to take us out to a larger vessel. I take Samira's elbow, help her to her feet. We tie our sandals to our waists and wade out, the precious pages of my life, of Zenobia, in my pack.

We travel the short distance and I glance across the river to steep mountains on the opposite bank. Once aboard, I look back. One last look at Emesa. Afternoon sun hovers on ruins, long shadows cast as the wind pulls our boat gently north and the city drifts further away. Darkness creeps in and I feel sadness. The last time I left the buildings were still whole, the streets bustled with people, and temples stood proud.

A memory always there, hidden in the years.

Samira is beautiful. Even with the dowdy clothes and lack of thick kohl around her eyes, she appears to me other-worldly. Perfectly proportioned features, a figure already shapely, and a sureness gained since I last saw her at our own Tripolis. Startling given her age, just thirteen years; my age when I first met Julius.

I doubt I look much of a warrior huddled in the boat, but I bear scars and carry muscle accumulated from years of training and fighting and living hard on scraps from the land as my warrior band faced enemies beyond the cities and settlements.

We travel for hours, sleeping through the night. In the morning, other ships come into sight. There are many on the river, yet ours seems different in ways I cannot fathom.

It is the captain's glance in passing; of greed in yellow-tinged eyes.

I rove the deck. Samira sleeps beside me. I slide a hand beneath my cloak for the handle of my dagger as watching eyes hover. Every impulse tells me to fight, to face the crew, but I dare not.

'You have a twitch?' Bamdad hisses.

'Where did you find this ship? Persia?'

'Fuck you, Zabdas.'

'We are not safe.'

Bamdad looks about him, keen eyes seeing clearer than before.

'They watch you,' he says.

'Safe passage but for me? Fucking wonderful. We are on a ship and it seems there is a price on my head.'

'Higher price on mine, I wager.'

'Unlikely,' I say.

Samira stirs. Eyes still closed, she says, 'I wondered how a slave became a warrior.'

'We are driven by our desires, not always our ability.'

I watch men move across the deck. Feel Bamdad reach for his own blade.

'Odenathus' mother was forceful. It surprises me he would give her so much rein in the palace.'

'Julius knew when he warned Zenobia what lengths Mina would go to achieve her desires. She would shriek at Odenathus, loud and publicly. When not shouting, she whispered in his ear attempting to influence. And if he refused her, she claimed it the will of the gods and sent for a priest of Emesa to persuade him. But the people loved him. He held their frontier for years, brought riches to the city, rode out to battle ahead of his army.'

'They loved him, even though he listened to her?'

'Mina had a fiery temper and iron will, but her persuasions were mostly well informed. I hated Odenathus for sending Julius south, away from Palmyra, but his people needed a protector, and he gave them what he could.'

'What are we to do?' Bamdad asks. 'Sit here recounting the past, or address the present?'

'What is it?' Samira says.

'We are not amongst friends,' I say.

Samira falls silent. The touch of my sword gives me comfort. The feel, the weight of it. It is a part of me.

Seven men encircle us, knives clutched in hands. They hesitate, and I see their fear. Men commanded to face us, they do not enjoy this role. I know then I have more skill with a sword or knife, that Bamdad has more still. Yet they come.

I draw my sword, the first ring of iron on iron ripples across the deck. My cloak falls and I am armour and sword and dagger and shield. A warrior now, not a traveller. I growl, and the men growl back and Bamdad laughs a wicked, insane laugh that would unnerve the gods if they were sleeping. But they are not. I know they are not. They watch us as we amuse them, laughing and cackling at our misfortune. Then the men before us smile and I glance to Samira, a knife at her neck, and Vaballathus obscures my vision. Vaballathus covered in blood on the dusty ground, bleeding out on the sands of home, no breath, no life, no tomorrow.

My blade clatters on the deck.

Samira whimpers.

A punch to my stomach, I keel in pain. Retch. Feel a blow to my face and my nose breaks, mouth filling with blood. I sink to my knees, take blow after blow, kick after kick.

'Grandfather,' Samira whimpers.

Gods' strength, Bamdad, I think, what a mess we are in.

Darkness rolls before my eyes and a man approaches, tall, wavering in and out of focus. The captain.

'I thought myself the luckiest of men when I saw this beauty board my boat.' He strokes Samira's cheek, hand moving down her neck, her shoulder, her breast. I am fire and heat and hatred but I can do nothing. Tears well in Samira's defiant eyes, yet she does not flinch or speak. 'You will be enjoyed and you will fetch me a high price. But you,' he says, turning to me, 'are the true prize.'

I spit blood onto the deck. 'I am yours. Do as you will. Let her be and I will not fight you.'

'Fight me?' He laughs. 'You cannot fight. You cannot move, my friend.'

'She is untouched. She will fetch a higher price if you leave her so.'

'I have no need of the coin she could make. I have you. Do you think the Tanukh have no friends? Your defeat over Jadhima is well-known, and now there is a price on your head that will buy me five more boats.'

He pulls Samira toward him.

'She could have had a man in her already.'

A shout from the sailor at the wheel and the captain says, 'Take them down.'

Samira disappears into the belly of the boat. I follow, a knife at my back, stumbling down steps and falling to the floor. Wood thumps. Blackness. I can see nothing. Where is Bamdad? Rotting souls fill my nostrils. Samira finds my hand and grips.

'Bamdad?'

A groan.

'Are you there?'

'I am, my friend. Rubetta, is she with us?'

'Here,' she replies.

My eyes adjust. Figures grow out of the darkness. Dozens of people crammed into the small hold down in the bowels of the ship, filthy and covered in piss and shit. A fucking way to keep slaves, I think, how many will survive to reach their destination? Children shriek and whimper. Pleading faces look to me, as if I can somehow save them.

'Do we travel downriver or upriver now? I say to Bamdad.

'Gods know,' he replies. 'I am sorry, my friend, I did not know.'

'The price is on my head alone.'

'Of course. The rest of us are not worth a shit.'

I laugh at that, though I know not why. Stuck in a hold in chains and still he can joke.

For hours we sit in gloom. Breath comes shallow and painful from the blows I have taken and the pain in my ribs, perhaps broken but I hope not. I have known worse.

Samira shuffles closer and looks at my wounds.

'Bruised only,' I say.

She takes a corner of her tunic and wipes the blood from my face. Does the same for Bamdad.

'How do you fare?' I ask him.

'Not as badly as you,' he says. 'I heard them say the Tanukh want you alive. They must want to make polite conversation over a game of dice.'

'I will lose if they do.'

'You always lose,' he says. 'It is why I have more money than you.'

'Hardly.'

'You think we can buy our way out?' he asks.

'Perhaps.' I am trying to think, to form a plan, gauge our options, but the pain makes it difficult and we have Samira with us. I brought her for a promise made long ago and now wish I had not. This is my choice, my decision. She is with me because I wanted this.

'Not much fun, though, is it, buying your way out?' Bamdad says.

'Never is,' I reply with a weak smile.

'Tell me of Teymour,' Samira asks. She is diverting me. Does she think my injuries worse than they are?

'You were reading this tale,' I say. 'It was not meant to be spoken.'

'Teymour was an arse,' Bamdad interjects.

'Helpful, Bamdad. He was a ruthless man, loyal to Julius. His heart, I learned, belonged only to Zenobia. But they could never be together, even if Zenobia had shared his affections. Teymour was a soldier, Zenobia a descendant of Cleopatra. She would rise higher than him, and she would see him fall.'

'That is an elegant phrasing, Zabdas, I applaud you,' Bamdad says, chuckling.

I winced with pain. I think of the pack taken, the pages of my tale wrapped inside, the captain reading them, the words of a life I have begun to divulge. Perhaps it is better to keep stories to the spoken word; never enshrined, always living through the repetition, the changes, embellishments and interpretation of others.

CHAPTER 9

Zabdas - 256 AD

I SLIPPED IN THE dust, sword a finger's breadth from my face, I rolled and pulled myself up. I struck again, my sword slippery in hot hands, lost in a world of fire and rage and competition. My arm burned from the weapon's weight. I pushed the pain to the back of my mind. Sweat poured down my face and I gasped for breath, desperate to master anger and frustration. I sliced forward and my opponent blocked, again and again, although I sensed him tiring with each stroke. The ground reflected bright white as I cut. My sight adjusted and I ducked. Pulled up, parried and slashed tirelessly, yet nothing gave. I found no relief, only weakness.

Each morning I woke and followed the regime of all soldiers. I trained. I worked each muscle in my body, stretched every organ and limb, became the best I could be. And never did it feel enough. In battle the weak fall, and I was afraid that would be me.

I heard men say not caring whether you live or die makes a man immortal; I said it made a man careless. But I had yet to see battle. In battle, I wondered, what would I see? How carefree would I become, how lost? I had never killed a man. I trained each day, but I was not sent to the frontier as other men were. I saw the rising sun on my sword in a training yard.

I thrust and cut again. The fight would not last. My opponent's strokes were sluggish. I finished with a series of strong, quick lunges. Karim fell back hard on the dusty ground.

A voice. For a heartbeat my concentration evaporated. I glanced over my shoulder, then a heartbeat more and I found myself in the dirt, forearm shading my eyes from the sun, groaning.

'Not often I see you on your back,' Karim said. He offered a hand and I took it and pulled myself from the ground. 'A win for me!' He beamed. A little older, he was taller and stronger, but I was quicker, and usually won.

I grunted, annoyed. Realised I had shown it and groaned again.

Two years since Julius' departure. It felt as raw as yesterday.

I trained as he arranged for me, focussing on becoming a soldier and one day soon joining him in the south. Or hoping for his return. What I would have given for that, to see him again in Palmyra, enjoying the gardens of the palace or his home. To have him read to me.

I brushed myself down as a king's guard approached.

'What does he want?' Karim asked.

'I requested a transfer to Al Quatif. So I expect he will inform me I am on night-watch.'

'Again?'

I shrugged. Karim did not understand. He would say nothing and stay from the frontier as long as possible, but I wanted to be with Julius, to fight for what he fought for and to have a place, an occupation.

'Zabdas.' The soldier gave me a curt nod. 'Commander Worod requests you on night-watch. You are to attend the main wall, east gate, before the sun sets.'

He turned and walked away. No more needed saying. I had performed the very same duty for the past six weeks.

'Again? I do not understand you, brother. It will not change anything.'

'I want to fight with Julius.'

'With Julius! All you ever talk of is Julius. Is it worth the time you spend on the wall when you should be in your bed? You can barely stand, brother, you are so tired.'

'Leave it be, Karim. I will ask until I am transferred or Julius returns.'

'Dolt.'

'Perhaps.'

'Petition the king. You are cousin of Zenobia, can she not persuade him?'

'I already petition the king directly and still he will not let me go.'

I picked up my boots and tunic.

'I must go.'

My requests were numerous. Each time the king ignored me, each time I was ordered by Commander Worod to take night-watch. Two years pushing myself to the brink of physical capability, taunts by my superiors, the slave mark burning upon my arm in the hot sun. I was a solider now, despite the mark of what I had been in a past life, yet I alone of my brothers that season had not been despatched to the frontier.

The men followed paths. Some dictated by birth, others seeking fortune and position. Many did what was expected, and others because they knew no other way. Meskenit followed the path of love, and accepted her husband's decision to travel south, and Teymour with him. And I understood both. But I could not understand Julius, and his choice of loyalty to country and king. He had despised Odenathus' decision to stay under Roman rule, yet now he fought for him, for Rome and for the greater good. And I hated myself for not feeling the same, not understanding what it was to believe in something greater than oneself. Instead I was obsessed by the thought of having a father again, and I could not hold back. I wanted Julius to be proud, for me to be his equal. Perhaps it was a test, to be given my greatest desire and have it ripped from me.

My veins ran hot. I struggled constantly to control my fear and sadness. But what burned most was guilt. Zenobia had been in the palace as I trained. Any distress she might have felt eluded me as I submerged in self-pity. She showed no emotion, but she must have felt something, and I should have seen it.

Julius was *her* father, not mine.

I stood on the city wall, looked out, wished my punishment more active so that I might stay awake. Cleaning the bathhouse? Perhaps not. Linen cloths clung to my face, protection from fine black sand and grit. I could barely see nor hear as wind whistled in my ears and stung my eyes. I had stood in the same position for hours and my legs had grown numb and I needed to piss. I walked to my left, to my right. The wall dropped the depth of several men. At my back, a ladder tormented. I had only to step down the rungs and I could go into the warmth, to drink and gamble the last of the night as my fellow soldiers did. No. I must stay; to disobey orders would be punishable by death.

Beside me, a torch flickered. Deep in my pocket, flint provided the means to re-light should the flames go out. I wished it were for warmth or even for light. To my right, a large beacon of dried timber, cotton and foliage lay dormant; my task to light the beacon and warn our soldiers should anyone approach the city. A pointless task. One that saw a man cold and hungry and wishing for his bed.

Nothing stirred. Nothing but wind-whipped sands. Tiredness crept upon me. My eyes closed as I fought to remain alert. Stiff, cold fingers clutched a spear without thinking. Weeks of the same routine took their toll. During the day we performed our drills and duties as usual, but most were expected to stand night watch a day or two, before recouping lost sleep.

I thought I heard my name as the wind whispered songs of

long ago. Night spoke. I shook my head, eyes conjuring shapes on a black horizon.

'Zabdas?'

Again, my name. Tired ears deceived me.

'Zabdas?'

Clear and strong. I tried to turn, to look around and see who called, but exhaustion overwhelmed and I could do nothing but stare ahead.

'Zabdas, is that you?'

The wind whistled more than my name. With great effort I summoned the energy to turn and look down the ladder. Zenobia ascended.

Awake, fully awake. I turned my back and looked out into the darkness once more. I did not wish to see her, to look upon her face and be reminded of Julius, of what I had lost, of what had been the past two years. To know she could have persuaded Odenathus to send me south but chose not to.

'Zabdas,' she shouted, 'I have sent messages. You did not return them. Why not? It has been weeks since I saw you last.'

The feeble torch provided little light, but it was enough. I turned to find her face creased with annoyance.

'I am kept here by Commander Worod, despite petitioning the king to be despatched south to aid your father. Why is that?'

'If Odenathus says you are not to go, then you should cease petitioning him. Perhaps your commanders do not think you ready.' She spoke with little compassion. I bit my tongue to avoid retort.

'Two years sweating on the training grounds in order to become a soldier, Zenobia. I took every opportunity given to become more than a slave, more than when your father found me. All so I could go south to be with him. What else can I do?'

'It is why I am here.'

My stomach lurched. 'You have word from him?'

'I have received ...' she began, but a rumbling disturbed the winds and we both turned to the blackness beyond the walls.

Nothing but blackness.

I picked up the torch and touched flame to dry tinder. The rumble turned to a rhythmic beat that soon filled the night. Horses. How many I could not tell. Yellow flames gripped and writhed and lit the night. Surprise and curiosity held me there, watching, waiting to see who approached. Never once in my nights on the wall had I known the gates open after dark.

The horizon began to move, shimmering like water.

The fire burned, brighter and lighter. Men shouted from below. Soon more fires raged along the walls. A horn sounded within the city as firelight flooded the night.

'Behind the wall,' a rough voice yelled.

Worod, the city commander waved us down. If enemy approached they would see us, glowing watchmen in our own firelight.

Worod ran the length of the wall toward the gates, shouting the command over and over. We all backed down behind the safety of the stone. Zenobia peered over, waiting for the first recognition of those approaching.

'Friend or foe?' she said.

'We will find out soon enough. We are prepared for any attack.'

My words were true, we were ever prepared for attack, but still I felt my stomach clench at the unknown.

Behind us, behind Zenobia and the long line of soldiers atop the wall, a din sounded. A rustle of movement as the city woke.

Citizens came out of their homes half-dressed, bleary-eyed and confused.

'The beacons!' they shouted. 'They are alight!'

Soldiers ordered people back to their beds, away from the wall, to keep silence. Few obeyed. They waited as we waited, blankets clung to shoulders, children crying or dancing or chasing, not realising the danger they may be in.

Darkness intensified the wind and pounding hooves. Daylight would have lessened fear, I thought, and we might have seen who approached. The city behind us would have been alive with trade, and I would not have been stood at the wall to witness the approach. I could not see their distance. I could see no standards, no colours.

The beacons roared and each one lit brought more people running. Archers swarmed into position. Everything precise; every move executed perfectly. So much happened, but only a few moments passed and we were ready.

With my spear in hand and a sword at my waist, I waited, Zenobia beside me. I felt frustration, stuck in Palmyra when she could have changed this. She could have done something. I had fallen in love with the city when first I saw it, but now … now I wanted only to leave, to be in the south. Two years in the palace, she could have spoken with the king, changed his mind. Tears pricked. The wind, I thought, but I knew it was not. The years and training had tired me, matured me. I was no longer a boy and I had my freedom, but with it I could do little. Was that Zenobia's fault? Perhaps not, she too was bound to Palmyra, away from her father and her mother. With an apology on my tongue I looked for her. A few feet away she stood talking with Odenathus.

He wore a tunic tied with a belt, hair dishevelled, and a sword hanging limp at his side. His injuries had faded in the two years since I first met him, and he had been contemplating his return to the frontier. It would be soon, I hoped.

Zenobia returned to me as Odenathus pushed through the crowds.

'He will not say,' she said, 'but it is clear he has no knowledge of who approaches.'

Time had seen Zenobia grow tall and slender, thick hair framing her face in lustrous waves of raven black. Since her father's departure we had spent little time in one another's company, and each time we did she seemed older, more mature, more determined.

Commands sounded and the archers touched arrows to their

bows. Despite her cloak Zenobia shivered. More commands and a ripple of talk.

The men approaching were Bedouin warriors. Our warriors.

As the gates opened and the crowd swarmed, Zenobia and I pushed through. I could see Odenathus framed in the gateway. He wore no armour, no rich cloths, yet still he looked like a king. He stood with authority and I imagined myself bowing to the man I disliked. Worod hovered in his shadow, fully dressed and adorned with jewels.

A small unit of soldiers, six in all, slowed. Their heads lolled, their horses bloodied. Crimson swords and spears hung at their sides. Faint smiles crossed their faces at the recognition of home, but they were shadowed with what had passed.

One man spurred his horse forward, slid with difficulty from the saddle and stumbled forward to embrace the king. They parted and the city fell silent.

Odenathus clutched the man with rough hands.

'Herodes!'

Defiant eyes looked up into the king's.

'Father.'

Odenathus patted his son's shoulders and beckoned the soldiers to follow him. Slaves intercepted horses.

They had travelled as darkness fell. The king must have known they brought ill news; the expressions upon their faces, what else could it be? Worod, small compared to the other two men, put a hand on the king's shoulder and whispered. A moment later he dismissed the night-watch and installed fresh men.

Odenathus walked back through the city, the six warriors around him, crowds following behind. Zenobia and I joined them. Gossip filtered through the streets. What was the fate of husbands and fathers and brothers? Who lived and who did not? Were the enemy close? Prayers were cried out to the gods.

At the palace steps the king climbed to the top and turned to his people. His face tired yet hardened, he said, 'Citizens of Palmyra, people of Tadmor. Our warriors return from our frontier. From bloodshed, terror and death. They have seen the Persians, have faced them in battle, smelled the breath of the enemy, and stood and fought for your homes, your families, your trade and your wealth. They protect mighty Rome from eastern enemies. They have our respect and honour. I ask that you leave them in peace this night. They have travelled far, and need rest.' Odenathus spoke with a force that forbade disobedience. The atmosphere tensed. The crowd listened.

Next to Odenathus, Herodes' head hung with exhaustion, face pale, muscular form limp, dirt and blood and the remnants of battle upon him.

'Go back to your homes,' Odenathus continued. 'The defenders of our city shall have rest and recuperation. Tomorrow, I shall speak with them.'

He scanned the mass of faces, his gaze a personal reassurance. Then he retired.

Zenobia clutched my arm and pulled me up the steps behind them.

'What are you doing?' I asked.

'I wish to know what is happening.'

'What do you mean?'

She grazed me a look of exasperation.

'I have not been open with you, Zabdas. You moved out of the palace.'

She did not sound hurt, her voice betrayed nothing, yet I sensed her disappointment. I had rooms in the palace beside Zenobia's, but I had chosen to move to the barracks so that I might forget my frustrations at staying in Palmyra and instead immerse myself in the army.

'My father did not simply go to war at the king's bidding as you believe. He made a bargain with Odenathus: if he agreed to become a general once more, and lead men to the Euphrates, I would have my father's voice on the Palmyrene council. I was to put forth my father's opinion on all matters, sit in their meetings, oversee documents sent to Rome, listen to the tax levies on grain, spice and silk …'

'Apologies, Zenobia, I did not know.'

'Apologies are not necessary, Zabdas, but I have missed your company. We are here in Palmyra together, are we not? And you are my cousin, I would have your support.'

I thought back on Julius' departure. He had requested I meet with him before he left. Perhaps he would have explained, but I was too hurt to see him, too afraid of saying goodbye.

'The bargain is a delicate one,' she said. 'Odenathus never wholly agreed. A woman on the council would not be well received by other councillors, Herodes in particular. My father sacrificed his retirement so that his dream might ignite, that I could have some weight in this city and make a difference.'

I could see Odenathus, Worod and the soldiers up ahead.

'The king said no one would be questioned until the morning.'

'Odenathus' army returns in tatters. He will not wait.'

She looked to the ceiling and rubbed her forehead.

I glanced back, through the open doors of the palace, to the street and the crowds beginning to disperse.

We filed into a dark room as slaves lit lamps and men took seats. Zenobia remained standing.

Odenathus looked at her long and hard before his eyes flickered to the men in the room.

'For the benefit of those who have been at the frontier, I introduce Zenobia, daughter of General Zabdilas, and Zabdas, nephew of the same. Now, let us speak of the matter in hand. Herodes?'

Heads turned to Odenathus' son. He reclined in a chair, giant-like. A crooked nose sat upon a square face, much as his father's but for the lack of scars and arrogant squint of his eyes.

Herodes regarded Zenobia and me, wondering perhaps if he ought to speak in front of us, licking his lips as if the very taste of our presence offended.

Servants came with bowls of water and cloths and set them down at the side of the room. Herodes stood up, walked over to one, washed his face and hands, and turned back to the room.

'The daughter of General Zabdilas?' Herodes mused. 'A legendary man.'

Zenobia's expression remained measured.

'Sit down, Herodes,' Odenathus commanded, anger lacing his words.

Herodes sat on the edge of his seat. He paused. 'The Persians have taken Nisibis.'

The five other soldiers hung their heads.

'How did this happen?' Odenathus demanded.

'We could do nothing, Father.'

'Nothing?' Odenathus shouted. 'Nothing? How in the name of Bel could you do nothing? There is *everything* you could have done. Do you know what will happen if the Persians reach Antioch? They will have our path blocked. No more trade with Rome, no more trade at all. They will take everything. This palace,' he said, moving towards his son, 'will be nothing more than an empty shell. Gods damn you, Herodes, I trusted you to keep the frontier safe whilst I was gone.'

'You should have been back months ago,' Herodes retorted. 'You claimed yourself well enough.'

'A man cannot be everywhere at once, Herodes.'

'The palace had greater need?'

Odenathus ignored the jibe. 'How many men are left in Carrhae?'

Herodes opened his mouth, closed it again. The other soldiers remained silent.

'How many?' Odenathus shouted.

'A few survived,' Herodes muttered.

The king pulled a hand through his beard. He looked to the floor, to the ceiling, and closed his eyes.

'My Lord—' Worod said.

The king raised a hand. He opened his eyes and I thought I saw tears. He bent over his son, their faces almost touching.

'It was a mistake to leave you in command of the army in

Carrhae.' Any early pride the king had shown evaporated. Herodes looked to argue. 'They were my men. Soldiers I have spent my life fighting beside. Men I would call friends. How many must die before you become a leader? Twenty thousand, fifty, a hundred?' A loud crack sounded. A gasp from Herodes followed.

'Get out,' Odenathus said to him. 'I cannot look upon you. All of you, get out.'

Herodes hurried from the room. Four of the soldiers followed. Only one remained.

Beard and face were thick with blood, bulging arms bore marks old and new, and he wore more remnants of battle than the others, and beneath them his mouth set in a grim line.

Odenathus said, 'I have known you many years, Zabbai, my friend, and I trust you more than I trust Herodes. Can I trust you now to tell me the truth? Tell me how my son lost the city of Nisibis.'

'Your son fought bravely, my Lord ...' he said in a husky voice.

'And yet?'

'He made grave errors. He ordered all troops north of the city. We heard rumours from the nomads that the Persians were moving to take Nisibis. He called men to join him from Samosata, Carrhae, Edessa, and Singara, where I was stationed.

'We warned him of the dangers if he consolidated the troops, but he insisted upon it. Once we arrived at the city, he gave orders to move a few miles north. If we had stayed behind the walls, we might have remained intact, but we would also have lost the surrounding land. He moved the army to the tip of the river, but we were not strong enough to hold the Persian force. Shapur himself led them. I have never seen an army so large. We were pushed back into the crook where the river splits, and it was there we were annihilated.' He rubbed his face with both hands and gave a small groan. 'I left reserves in Singara. Some managed to flee there. Then we rode for Palmyra to bring you the news. The Persians now number more than a hundred thousand.'

A hundred thousand.

Odenathus closed his eyes. 'A force larger than we have known.'

'What of the citizens?' Zenobia asked.

'I do not know,' Zabbai replied, shaking his head. 'The city was taken, that I know.'

'You could have sought refuge within the city, protected it,' Worod said.

Zabbai's mouth thinned. 'Once pushed back as far as the city, we were few and the enemy many. The citizens locked the gates. We could not retreat inside.'

Odenathus shook his head. 'They turned against you, their own countrymen? How could they?'

'Do we despatch men north?' Worod asked.

'There is little choice,' Odenathus replied. 'I will go myself. And we must warn Rome; they need to know of the Persian position. I pray they now send aid.'

'You do not have enough men to combat so many,' Zenobia said, her voice concerned.

'You know little of war, girl,' Worod replied.

'Perhaps you can enlighten me as to our position, Commander,' she replied. 'Do we have enough?'

His silence was reply enough.

'Call on the tribes,' I said. 'There must be hundreds in Syria. Call upon them for aid.'

'You are right, Zabdas,' Zenobia said, touching my arm. 'We must call upon our fellow tribes. We are all under threat, they must see this. They will suffer too at the hands of the Persians if we cannot push them back.'

'Rome will not listen,' Worod replied.

'We are in crisis, my friend,' Odenathus said. 'They will have to come or their eastern frontier will fall. When they do, together we shall finally crush the Sassanians.'

'They will not,' Worod said. 'You waste your time. They have not sent an army before, what makes you think they will now?'

'I have confidence.'

'But *how* will you persuade them?' Worod persisted.

'In the past I have sent men loyal and trusted to me. They have been insufficient to persuade Rome. But I have come to trust others.' Odenathus turned to Zenobia.

I could not hide my shock.

'You go to Rome?'

She placed her hand on my arm.

'I will. Odenathus and I have discussed it of late. Rome needs to be informed of the Persian position.'

'Your father left you safely in Palmyra,' I said, my voice quiet, weak, scarcely believing her words. 'I do not think he imagined you going on errands to Rome.'

'I will leave tomorrow.'

'Zabdas, you are to go with her,' Odenathus said. 'You will form her personal guard. You will travel more quickly without slaves and servants, and I know Julius would approve of your accompanying her.'

Odenathus' expression turned thoughtful.

'Zabbai, now that you are home, I would have you go too.'

Zabbai nodded.

I could not think. Zenobia, Julius; I could not keep them both safe thousands of miles apart. How could I embrace this new turn, this other path, and journey with Zenobia, forgetting the south? I could not leave her, and the king gave little choice.

'I will go,' I confirmed.

'Keep her safe,' Odenathus said.

Zenobia stood tall and proud, despite her youth, flickering with energy, no need of protection.

'Of course,' I replied.

'It seems we have our tasks set out,' the king said. 'Worod, Zabbai, in the morning we will begin uniting the tribes of Syria.'

His words told of an easy feat. I saw a huge undertaking. Each tribe needed to be found, persuaded, bribed or coerced into joining the warriors of Palmyra and the Roman legions already stationed in the region in a bid to scourge the land of Persians. My suggestion, but I did not now imagine it could be achieved.

Odenathus clapped my shoulder and smiled grimly, a familiarity I found uncomfortable.

'Everything will fall into place,' he said.

He glanced at Worod and Zabbai, but they posed no objection to his plans. He kissed Zenobia's forehead.

'You have my gratitude.'

She looked up at him, confirmation of the evening's events on her face, the exchange one perhaps of friendship; the gratitude of a man to the daughter of a friend. But I knew the meaning of the look, the kiss. Zenobia had secured her position in the senate hall and the king's affections.

Surprise hit me, then complete understanding. I had not seen it before because I had not been in the palace. Would it have made a difference had I been? I did not know. Zenobia knew she would rise, and she had. Her match was destined to be a man of political influence, but I had convinced myself it would be Herodes, the young prince of this beautiful city, and not the mature father, married once already.

Odenathus said, 'As you are here, Zabdas, I would ask for your assistance tonight.'

With little choice I nodded.

'Zenobia, go with Worod. He will ensure you have a suitable escort to Rome. I want at least a hundred men with her, Commander. Zabbai, get some rest. We will talk more in the morning.'

Zabbai nodded, a furrow to his brow, unrest in his eyes. He was a broken man. Friends lost to Persian swords and nothing to be done. Odenathus sent him to Rome to escape, I thought. He left, and Zenobia and Worod followed, leaving me alone with the king.

The king might have designed this, to threaten or to warn, his affections for Zenobia perhaps rendering him jealous of other men, be they cousins or not. Unlikely, I had been ordered to accompany her to Rome.

He called for a slave.

'I need the city's taxation records. And food and drink.'

The slave hurried to fulfil his request.

'The records are sent to Rome, but I always have a copy kept here for our own use.'

Two slaves returned, one carrying a jug and cups, the other a platter of food. They placed them upon the table and Odenathus accepted a cup of wine. I followed suit as he helped himself to grapes.

'Eat,' he said. 'Julius spoke fondly of you. A shepherd boy turned slave, turned soldier. What next?' he smiled, a genuine, large smile.

Errand boy to Rome, I thought.

An old man hurried in, scrolls in his arms, several slaves bearing more scrolls in his wake.

'Kouros,' Odenathus acknowledged him.

'My Lord,' the man replied, and attempted to bow.

He put the scrolls down on a table to one side of the room. We moved across. Pillars shadowed us and slaves hurried over with lamps.

'Kouros is my record keeper,' Odenathus said. 'Without him, the city's records would be in chaos. Births, deaths, marriages, taxes, levies, land. Rome requires everything to be recorded and kept safe. Now, Zabdas, I know you are a man of some mathematical skill, of log-keeping yourself. You work on the army's records, I am told, so you will have an understanding of such documents?'

I peered at the scrolls. Took one, unrolled it and squinted in the candlelight. They were not records, but catalogues of records.

'They make sense to me.'

'Good. We must extract everything that can be of use.'

'What are we looking for, my Lord?' I asked.

Kouros nodded in a bid for clarification.

'This, gentlemen, is our means of locating every tribe in the province. If a man trades, he is recorded. If he does not trade through Palmyra, he does not trade at all.'

I read and we searched, back and forth through scrolls and years. We searched and more men came to assist. I requested blank scrolls and began drawing up an endless list of candidates who could raise arms. We found corresponding records, obtained locations and wrote them down.

I did not think of Rome as we worked. I did not think of Zenobia. The task consumed us. Worod returned in the early hours, unrolling scroll after scroll, enthused by the notion that more fighting men might be found. Odenathus himself was not idle, sending messengers, despatching orders, tirelessly reading and writing and searching, as we all did, for precious information.

Hours passed and morning light drove through window gaps. My eyes were tired, but reading became easier. Roman-drawn maps of Syria were laid on the floor and every tribe marked upon them. Hundreds. Odenathus finally saw the enormity of our task. Many days travel would be required to seek the tribes, many more to persuade them, and even then, they may not come.

I left at midday and went to my palace rooms. Nothing had changed. They were the same rooms I had slept in whilst Julius was here. Bright light lit dust in the air. I walked through it, disturbing the particles, and looked out of the window to a rare view. People milled about their business, their night one of sleep where mine was not.

I turned back, surveying the empty space. I wished then I had stayed, slept in this bed, in the room beside Zenobia.

She was in her own room, bright light illuminating her hair and olive skin.

'Zabdas.' She smiled. 'When my father told us of Rome, I did not think we would travel there, to the centre of the Empire, you and I together. I am glad we have the chance to spend time with one another.'

I yawned and rubbed my face. My mind returned to the night before, of standing on the city wall, keeping watch, my tiredness. That weariness evaporated with all the commotion, but now it returned ten-fold.

'I am glad also,' I said, though I could not be sure I meant it. 'You were about to tell me news of your father earlier?'

She paused. Worry cracked her unreadable mask.

My own stomach lurched, dread filling the unknown.

'Teymour has been injured in battle. He may not live.'

A moment of relief that it was Teymour and not Julius.

'What has happened?'

She pulled out the note from layers of robes, unfolded and handed it to me.

'The Tanukh tried to take the Euphrates. My father commandeered a number of vessels and blocked the river to stop them raiding the north. There was a night attack. Two boats were boarded by the enemy and as they struggled for command Teymour was stabbed in the belly. My father's men still hold the river, but his letter is dated three weeks ago.'

I crossed the room and embraced her. We had not seen Teymour in two years, but he had written as often as Julius with news, and Zenobia had always passed it on. I knew by her face she worried for him.

I tightened my embrace. Whispered, 'The gods will not forsake him. He will live.'

Damn the gods. I would have gone south in that moment, with or without the king's permission, accepting whatever punishment I might face, but we had orders now; and Zenobia a task that had come full circle. The same task that was once Julius': to travel to Rome and plead for more troops, to describe the horrors of the east and tell of the grave blade-edge upon which we balanced. To stand before the most powerful men in the Empire; the greatest men in the world, and give them news foretold for centuries.

The east was about to crumble under a new ruler.

CHAPTER 10

Zabdas - 257 AD

No FURTHER NEWS CAME from the frontier. Not east or south. I thought of Teymour bleeding life from his wounds, wondered if we would see him once more.

Zenobia, Zabbai and I left Palmyra with more than a hundred men, Rome our destination; the land where fineries of the east concluded their journey, to witness the very heart of the greatest empire, and leave behind the frontier, besieged with enemies, clamouring for a scrap of Rome's vast, incomprehensible wealth.

Each night we erected long, low, black tents of goat and camel hair; easy to assemble and disassemble, quick to move should we need to. Each night I slept inside the entrance of Zenobia's tent. Our Bedouin escort with their swords and light armour deterred those who might cause us harm, yet we stayed no more than a night in one place.

Zabbai led our path, though Zenobia held a certain power. The men sensed her closeness to the king, noted Zabbai glance to her for permission or reassurance. Respect, I thought at first, then I wondered did they fear her, but I could not see it.

Without the cargo that burdened trade caravans we made a fine pace. Still it took longer than we wanted to reach the west. The landscape changed as we moved onward, subtle differences in architecture and climate. Syria could be warm even with winds, and only the darkness brought an icy chill. Further west the temperature dropped, yet we were not in the coldest months. We wore thick cloaks, two at night, and Zenobia braved the conditions without discontent.

We had travelled by land to Antioch on the west coast of Syria, then across the Mediterranean. Ianuanius, as the Romans have it, saw us in to a new year, but Februarius arrived and conditions became colder still. Constant drizzle and occasional snow flecked our cloaks; an icy reminder we were no longer home.

I longed to see Rome, even bearing our grave message. Zenobia was unmoved by my eagerness to fulfil our mission and return east. But Zabbai, so patient and methodical, appeared anxious. These lands were unknown to him, far from home. Zenobia said we were a part of them, of the great and mighty Empire, just as the cities and towns of Hispaniae and Britanniae were in the west. Why should we be afraid?

Zabbai pondered the diversion of forces from Thraciae. They must suffer the Goth enemy too, he said. Food shortages would be common, farms further north raided. No, he surmised, Rome could not spare those soldiers.

We clung to the southern lands, far from the enemy. Yet they suffered piracy from their own kind.

Would Rome listen? I heard talk of the Empire's options. Rome could cut off its territory at Byzantium, where the land became a bottleneck, and could be more easily defended. They would forfeit the whole of Anatolia, Asiana and Syria, and grain from Egypt would cease; a whole third of the Empire's grain supply each year. And Palmyrene trade would end.

We secured passage across the waters, and met no resistance the morning we saw Italia on the horizon. Sunlight shone on calm waters. I felt the familiarity of Zenobia by my side. Memories warmed me; of standing next to Julius, gazing at the shores of Syria, seeing the place that became home.

'I received a note,' I said, thoughts spurring words, 'from your mother, just over a year ago.'

'What did it contain?'

'It was about a slave-girl of your house. Farva.'

'I know the one. My sister wrote she died in childbirth,' Zenobia said with indifference. 'She had a boy.'

'I believe so.'

'I have seen him when I travelled home. He grows strong. What do you want to know, Zabdas?'

'Nothing,' I said, afraid, unable to speak.

'Of course you must. You touched upon this subject.'

'Your mother wrote that the girl claimed him mine.'

On the edge of my vision I saw her incline her head.

'I never lay with her,' I explained. 'She propositioned, but I did not accept.'

Zenobia half smiled. 'Then you have nothing to concern yourself with.'

'I do not.'

'But it does not sit well with you? I hear you do not join fellow soldiers in brothel activities. That you have a fear of women.'

'Do I fear you?' I said, and laughed, a hollow, forced sound.

'I did not say I believed the talk. I think perhaps you are afraid of being a free man.'

We said no more. I reflected on the irony of the claim Farva had made; I was a soldier now, learning to defend and kill. To end life, rather than give. No, not to end, to protect. And I wondered vaguely if Zenobia had lain with Odenathus. Put it from my mind. I could not think of it.

We drifted toward land. My breath misted on the air and I wrapped my cloak tighter about my shoulders. Zenobia threw back her head, eyes closed, and breathed deeply before returning a hungry gaze on our destination.

On land, days went by with no trace of the city. Markers gave indication of distance, but bore no relevance to my aching limbs.

'It is possible they know of the Persian victories already,' Zabbai said.

'No one could have journeyed faster than us,' I replied. 'If they have, are we wasting our time?'

'The Roman commanders in Syria will have sent flag messages back. But we are not wasting our time,' he said. 'If Rome is aware that the Persians have pressed further into Syria, it is our task to discover their intentions and inform Odenathus and the Syrian army as soon as possible. If Rome sits back, then we plead our case.'

'We must exaggerate our weak position,' Zenobia said. 'Shapur could have taken Palmyra and be marching into Anatolia before we even reach Rome.'

Our position could be weaker still. I felt sick, my stomach rolling, the fear of what we would return to unsettling.

'Do you think the Persians *have* moved further?' I said.

Zabbai glanced at Zenobia before saying, 'I have seen his army, Zabdas. I watched the Persians take Nisibis. If unchecked, the whole of Rome could fall. They are a plague and their leader is a ruthless man who knows how to conqueror. He knows Rome is weak.'

'Rome cannot decline when the Persians rip a path into the heart of their empire.' I said.

Zabbai shrugged. 'We will see.'

Zenobia said nothing, her mind working.

Two days later, Rome was in sight.

We arrived at an entrance on the outer limits of the city, and our hundred strong escort was refused entry.

'No soldiers inside the city,' Zabbai said.

They set up camp on the outskirts whilst Zenobia, Zabbai and I negotiated access. We represented the Syrian government, we said, and had lodgings arranged within.

Buildings taller than I had known reached for the sky, larger even than the temples of Palmyra. Floors were constructed within buildings, Zabbai said, the poorer dwelling in compact apartments. Marble and mosaic were in abundance, and dull mortar made houses and roads everywhere. Republican buildings of great mastery dotted the grey scene. Magnificent, tall, dominating. Yet everything had been washed of colour, grey and hints of pale, defiant hues stroked here and there, nonetheless worn and faded. Streets rang with the sound of chariots. Instead of a bustling sound, of traders selling wares and soldiers keeping peace, an overwhelming noise rang, inescapable.

Every street forced me to look up to see the sky. No greenery present. How could anyone live here and find peace? The people were unfriendly; many a man caught my shoulder in passing, without apology or acknowledgment. Syrian women bore sumptuous dark skin of olive tones; here they were intriguing and pale, and many sported hair of pale gold and looked upon you with sea-blue eyes.

Rome was so full of people and wonders and buildings that I could not breathe. I wanted to return to Syria, to escape the noise and the traffic and the desperate, unstoppable rhythm.

I was not the only one unimpressed. Zenobia gazed without acknowledgment or comment. When asked her opinion she said, 'The greatest things in this world are rarely the most beautiful.' I agreed. This city might have been large, sophisticated and advanced, yet it lacked identity, as if every beautiful thing of ingenious design had been mixed in a pot and poured out onto seven hills. Rome was every exquisite culture imaginable, covered in a hard-setting grey slush.

Zenobia's Latin was extensive. She spoke to the guards at the city entrance, then to errand boys. Zabbai and I waited as she murmured to them, passed them coins, then gestured we follow one.

'Where are we headed?' I asked.

'To see an old friend of my father's. A man named Regulus. Let us hope he can secure an audience with the emperor.'

Slaves brushed doorsteps. A man's voice shouted, drunk and obscene as servants with bowed heads crossed our path carrying messages from one house to another, and togas whipped in and out of sight.

I felt as if we had crossed the entire city when the boy came to a halt and gestured a door.

'Gratitude,' Zenobia said, dropping more coins into the boy's outstretched hand.

Zabbai stepped forward and tapped on the door.

'How does Julius know him?' I asked.

'My father stayed here many times when in Rome.' She glanced skyward. 'It is getting late.'

The door creaked open. Two bright-blue eyes peered at us.

'Can I help you?'

'I seek Regulus,' Zenobia said. 'It is a matter of importance.'

The soft slap of sandals.

'Who calls?' Another voice, older and more croak-like than the first.

The girl opened the door. A man with greying hair and a stick to aid him walked toward us.

'Who are you and how I can help?'

'You are Regulus?' Zenobia asked.

'I am. And you are?'

'You know my father,' Zenobia replied. 'Zabdilas.'

Eyes alert, the old man checked himself, leant further on his stick to peer at Zenobia. He studied her, but she did not flinch. Lines of age changed shape, moulding to a grin, and misty-yellow eyes filled with joy.

'Tell me I am not deceived? If I were to have laid a bet on who knocked at my door, I would be missing a small fortune. Tell me you are Zenobia, daughter of Julius Zabdilas?'

Zenobia smiled back and I reflected she had not done fully in months.

'My father talked of you often.'

Regulus' cane clattered to the floor. He beckoned Zenobia with both arms. She held him, comfortable and relaxed in his embrace, his soft beard resting against her black hair.

'My dear girl, tell me how your father is? It has been a long time since he last wrote.' He glanced to Zabbai and me. He said in Aramaic, 'Forgive my rudeness. I should not have assumed you understood everything.'

I had understood, but smiled nonetheless.

'Goodness, what has hospitality come to? Come in, come in. My house is modest but the least I can do is let you sit down.'

The girl who answered the door led us down the hallway to a sitting room, where furniture was intimately arranged and scrolls lined the walls. From Cicero to Ptolemy, Aristotle to Aurelius, great philosophers had their place on the shelves. No statues stood atop pedestals, but models of unknown devices, made of metals bent and twisted.

'Please, sit,' Regulus said, beaming. 'I still cannot believe you are here, Zenobia, in Rome! How frightful it must seem, compared to Palmyra, a desert oasis. I have longed to visit, but alas I think I may now be too old for the journey.'

Servants appeared with trays of refreshments.

'You may leave us now, Aurelia,' Regulus said, and to us: 'A student. Or ward, rather. The bastard daughter of a general, no less. Her mother was an old friend of mine, but there was little I could do to help her when she fell ill, except to agree to put a roof over her daughter's head when the end came.' He flicked a hand as though it was nothing. 'I have made my enemies over the years, but I should not wish one of a woman close to death. So, you must tell me of Julius?'

Zenobia's smile faded and hard resolve returned.

'Odenathus sent my father to fight the Tanukh tribe in southern Syria.'

'The Tanukh? But your father defeated the Tanukh years ago. He told me as much himself.'

'They have a new king now, a man named Jadhima, intent on taking the Euphrates and Palmyra's trade. My father left two years ago, and I have not seen him since.'

Regulus shook his head.

'The Empire falls into dark times. We hear of new enemies rising and old enemies returning every day. There was a time when Rome knew only victory. Now everything is in chaos. Chaos!' he repeated. 'The gods do love it!'

I was barely listening. My eyes and mind were fixed on the pale girl with paler hair and bright eyes. I had been used to Zenobia's eyes, of my people's eyes, dark and mysterious. Yet hers were blue and innocent; the sea in daylight under a radiant sun.

'The east is not chaos,' Zabbai said. 'Odenathus holds the frontiers well, or as well as he can under the circumstances. We do not have enough men.'

Zenobia hushed Zabbai with a hand. 'Before we left Syria, we heard that one of my father's friends, Teymour, had been injured during battle. I believe you knew him?'

Aurelia glanced to me, her cheeks growing red, a nervous smile upon her lips.

'I believe I did. A quiet fellow with a surly face, but amiable once you got to know him. I am sorry to hear of this, Zenobia. I thought your father well. The last time I heard, he searched for the Black Stone of Elagabal.'

'Two years ago you would have been right,' Zenobia said.

I smiled back at Aurelia. I could not help myself. She had an innocence rarely witnessed. A bastard born, I pondered, yet she was exquisitely beautiful, soft hair, a heart-shaped face.

'Did he find the stone?' Regulus asked.

Zenobia shook her head.

The old man sighed. 'That does not surprise me. He asked if I knew of anything that could assist him, anything that might give a clue as to its whereabouts. But one hears little when people believe the Stone is in Edessa!' He caressed his cup. 'Does Odenathus still believe it will save him from the Persians?'

'Mina does, the king's mother.'

'Fools. They are all fools! I told him as much when I saw him last. He mentioned his disagreements with Odenathus. I have been involved in the politics of Rome for many years, but even so I sympathise with your father's beliefs. Things here are not smooth, they are constantly changing. I think your father may be right. The Empire is on the brink of financial crisis. Whole legions are hit with plague as they attempt to defend against invasion. Emperors come and go with the wind. All backstabbing and murder and I make no joke! The best thing Odenathus could do is sever himself and secure his lands. Julius was right. He is always right. A fine man, your father. He said the king rules with passion. He is proud of him. I think he likes Odenathus a great deal, but I think Julius the wiser of the two.'

We all sat in silence a moment, but the girl, Aurelia, had moved closer, so close I began to feel the warmth of her, my skin pinching at our proximity as I looked around at our silent group, wondering suddenly if they looked at me, at us, knowing my thoughts.

'How is your sister? Hebony?' Regulus went on.

'She is married now, and with child.'

'Wonderful, wonderful! You must give her my congratulations when next you see her.'

He turned to Zabbai. 'You are a general, no?'

'I am.'

'The scars give you away, my son. And you,' he said to me, 'who might you be?'

I wrenched to the present and the conversation in the room, unsure of the words that had a moment before been spoken.

'Apologies,' I said, 'it was a long journey.'

'Of course,' Regulus said. 'I was asking your name.'

'My name is Zabdas.'

'You give little away, my boy. Are you a soldier?'

'A soldier and Julius' nephew.'

Regulus looked a little surprised, glanced to Zenobia. 'The boy your father has been looking for, he found him?'

'In Yemen,' Zenobia said. 'A slave.'

'Oh dear. Gods do like to play games,' Regulus said. 'I am

glad he found you. He always wanted a son. Very good. Well now, we have the formalities over with, I think it best you tell me what you are doing so far from home.'

'My father has never been a man of chance,' Zenobia said. 'If in Rome, I was to seek your help.'

We explained how Persian forces breached the Syrian frontier, that our armies were no longer large enough to sustain a defence and would soon be crushed beneath the weight of invasion.

'Disastrous,' Regulus said. 'I can scarce believe they have taken so many cities. I have heard murmur the threat increased. Indeed, the message came through only a week or so ago that you were pressed still further. The senate suggested you could hold, as you had always done.'

Zenobia shook her head.

Zabbai said: 'That is no longer possible. Too much land has been taken, too many soldiers killed. I was there as Shapur defeated us and took our cities. I watched his hundred thousand strong army swipe ours from the north. He has amassed a substantial force; far greater than ours.'

'And what is it I can do to help you?' Regulus asked.

'We need an audience with the emperor. He is in the city?' Zabbai asked.

'Valerian Caesar is at present. Ideally a campaign needs to be put in motion. For that he would be the best man to speak to, I should imagine. The senate will sit and talk of it much so I think a military man is your best option. As an ex-member of the senate I still have some sway, but not much. I will do my best, of course. It seems I have some messages to send. Aurelia!'

'You wish to stay here tonight?' he asked.

'Our men are camped outside the city,' Zabbai said. 'We will stay with them tonight.'

'I will return tomorrow, Regulus,' Zenobia said, 'to see what news you have. Much gratitude, for everything you have done.'

'Send word of your location, in case I need to reach you. Aurelia, my dear, fetch a messenger.'

We wished Regulus luck, offered him thanks, and left. Gods willing he would gain audience with the emperor.

'You think he will succeed?' I asked Zenobia.

'My father believed Regulus could be trusted to do everything in his power if the need arose.'

She pulled her cloak around her shoulders and took a long, deep breath. I yawned. I longed for home, just one night back in Julius' house with his family, my family. I thought of my promise to Meskenit two years ago; that I would keep Julius safe. How I had failed her. Julius was at the Euphrates. I was here. He had Teymour, but Teymour was injured, perhaps now dead.

A breeze dragged across dirt and sand and grassy hills. It pulled Zenobia's hair back from her face, the long, strong nose and black kohl eyes. Did she think of her family, of her father, of Syria's danger? Did she trust the man, Regulus, on her father's word? I could not tell. I could never decipher her thoughts, her words, her posture or expression. Perhaps she had misgivings, fretted whether he would gain audience with the emperor, or queried the character of this man, but in those moments I did not know if she questioned herself, doubted her ability to persuade an emperor, to gain an army, to ride home ahead of legions. She did not show it. Her almond eyes held confidence. Her persona always the same: untroubled.

Sunlight vanished behind the tiled roofs, streets grew dark and grey, and night fell entirely as we reached camp.

The following day, the three of us returned to the house of Regulus. The air hummed with activity, messengers coming and going, slaves rushed back and forth, carrying stylus and parchment and scrolls.

'Ah, Zenobia, come in,' Regulus said as we entered the sitting area. 'I wondered what time you would arrive.'

Zenobia, Zabbai and I sat down. Aurelia offered us refreshments. Her pale cheeks and golden waves were striking beside

Zenobia's black hair and dark complexion. Zenobia was sure and determined, but Aurelia's shoulders curled, her head turned slightly away. Her attitude one of timidity.

Regulus rolled a parchment, slipped a ribbon around it and sealed it with a disc of wax. 'Aurelia, please wait a moment.'

He eased himself to unsure legs, and moved slowly to a writing desk. He pulled a blank papyrus toward him, scratched a few words, and handed it to the messenger.

'Kindly see the messenger out would you, Aurelia. Thank you, my dear.'

They left and Regulus turned his attention to us.

'Well, I have made petitions on your behalf and I am hopeful that I can gain you an audience with Valerian Caesar in the coming weeks.'

'Weeks?' Zabbai said, and I felt my own energy ebb. 'Gods be damned, we could be crushed before we reach home if we left this very day. Can nothing be done?'

'I am afraid not. The emperor is in great demand. You are fortunate he is in the city.'

Zenobia pulled her gaze from Regulus, stole a glance at me. Frustration hung on her face. Regulus' respect and weight could no more gain a meet with the emperor than those who had come before.

'Is a few weeks realistic?' Zenobia asked. 'Or does the emperor have no desire to see us?'

'It is hard to say, I am no longer at the centre of politics, an old man only. Perhaps we should rest. There is little more we can do but wait. I can scarcely believe I have been the centre of such a whirl of information.' He grinned. 'Do not fret. Nothing more can be done today.'

'You are right,' Zabbai said. 'We must wait.'

'Stay here, until you are called up,' Regulus suggested. 'I would enjoy your company very much.'

'I must return to my men,' Zabbai replied, but Zenobia agreed to stay, and I with her.

We ate, and talked and drank, through the late afternoon and into the evening. I enjoyed Regulus' house, his curiosities, groaning library and hospitality. It was as if I were back in Julius' house.

'You are as beautiful as I expected you to be, Zenobia,' Regulus said, his eyes watery. He took a long sip of wine and studied her. 'A descendant of Cleopatra Selene. I should have expected no less.'

'You are kind, Regulus. Perhaps one day you will do me the honour of visiting the Palmyrene court. You would like it.' She smiled, warm and sincere.

'Perhaps I shall make the effort.'

We retired. I rolled from one side of my bed to the other, unable to sleep, staring at the blank walls of the room. I thought on our company outside the city. I lay in comfort as they lay in tents. I could not imagine our audience with the emperor now. With Valerian Caesar. Day would turn to endless day, weeks to months. Success was impossible. And yet I could not imagine returning defeated. We had to return with troops. We could not fail.

Morning came and with it the sound of the city. The noise seemed louder than the day before and my head pounded from too much thought and too little sleep. I left my room and found Zenobia and Regulus talking, but I did not join them.

I walked through to the rear of the house, looking for a water pump. I entered a communal area, women washing clothes, tradesmen hurrying back and forth, the smell of bread baking filling the air.

'Merchants arrived from Syria this very morning. They talk of the Persian threat. They say you are close to collapse, that you have lost cities already. They claim the Persians raid and trade suffers.'

My heart jumped. I turned to see Aurelia, a bucket beside

her. She ladled two cups of water and offered me one. I drank, cold and clean and when I had finished she offered more and I splashed my face and neck.

'They are right,' I said. 'Our king sent us to Rome to beg for reinforcements. He has lost thousands of men the past few months. Cities too,' I conceded. 'He cannot hold for long.'

'Regulus will do his best,' she said, voice soft as golden hair. 'Though I daresay by midday the whole of Rome will know how close you are to collapse. The mob talks.'

She passed me a cloth. I dried my hands. Merchants talked, I thought, and wondered if we stood on firmer ground, that the emperor would now have to act.

I handed the cloth back to Aurelia.

'I have never seen the east,' she said. 'It is as glorious as they say?'

'I saw Palmyra for the first time when I was thirteen. It is a beautiful city. Marble and statues and stone, mosaics in the streets, spice and silk and anything you can imagine in the marketplace. The people are friendly, too; the merchants proud. Palmyra thrives.'

'You love your city,' she mused. 'Is it more beautiful than Rome?'

I thought to say no. I did not wish to offend the Roman girl, but I could not lie to innocent eyes. We walked back into the house and I said, 'I think it so. Where I am from, luxuries are commonplace. Every corner of Syria is beautiful beyond comprehension. Palmyra was not always my home, but I am honoured to call it so. To see it fall ...'

'Where did you live before Palmyra?'

'I was born in Egypt.'

'Why did you leave?'

The slave mark upon my arm burned and with it shame grew. I could not utter the words, the story of my past, and explain how and why I found myself in Palmyra.

'My family are in Syria,' I said. 'Julius, Zenobia ...'

'You are fortunate indeed.'

She reminded me of Zenobia when I first met her in Julius' home; her expression free of worry and full of youth.

'And you,' I asked, 'you are a student?'

'Regulus teaches me languages, philosophy and mathematics. I have been in Regulus' house a long time. He is a private man, and I think perhaps I care for him more than he cares for me now. I am loath to ever leave his home for he is the best of men.'

We stood in the corridor. I could hear Regulus and Zenobia's muted conversation.

'Your father, why are you not with him?'

I could have kicked myself for the bluntness of my question, my ignorance of the politics of her birth, but she answered freely enough.

'My father is Dux Equitum, Commander of the Cavalry in the north. He fights the Goths. Right now they celebrate another victory.' She grimaced, as if war had no place. 'My father knows I reside in Regulus' home, that I am tutored by him, but he has never visited this place, never once wondered what his bastard daughter might look like or whether she bears any resemblance to him at all.'

'I am sorry for that.'

'There is no need. It is as it has always been. I will never be recognised by him. And you, Zabdas, you have always been a soldier?'

My name on foreign lips, the roll and mispronunciation, warmed me.

'Almost always,' I said evasively.

My past weighed heavily and I craved the touch of Aurelia's skin. That it might offer comfort, gentle and warm. It seemed her mother had secured her an education, as Julius had Zenobia. And yet neither Zenobia's nor Aurelia's past was mine.

'What do you not say?' she asked.

I sighed. A soldier, a cousin to Zenobia, a man now, but still …

I rolled down the leather cuff I wore on my arm, the slave mark beneath. Hebony's concoctions had seen it fade, yet it was no less visible. A lurid mark of the rank I had once held.

'You are a slave?' Her face fell, eyes shocked. 'A slave.'

She could not take her eyes from the mark, the brand of the man I was, and I could not escape it any more than I could wash the burn from my flesh.

'I was,' I said.

'But no more?'

'I was not born a slave.' For a moment I felt different, defensive. 'I was taken a slave when my parents were killed. Five years old,' I said, and I was angry. Not at her, not at this beautiful creature before me, but at what had been, the inescapable brand I had been given. 'I am Zenobia's cousin. Her father found me and took me back to Syria.'

She smiled. Reached out. I pulled my arm away but her fingers were upon it, the inside of my arm, my wrist, tracing the scars.

I had not shocked her, she did not recoil. I watched her face, pale and soft and delicate, eyes downturned. Long, soft lashes resting on pink cheeks.

We would be leaving soon, I told myself. And it pained me to think it.

Regulus bustled in, grinning.

'There you are,' he said. 'I have had word. You have been granted audience with the emperor in the morning.'

I felt Aurelia beside me. If the emperor saw us in the morning, we could well be leaving by the afternoon. I should have been overjoyed at the news, but I was torn. I craved a few moments more with this Roman girl.

Regulus sent a slave to fetch Zabbai. He arrived the following morning, relief evident.

'We have what we came for,' he said.

'We have an audience,' Zenobia corrected. 'We need soldiers.'

We set out, a slave to guide us, walking through streets that looked almost like those of Palmyra. Clean stone paved our way, the finer dressed citizens dotting about here and there. Even the slaves wore better clothes, washed and clean and cared for. Soldiers ushered beggars on, and litters carried many aristocrats down into the city.

At the house of Valerian Caesar, armed praetorians granted entrance. A servant greeted and exchanged words with Zenobia. She handed him the scroll from Odenathus and he nodded and disappeared from sight.

In due course the servant scurried back. We rose and followed him through the enormous house. The interior bore resemblance to Julius' home. Floors of polished marble reflecting whole rooms and carefully positioned statues rang of good taste.

We came to a halt. A doorway of solid wood blocked our path. The servant opened the door fully, stepped aside, bowed, and announced:

'Zabbai, commanding officer in the Palmyrene army and Zenobia Julia Zabdilas, Zabdas Zabdilas.'

We filed past, into the room, and the servant closed the door behind us and left. Inside, praetorian guards stood either side of the door. Shelves lined the walls, books, maps, plans, official documents, the odd ill-placed bust and figurine. My eyes came to rest on a man behind a large desk, his head buried in scrolls, two more praetorians behind him.

The man continued to write. Moments passed and Zenobia glanced to me, a look of puzzlement and exasperation. Eventually he looked up. He was middle years, a hunched figure, lean but not strong. He stared long at each of us, then set his stylus aside and sat back in his chair.

'You requested an audience with me and have travelled far. This scroll states you have important matters to discuss. Odenathus is a most trustworthy and valued king. I do not have much time, but you may speak freely of what it is you require.'

His voice surprised me, high-pitched, unnatural. He spoke Latin, but as with Regulus and Aurelia, I understood most of what had been said. He was not as I imagined. No superiority in his presence or command in his tone. His long, thin face home to sunken eyes and drooping cheeks.

'Greetings, Valerian Caesar,' Zenobia said, inclining her head. 'We appreciate you are a busy man and I thank you for taking the time to grant audience.'

He leant back further in his chair and said, 'And you are Zenobia Julia Zabdilas. Have we met before? I cannot remember a woman travelling from the east to request audience in the past.'

'This is my first visit to Rome.'

He bit the skin on his fingers. 'But you are familiar. Not in looks, but you remind me of someone. A servant, perhaps,' he said, and I wondered if his words deliberate.

'My father visited this city many times. It is him you will recall.'

The emperor's eyes grew small.

'Indeed, it could be.'

His gaze wandered around his room, as though he did not recognize it, lost in thought, our presence no longer focussing his attention. Then his eyes flicked back to Zenobia.

'Zabdilas?'

'Julius,' Zenobia said.

'I am sure I recall a man of that name. There are many names which begin with a 'z' in Syria, no?'

Zenobia inclined her head.

'Take a seat,' he said, gesturing chairs on the opposite side of his desk.

Zenobia sat and Zabbai and I followed.

'Caesar, we are here to plead for aid,' Zabbai said.

Valerian's eyes sparked. We amused him.

'The Persian king, Shapur I, continues to press the east hard,' Zabbai explained. 'But Syria can no longer hold his armies.

Much land has been lost. We require aid or the east shall fall. It may already have.'

'I have reports from my commanding officers in the east. They admit land has been lost, but they are confident the frontier can be held for the time being.'

'I doubt that,' Zenobia said.

'You have a map?' Zabbai interjected, before Zenobia could say more.

'What? A map? I ... of course, here.' He gestured a slave who retrieved a scroll from one of many pocket shelves. I moved desk clutter aside. Once unrolled, the scroll displayed a great web of countries, and dotted across the lands, cities were marked like flies. On the left: Britanniae, Hispaniae, Galliae and Viennensis. On the right: Pannoniae, Moesiae, Dacia, Thraciae, Asiana, Pontica and Oriens. Below, Africa and Egypt sat on the opposite side of the Mediterranium. In the centre: Italia. Every piece of land, every island under Roman control, contained on one scroll. Palmyra a beetle in the desert.

Zabbai moved to the right of the map, and peered at a black speck.

'This *was* the border between Syria and Persis.' He swept his finger across the map.

Valerian sat up, stiff in his chair, brow creased, but said nothing.

'They have crossed the Euphrates here and here,' Zabbai went on. 'They have taken Nisibis, now they are heading for Carrhae and on to Edessa, then every other city in Syria. After Syria they move into Asia Minor.' He dotted his finger at various places. 'Your legions fail to hold them, and Bedouin warriors face the rising of the south. The Tanukh press the river hard. Odenathus concentrates a sizeable portion of the Syrian forces there.'

Valerian sank back in his chair, features composed in thought.

'We need more men,' Zabbai said, 'to push the Persians across the Tigris. If your legions stationed in Syria have not already requested reinforcements, they should have. They are pressed as we are.'

Valerian looked at the map. Shook his head.

'I must think of the military front as a whole. The Empire is vast and under a greater threat than ever before. In the east we encounter the Persian threat, as you say, in the west the presence of the Saxons, Franks and Alemanni. The Vandals and Goths hit hard in the north. These are just a few of the pressures I face, and all are larger and more formidable than we politicians have previously understood.

'So,' he said, as if concluding the conversation, 'we move to a time of defence rather than attack. Conquering will no longer be an option for the present; that has been obvious for some time. Our leaders in military circles need to do everything they can to hold and defeat our enemies, but where the danger is less, so must our concern be.'

'You must understand,' Zabbai said, 'King Odenathus cannot hold the frontier, and your forces in Syria are next to none. Shapur's forces have grown strong, and meanwhile the Tanukh attempt to take the southern Euphrates. Our scouts tell us the Persian army number a hundred thousand or more, whilst our own numbers diminish. If Rome does nothing the east will fall, and with it your trade routes.'

'There are Roman legions already in Syria. My own men tell me our client king can hold the frontier with the legions already deployed there. He has done so for years.'

'I beg you,' Zenobia said. 'The east will fall.'

Valerian scratched his forehead. 'My son will continue targeting his forces to the west, as he has been doing these past months. Meanwhile, I will join the armies facing the Goths, and Odenathus and the eastern based legions will continue to defend against the Persians until one or both of the other fronts are stable enough to withdraw and move forces. This is the best I can offer. I have already talked with my advisors, and this is the most beneficial option.'

Zenobia leaned forward. 'Caesar, we are here to express the

precariousness of our situation. Perhaps, if you yourself cannot lead men east, you can spare legions to assist the defence?'

'It is not that simple,' Valerian said stiffly. 'Arrangements and details of the campaign in the north take time. Until then, legions cannot be despatched elsewhere. I cannot send men east until I have secured the north.'

Valerian flicked his hand and a slave moved forward and rolled up the map. The emperor did not look at us, but waited as if expecting us to leave.

Zabbai's eyes widened.

'Caesar, I must implore you to reconsider. Our request is necessary and urgent. Speed is vital. We cannot wait. I have seen the frontier myself. I have seen the Persian force raze whole cities, watched as the men and women and children within were slaughtered.'

Valerian flushed. 'My commanders, too, have seen your frontier. They believe it can hold. Your king should think the same if he knows of war.'

Zabbai replied, 'King Odenathus has long protected your frontier. He knows the eastern force better than any man, living or dead. His decisions are made in your interests, and he made the choice to send us here to request aid.'

Zabbai stared at the emperor a moment, impatience and frustration evident.

'You will do nothing?' he said.

Valerian did not respond and Zabbai stalked out.

'Your time has been greatly appreciated, Caesar,' Zenobia said. She bowed, elegant and courteous, and we too left.

We walked back through the gates of Valerian's villa, the sun high and the streets warm.

'My father was right,' Zenobia said. 'Valerian is a fool. A puppet to the senate.'

'What do we do now?' I asked.

'I do not know. If he will not change his mind, then there is little to be done. We must return to Syria, hope that Odenathus has secured aid from the tribes.'

'I am going back to camp,' Zabbai said.

Zenobia nodded. 'Zabdas and I will return to Regulus and inform him of the outcome of our meeting.'

The proud villas behind, we roamed through modest dwellings. Quaint buildings, flowers thirsty for the weak sun, dogs sniffing and pissing in the gutters.

'Valerian thinks our plight small compared to his other troubles,' I said.

'*Mehercule*! I wish I knew what to do now, Zabdas. We have failed. I have failed. I, who assured Odenathus that I would succeed where my father could not. We were never going to gain reinforcements. I was convinced, sure that on the brink of invasion, Rome would have no choice but to listen.'

'And so we pray to Bel and every other god and hope that we return to cities and sand and not a bloodbath.'

'Look at this.' Zenobia gestured about us, the stone buildings, paved streets and masses coming and going. Trading as we traded, drinking as our soldiers drank. 'They enjoy as we enjoy, have what we have, and yet our lives will be stripped from us. We must have Rome's support to secure our frontier.'

'We cannot, Zenobia.'

Determination etched her olive face, a half smile forming on her lips.

'My father would have us sever ourselves from Rome, but we have not. We are still part of the empire, Zabdas, and if we are to remain within it I will have Rome send the soldiers we are owed.'

CHAPTER 11

Zabdas - 258 AD

REGULUS SAT WAITING. HE tapped his cane against the edge of his couch, his hearing failing, I thought, as he jumped too late at the sound of our approach.

'Did you see him?'

'We saw Valerian,' Zenobia replied.

'Do not keep an old man in suspense. What did he say?'

Zenobia knelt down beside Regulus and took his hands in her own. She stroked them, as if they could give her the same comfort she gave Regulus as his misty eyes grew soft and sad.

'The emperor has corresponded with his own commanders, spoken with the senate, and concluded that Syria can hold with the forces it has for the time being.' Zenobia leaned forward. 'Regulus, Valerian does not understand the severity of our situation. We are close to falling. We may have already.'

Regulus shook his head. 'I had hoped Valerian would listen. But I should not have expected so much. Not from a man like him. He is an emperor by default. He did not defeat his predecessor, Trebonianus. It was Aemilianus who did that, and sometimes I think he would have made a better leader.'

'He became emperor by default?' I said.

Regulus tapped his cane on the side of the couch rapidly, then set it aside.

'Valerian commanded forces in Raetia and Noricum when

Aemilianus attempted to usurp Trebonianus as emperor. Aemilianus' men killed Trebonianus and his son whilst Valerian's own men proclaimed him emperor. When Valerian arrived back in Italia, Aemilianus was killed by his own men, and they joined Valerian's forces. Valerian is a man of the senate, and had their support, you see.'

'And so Valerian became emperor,' I said.

'His son is much worse. The stupidity of the father is replaced by careless self-importance. He fights whilst Valerian makes ill-advised decisions here in Rome! Listen to me; yesterday's man complaining of today's politics. An old fool!'

'You are no fool, Regulus, of that I am certain,' Zenobia said. 'What can be done? We cannot return to Syria with nothing. Can you persuade the senate to change the emperor's mind?'

Regulus sighed and clasped his hands across his stomach.

'They are not men I know well, Zenobia, not anymore. They are another generation. When I was younger, politics was all-important. The Empire was ruled from the senate house. Now it is ruled on the battlefield and a public vote of popularity. No, they will not listen to me. It has been many years since I last held any real power.'

'The senate respect you,' she said.

'Ah, well, some. But most are men close to Valerian, of the same mind, to take what Rome has left before they die. There is no future with them. They do not think of what the empire has been or what she might one day become again. Valerian has made up his mind, if he will not send more forces east, neither will the senate. You need to persuade the commander, not the old men who have no authority over the army.'

'Persuade him, persuade them, Regulus. They must listen.'

'I will fail, my dear, as you have.'

Zenobia leaned forward. 'You will not. You cannot.'

Regulus appeared thoughtful.

Zenobia looked back, defying him to decline.

'The Empire's fate hangs in the balance, Regulus.'

'No, no. Do not talk so. I am too old and much too sentimental to risk my comfortable position to the wrath of those with power.'

Gods, I thought, would no one help? Would not one man step forward and raise his spear or sword and pledge their aid to us?

'Do it for Rome,' I said.

'I stand to lose everything I have gained if I stand against Valerian now. There was a time when I held the better hand, but he is emperor and wears the purple, he commands the armies. Did you hear what he had done to those poor Christians? Had them massacred, that is what! Free people made slaves or executed for *religion!*'

Zenobia's posture remained unmoved.

'I do not want to fail. We cannot fail, Regulus. Is there no other way? No other we can persuade?'

Regulus shook his head. 'No. Valerian is emperor. He holds imperium. But ...'

'But what?' Zenobia demanded.

'There is one man who shares that power. Valerian's son, Gallienus, is co-emperor after all ...'

'He is,' Zenobia said impatiently, 'but he is at the Danube. And he could not go against Valerian's decision. Could he?'

'Actually, Gallienus is not at the Danube. News has it he made progress and met with some success. He is on his way back to Rome as we speak.'

'Gods, you did not mention this before!' I said.

'We must speak with him,' Zenobia replied.

Regulus looked thoughtful.

'You could try to persuade him, but his father has already made the decision. It would mean his son persuading him otherwise, contradicting him — or overriding him — and it could take some time to gain an audience with him.'

Zenobia shook her head. 'It cannot wait. We will ride out and meet him. Speak with him outside of Rome, before he has chance to speak with his father and become drawn into the politics of the city.'

'Do you know his route to the city? Is it possible to discover where he might be?' I asked.

Regulus frowned. 'I should be able to. The gods know I have enough contacts in this city. I may not have persuasion, but information is a little easier.'

A servant saw Zenobia and me back to camp. Thick grey cloud blocked the moon, our path lit by torches burning along the city wall. Regulus did not seem hopeful of our meeting Gallienus, of persuading him, but my hopes ran high as we walked in the fresh evening.

'We leave for Syria in the morning,' Zabbai said as Zenobia and I stooped into his tent. 'We must report back to Odenathus as soon as possible. Inform him that Rome has no intentions of sending reinforcements east.'

'We go west first,' Zenobia replied. 'I am told Co-Emperor Gallienus returns from the Danube.'

Zabbai faltered, his expression confused. He scratched his beard and took a step toward Zenobia.

'And what do you hope to achieve?'

'Gallienus is an emperor, but he is also a soldier, like you. He is our second chance. We explain to him, convince him of the eastern situation, and we could have the army we need. You have heard of his victories in the west, as I have. If he led men against the Persians, can you imagine?'

Zabbai barked a laugh. 'He is the son, emperor only in name. Valerian turned us down. He trusts his own generals and commanders. You heard what he said and we waste precious time.'

'I will go, even if you will not. It is worth the chance.'

Zabbai grabbed Zenobia's upper arm, squeezed bracelet into flesh. She remained impassive.

'Gods, Zenobia, you have no idea. You think you were sent

here to bargain with the emperor?' he spat. 'You think you are here because of your station, because it was once your father's role? He failed, just as we fail now. Or perhaps you think you are here because you lie with Odenathus? You are a woman, Zenobia, and nothing more. You have a cunt and breasts and charm. That is not enough. Not in Palmyra and not in Rome. Odenathus plays you and you do not see it.'

'Stop this now!' I put a hand on Zabbai's shoulder.

He shrugged me off. Zenobia looked him in the eye, no emotion, no tears, no embarrassment. Her face betrayed neither trembling lip nor faintest smile.

'You think no one knew?' he sneered. 'I have been the king's confidante for many years. The day will never come where Odenathus takes you as a wife. You whore yourself to him, play with his affection. How much gold before you are satisfied? How much power? I, too, spoke with Odenathus before we left Palmyra. You are in Rome because he wanted rid of you; because he never wanted you on his council. Because despite your father's wishes, Odenathus will not give up or share power to *you*.'

'Enough,' I said, pushing Zabbai back. He took a step and his words ceased.

I had not seen it. I thought Zenobia here because of her father. Zabbai had known Odenathus' intentions, kept them to himself, humoured Zenobia. He had done his duty, followed orders, and shown her respect. And I had not seen it.

'Whom Odenathus chooses to take as his wife is irrelevant,' Zenobia said, her voice level. 'Do not question my authority, Zabbai.'

'You threaten me?'

'I threaten no one. I respect you a great deal. Odenathus speaks highly of you and no one in the army stands above you. I would see the same respect that I have for you, that is all.'

Zenobia bowed her head and left before Zabbai could answer.

The still night hummed with our hundred strong camp.

Outside the walls of Rome we were exposed, but I felt safer than within.

'Gallienus is four days from Rome,' Zenobia said. 'If we ride now, we should meet him in less than two.'

'We go without Zabbai?'

She glanced back at his tent and sucked a quick breath. Shook her head.

'We go alone.'

Our guide led a path out of Rome. He had been appointed by Regulus, a man who knew the area and could be trusted. Zabbai stayed behind, but sent with us two of his men for our safety.

What could we say to persuade Gallienus? I pondered. I could think of nothing. The heavy grey sky grew dark and broke with rain. I wiped my face, struggling to see. It ran down Zenobia's face and neck, a tide upon her skin, yet she did not brush it away. She embraced it and her hair welled and clung to a sodden cloak.

'Will this work, do you think?' I asked.

'He is a lord of war, but that is all I know of our second emperor. Regulus' opinion was not high, but if Gallienus is an arrogant man, he may see sport in standing against his father. We can but hope.'

'And if he agrees with his father, and refuses to assign reinforcements to the east?'

A purposeful look. 'What makes you think I know all the answers, Zabdas?'

Because she was ever sure, I thought, but did not say it.

'I never said you did,' I said instead.

'No,' she mused, 'you did not. Let us hope we can speak with Gallienus.'

Two days ride. Two nights sleeping in our low black tents. On the morning of the third day we found Gallienus' men blocking the road ahead.

Two men rode out, banners fluttering in a weak wind, to greet us.

'I seek an audience with Emperor Gallienus on a matter of urgency,' Zenobia said, back straight, confident.

They looked to each other and smirked.

'What do you want with the emperor, girl?' one asked.

'I am a consul of Palmyra, Syria. My business is with the emperor alone.'

Body thick with mud, face weary, and boots in need of repair, the soldier jerked his head. 'Come with me.'

The soldiers escorted us forwards, down the lines of men, until we stepped in line with the marching soldiers.

'What is it?' one asked. He was as dirty as the rest, marching on foot, face brown and lined and tired.

'You have a request for audience,' the soldier replied.

The emperor looked over to Zenobia as if I were not there, and his face lost ten years as his frown smoothed and grim expression turned to surprise.

'We will be making camp soon,' he said. 'I will speak with them then.'

The army moved for no more than an hour more. Shouts sounded, legionaries stopped, orders were given, a camp organised and trenches dug.

The two men and our escort erected one tent and Zenobia and I the other. She was able-bodied, constructing quickly and efficiently. She did not speak, and I knew she thought on her words to Gallienus.

We ate amongst the Romans. Chatter and drinking and games filled cold night air. Zenobia drank with them, tossing dice and winning. If she charmed the emperor as she charmed the men we would have no trouble persuading him.

The camp settled. Noise and fires died and men drifted into

peaceful slumber.

'The emperor will see you now,' a soldier said, and jerked his head for us to follow.

We walked a long line of tents, taller than ours, but still the soldiers stooped in and out. We paused outside one, six soldiers standing sentry, and I felt a flutter of apprehension, our mission riding on the next few moments; our second and last chance.

We ducked inside. Gallienus sat behind a table as Valerian had sat behind a desk in Rome, the tent otherwise bare. They were different in approach. Valerian did not wish to see us, made no pretence at humouring us, and believed what he had wanted to believe, what his own commanders told him. Gallienus sat with a serenity I had not imagined a man of war to emanate. Scars marred his face, cutting through a short beard, no thicker than my own. He stood up and genially gestured we take chairs opposite him. An aide stood to one side, four soldiers lining the walls, and the soldier who had come for us sat down at one end of the table.

'My sincere apologies,' the emperor said. 'You caught me on a long march home. I am not entirely sure who it is I address,' he smiled, eyes flicking between Zenobia and myself.

'We are honoured to be in your presence, Caesar. I am Zenobia Zabdilas, consul of Palmyra, and this is my personal guard and cousin, Zabdas. We were sent to Rome on behalf of King Odenathus …'

'Of Syria?' Gallienus interrupted.

'Palmyra, indeed.'

Gallienus relaxed into his seat and traced a wide scar close to his ear.

'But you are not in Rome. You are west of Rome, seeking an audience with me.'

The man sitting at the end of the table gave a low snigger and leaned forward on the table.

Gallienus appeared amused as he waited for a response.

Zenobia remained unmoved.

'Indeed, Caesar. I am here to plead for reinforcements ...'

'Wait a moment,' Gallienus said, and my patience tore. 'Two questions. Firstly, why come to me? My father is at this very moment in Rome. Surely he could have listened to your plea?'

Zenobia did not hesitate. 'We have pleaded with your father already, but alas to no avail. Roman commanders report that the east can hold for now, as it always has, against the Persian invaders. He makes his decision based on this.'

Gallienus closed his eyes momentarily.

'I see. And so you have come to me in the hope that my opinion might differ?'

'Precisely.'

Gallienus chuckled, and the man at the end of the table laughed, too.

'I admire your honesty.'

'You had a second question?' she said.

Gallienus tilted his head and studied Zenobia.

'Why would a woman come with only three soldiers and a guide? Surely you travelled from Syria with a larger escort?'

Zenobia shrugged off her cloak.

'We came with an escort of more than a hundred men. Our leader and company felt we had done all we could having spoken with your father.'

The emperor's smile evaporated.

'I see. This man, this leader with whom you came, he thinks my father holds imperium, hmm?'

Zenobia said nothing. Clever, I thought. She touched on delicate matters.

After a while Gallienus said, 'What makes you think my answer will differ from my co-emperor's?'

'You are a lord of war,' Zenobia replied. 'You know enough to understand and sympathise with Odenathus' position and the problems he faces. The Persians threaten Syria, but it is also under invasion from many other tribes, including the Tanukh.' She leaned forward and they held one another's gaze with ease.

'My king has held the Syrian frontier — your frontier — for many years with success. But our enemies become more powerful, and yet the legions in Syria remain the same. It has become increasingly difficult to continue to maintain control. Numerous cities have been lost. My own father led men to the Euphrates two years ago. He came out of retirement to protect the Empire.'

My mind was filled with Julius, whether he still held the southern frontier, and if he were dead or alive. I felt the draw of home, a heavy pull in my stomach. I craved, then, to return to Palmyra.

'My father will have seen your problems in the east as part of a greater problem, as part of the Empire's problems; something that weighs heavily on us both. When he and I became colleagues, Rome was close to collapse; it still is. Maintaining and securing the frontiers is a huge problem. A massive undertaking. If Valerian Caesar thinks you can hold, he makes his decision based on how much pressure he is under elsewhere.' Gallienus barely looked at me as he spoke, eyes fixed intently on Zenobia. 'It is an easy choice to make, when the people whose lives are immediately at risk are not people you know, when there are enemies closer to home. Believe me, I understand the troubles your country faces, and I have a great deal of respect for Odenathus. He is an incredibly loyal man.'

'He is the best of men,' Zenobia replied. 'You could not wish for a more trustworthy ruler to a client kingdom.'

A mild hint that Odenathus could turn against Rome without notice was not lost on the younger emperor.

'You can leave us now, Posthumus,' Gallienus said to the man sat at the end of the table.

'Caesar,' Posthumus acknowledged.

He bowed and stooped out of the tent. Only the guards, Zenobia, Gallienus and I remained.

'I understand,' he said. 'Odenathus has my full support in all matters, but whether it is physically possible to push more legions to Syria's frontier is another problem entirely. That may be difficult to accept, but it is also quite probably the case. I know my own men are stretched.'

'Give me a day,' Zenobia challenged, 'and I will change your mind.'

Gallienus grinned, boyish and amused. He rose from his seat, took Zenobia's hand and assisted her to her feet.

'I have no doubt you would try. Your escort waits for you in Rome?'

'They are camped on the outskirts of the city.'

'Then you can travel back with me. And you can have two days to plead your case.'

Hope gripped once more.

The following morning we set off back to Rome. Zenobia accompanied Gallienus. They both walked, despite his offer of a horse. She described the horrors that had been relayed to us by our own soldiers; how our frontier was collapsing, cities pillaged, citizens taken as slaves, trade routes threatened – a reminder of Rome's own grain supply.

'It is why Rome can never let Palmyra fall,' he said. 'Without produce from Egypt, Rome would starve.'

'And yet we are so close to falling ...'

'So you keep reminding me. Tell me, Zenobia, how did you gain your position within Palmyra? It is most unusual for women; particularly in the eastern courts.'

'My father is a stratego in the Palmyrene army. A well-respected man. Whilst at war, I am his voice on the council.'

'Ah, I see. I thought perhaps ...' He paused, as if unwilling to finish his thoughts.

I could not see Zenobia's expression, but she made no attempt to pursue his unfinished words.

'I am concerned,' Gallienus went on, brushing arms with her, 'that at least a third of the Empire's grain supply comes from Egypt through Syria. There is no denying that. You are right of course, and it is a very real threat.'

'That is my concern, also,' Zenobia replied. 'If Syria falls, and the supply routes forfeit ...'

'Indeed. It is an important frontier to protect; a vital trade route. Odenathus has held well and for a good long time. But I know he has petitioned many times in the past. The senate has voted on numerous occasions. In reality, that is quite possibly why my father believes he can still hold. Jupiter's whiskers, we have so many other problems, Zenobia.'

The leather beneath Gallienus' armour creaked. We walked fast, yet he broke no sweat, his breath was not laboured, and his stride betrayed no ailments.

I watched as the connection between the emperor and Zenobia grew. She spoke differently; coldness dropping away replaced by understanding and warmth and agreement. Her diplomacy reminded me of Julius, and the gentle way he spoke. I hoped she knew what she did, and it seemed I had no cause for concern. Two days later, when the city came in sight, Gallienus agreed that Syria's security warranted attention. He would discuss the matter with his father.

Our position changed the way a storm in the desert changes the lie of the land, creating drifts where before the sands were flat. The decision to send more forces east was no longer that of Valerian alone, but also of Gallienus, a man known as The Hero of War.

Zenobia would not return to our camp. She would stay in the city, with Regulus, until word came from Gallienus. I agreed readily enough, swayed by my desire to spend time with Aurelia.

Back at Regulus' house, we discovered he had continued to send messages to anyone and everyone he held acquaintance with and trusted during our absence.

'He promised to speak with his father?' he said of our news. 'My my, you have done well, Zenobia. I have sat here worrying a great deal. I scarce believed you would get to speak with him, least of all persuade him to address the matter. Let us hope the gods are with you.'

'We do not need many. If Gallienus can persuade his father to spare just a few thousand, it will be enough,' Zenobia said.

'Indeed, indeed. At least to provide a solid defence.'

'Exactly. For a man of the philosophical world, you know a good deal about the military.'

'As do you, Zenobia,' he replied.

Zenobia smiled. 'My father talked much of life in the army.'

'He spoke of it when he was here, too,' Regulus replied, and I felt a pang of jealousy. Both Zenobia and Regulus had talked to Julius of his life in the army, of war, or soldiering. They knew him far better and for longer than I. They could recount experiences, phrases Julius said, things he had taught them. I barely knew him.

Our immediate excitement waned. News from Gallienus failed to appear. My patience wore thin as despair grew.

'Perhaps obtaining reinforcements was just a dream,' Regulus would say to Zenobia.

She would laugh, shrug his comments away, until one evening, almost three weeks after our return to Rome, and still no word from Gallienus, she lost her restraint.

'Are we not all dreamers, Regulus? We dream to improve, to aspire, to become more. We dream of peace and happiness and family, of wealth, land and power. Every one of us in this room is free. Free to eat what we like, to walk where we want, speak the words we wish to speak and worship the gods we desire. Zabdas knows what it is to lose freedom.' She grabbed my arm and pulled the band from my wrist, exposing the slave mark upon it. 'We all bear this mark, whether it be Persian or Goth or one of a hundred enemies. I dream of a land without threat and fear of invasion.'

Impatience, I think, encouraged her. Regulus took no offence. Too old and wise to be disgruntled over heated words.

And I think he admired her for them. When he accused her of being a dreamer, it had not been in jest. She was more passionate than anyone. Did he see that her ambitions would carry her far in life? Perhaps. She knew what she sought. She grasped with both hands and refused to let go, just as she had once told me to.

The morning after, she went to Gallienus.

'I will go with you,' I said.

She shook her head and wrapped a cloak about her shoulders, lifting the hood and masking her face.

'No. I need only a guide, Zabdas, and you do not know Rome. I must do this alone. I will be back before long.'

Regulus hobbled into the room.

'You need to be careful, Zenobia. If Valerian discovers you putting pressure on his son to change his mind, he will not be pleased.'

'Do not worry, Regulus, I will be discreet.'

'It is not worth risking your safety. Gallienus will send word as soon as he can,' Regulus replied.

She lifted her hood back.

'He has yet to send word. Palmyra is my home, but I share it with thousands. Should we all lose our homes because one person was too afraid to push for aid?'

Regulus nodded. I could not. She replaced her hood and left.

'Be careful,' I called after her.

'She is strong, Zabdas. She will return to us safe, I am sure,' Regulus said, and disappeared into the depths of his house.

I wanted to believe his words, but my heart felt terror, an iron grip on my stomach. Alone, she would go to Gallienus, request an audience. What else? My thoughts turned bitter at the connection they had, the flirtation between them. There was more, I thought, but could not be sure.

Hours passed. She did not return. I paced, staring without comprehension at mosaic floors and out at a crisp blue sky. What had happened? What fate had befallen her? My heart pounded. I sat in a house, in safety and luxury, yet I felt on a battlefield, the apprehension of the enemy present.

Regulus joined me, and together we sat in silence. We paced the small garden without a word, staring absently at the flowers and plants, before resuming our seats. Aurelia offered food, but I felt no hunger. She touched my bare arm, and warmth spread in a radius from where our flesh met. For a moment I relaxed, but it was short-lived. A knock at the door stirred everyone. Aurelia answered, only to discover a messenger for Regulus on a personal matter. Was Zenobia sitting in the same room as Gallienus? Had Valerian discovered her liaison with his son and co-emperor? She was my family now, my cousin and my friend. I should have gone with her.

Midday came and went. Light began to fade, and with it my hope of Zenobia's return. I sat in the garden numb to the cold. I thought about returning indoors, but felt no inclination to move. And then Aurelia joined me.

'Regulus believes Zenobia will return soon,' she said, her voice little more than a whisper.

'I pray to the gods she does.'

'If Regulus believes it, then she will.'

I looked into the water behind me. The grubby reflection of a lean boy, sun-dark skin and hair as black as raven wings, stared back. Next to him, a girl, shimmering hair illuminated by the glowing moon. The reflection smiled. Although I did not feel it, the boy smiled back. Her hand moved towards me, warm fingers gripping, and I closed my eyes, heart hammering, a rush of excitement and longing and need. I wanted her. When I turned I found her soft, open mouth with my own. My fingers released hers; I pulled her toward me, held her close, her body pressed against mine. She wrapped her arms around me. I willed the moment to last a lifetime, encompassed in this world. The two of us, letting every morsel of grief and despair wash away. Experiencing new pleasures.

I kissed her again, mouth sweet and soft and skin perfumed with rosewater.

Voices sounded. Zenobia had returned.

I pulled away and looked into pale eyes.

'Go,' Aurelia said.

I ran into the house. Zenobia was safe, unharmed; exactly as she had left that morning. My heartbeat slowed and relief flooded. A moment and I noticed Zabbai beside her.

'Zabdas, it is good to see you,' he said.

'And you,' I replied, earlier words brushed aside by good news.

'Please, continue,' Regulus urged Zenobia.

Zenobia smiled. 'Gallienus meets with his father at this very moment. I believe he can persuade him, that we will have forces re-distributed to Syria. I sought Zabbai to give him the news.'

'That is wonderful,' Regulus said.

Zenobia slid her cloak from her shoulders and laid it across a couch.

Zabbai said, 'We can hope. Valerian is the supreme emperor. If he chooses to stand firm, there may be nothing Gallienus can do. You need to remember that Gallienus commands in the west. The east is Valerian's problem.'

'Have faith,' Zenobia said.

Zabbai grumbled, low and inaudible.

'By the gods,' Regulus exclaimed, 'we might yet have the answer we need.'

And we would return home …

I looked back to see Aurelia standing in the doorway, eyes pooling and pink. She smiled at me and I knew joy and sadness simultaneously.

'What happened?' I asked, turning back. 'Had Gallienus not already spoken with his father of Syria?'

'It has been months since Gallienus last saw him,' Zenobia said. 'They need to talk of other matters primarily, but he understands our situation. He assured me he would speak with

Valerian on our behalf. The city is already buzzing with the excitement of his return. And his victory.'

Regulus sat down and let out a long breath.

'Well, Gallienus is a more sensible man than his father,' he said, contradicting himself. 'And more successful in war. This is what the Empire needs; stories of heroes and victories, not another frontier under attack.'

'It does,' Zabbai agreed. 'Gallienus may be the man to provide just that. But I am still reluctant to believe he can change his father's mind.'

'Rome needs a true warrior in order to rid itself of enemies,' Zenobia said, ignoring Zabbai.

Regulus looked reproachful. 'It needs a leader, not necessarily a warrior.'

Zenobia nodded. 'If Valerian agrees with his son and decides to send forces east, how long until legionaries reach our frontier?'

Zabbai shrugged. 'It depends. He may take legions from Rome, or redistribute men already close to Syria. Either way it will take months.'

Night passed, then the day. Still we heard nothing. Celebrations in aid of Gallienus' return still filled the streets outside weeks after his return, singing and the smell of freshly baked bread, and traders knocked on Regulus' door offering goods.

In the evening Zabbai sat beside me as we ate, the atmosphere light and enjoyable, despite talk of our plight.

'Are all Syrian soldiers great warriors?' Aurelia asked.

'We have many,' Zenobia replied. She leaned close to her avid listener, touched her golden hair with interest. 'To be a soldier of Palmyra — a Bedouin warrior — is a great privilege. We have distinguished philosophers, too. And priest kings rule some of our lands.'

'And is your king a warrior or a philosopher?'

'A warrior,' Zenobia said. 'He fights as I am told the Greeks do, without fear of death. Palmyrenes fight for their families and their homes. They fight because it is an honour and duty. And they die with swords in their hands.'

'Do you fight like a Palmyrene, Zabdas?'

'He does,' Zenobia replied for me.

Embarrassed, I said, 'I have yet to see battle.'

Zenobia frowned. 'Your heart, Zabdas, can match any Palmyrene's for courage and honour. You are an Egyptian after all.' Although she paid me great compliment, Zenobia's words were firm.

Wine flowed. We spoke of great rulers, the Empire, Persians, Tanukh, Goths, Britons, food, philosophers, and slavery. We talked of everything and the night wore on and Zabbai clapped me on the shoulder and pulled me away from the rest of the group.

'I do not know how she did it, but Gallienus will be talking with his father. How in the name of Bel did you walk up to a marching army, demand an audience with the co-emperor, and return here victorious? For the love of the gods, her father never came close to securing aid.'

Swaying slightly, my head whirring, I said, 'I cannot tell you, Zabbai, for I do not know. I think she is blessed,' I slurred. 'She talks about the gods and Selene and their favour …'

'The gods! Ha!'

I nodded slowly. 'Who knows?'

'Not me, I can tell you. The men, they like her.'

'Everyone likes her.'

'It is more than that. They hold respect. They believe she can achieve anything.'

We retired, hoping dawn would bring news. I wanted a moment alone with Aurelia, but I could not find it, and so I bade her a polite goodnight. I could not stop thinking of her, looking at her, but every time she crossed my mind my heart grew heavy. She was Roman, she would stay in Rome and marry. But if she felt as I did, she would not wish me to leave.

My thoughts dwelt on her above all else. I became tormented by my own desires, my own inability to flush thoughts of her from my mind. It felt natural to want her. It felt simple.

I stirred from sleep, morning chill on my shoulder and the room dark. Pounding sounded. Half-dressed, I left my room to find Regulus, confused and bewildered.

Aurelia appeared behind him. 'There is someone at the door,' she said.

We hastened down the passageway. I stole a glance at Aurelia, tousled hair, pale skin, a blanket wrapped about her. Zabbai appeared with a knife in his hand, Zenobia beside him. Zabbai was fully dressed, perhaps having slept as such. Zenobia wore a light shift.

Thudding again.

'Roman soldiers?' Zabbai asked.

Regulus, expression fearful, shook his head. 'I do not know.'

'It could be Gallienus.' Zenobia said.

I hoped for the latter.

A slave moved forward and opened the door.

'Move aside,' the visitor said.

Regulus moved forward. 'Who are you and what is your business here? This is no hour to call upon good citizens.'

Aurelia tugged my arm, gestured for Zenobia and Zabbai to follow. We backed down the corridor and she pulled a tapestry aside, pushed us behind and let the woven wall drop back into place. Hidden behind a false wall, I could not breathe, musty smell overwhelming and the urge to sneeze tormenting. My eyes adjusted to the dim light and I looked to my companions.

'Stand aside, old man,' came a voice, harsh and authoritative, but I sensed a faint quaver.

The door banged open. Aurelia gasped and feet shuffled back down the hallway.

'What now?' Zabbai whispered, raising his knife.

Zenobia put a finger to her lips and frowned.

'I insist you leave my home,' Regulus said.

The other man spoke, quiet and inaudible.

'They are searching for us,' I mouthed.

Zenobia nodded.

I looked for another way out, a passage to another part of the house, to a hidden room or outside, but found only solid walls and cobwebs.

'Something has happened,' I said. 'It is too quiet.'

We fell silent. Zenobia's breath on my cheek. I leaned toward the opening, straining to hear. Nothing.

We seemed to wait an eternity in the darkness before footsteps sounded and the tapestry was pulled aside. To my relief, only Regulus and Aurelia stood before us.

'Apologies, my friends. They took some persuading to leave.'

Zenobia put her hands on Regulus' shoulders. 'What news? What is happening?'

'I am not sure,' he replied, a hundred years on his old face. 'It seems there is a warrant out for your arrest.'

'We need to leave,' Zabbai said. 'It does not matter why they want to arrest us. And you are in equal danger, Regulus.'

'Ha,' Regulus replied, 'I am in no danger.'

'Zabbai is right,' Zenobia said. 'This house is no longer safe.'

I opened my mouth to speak, to agree that we should leave, that Regulus and Aurelia ought to find another place to stay, with friends or family, until our presence had past. But I did not, for a knock sounded at the door.

Gallienus himself had come to the house of Regulus.

CHAPTER 12

Samira - 290 AD (Present day)

I CANNOT DENY I am afraid, that the men upon this ship drive fear into my heart and anger into my soul. Grandfather is injured. He tries not to let it show but I know he is as I dab blood from his nose with my skirts. He is not as young as he once was, and he forgets.

I think of the captain, his hand upon my breast, his breath upon my face, and bile rises in my throat. Bamdad is looking at me. He sees what I am thinking, and I am embarrassed by the look he gives me, of pity.

'I am all right,' I say to him. 'Do not look at me that way.'

'None of us are all right,' he replies. 'What a fucking mess.'

I recoil at his tone. Jovial Bamdad, never serious, always humorous, and I know then we will be lucky to survive.

I try to unfasten the manacles on my grandfather's wrists and ankles, to free him of his bonds, but it is no use.

'Leave them,' he says.

I sit back, despair filling me, but we cannot let them take us and claim a price for my grandfather and Bamdad. How can we escape, I wonder, and set my mind to positive thought.

Shouting above and orders flying back and forth across the deck and the chant of the oar slaves. So much noise I cannot concentrate. A splash. The anchor dropped? The people about us stir, children wailing and whimpering and crying as mothers try to comfort them.

The hatch opens and daylight pours into the black hole in which we huddle.

'Move, move, up you come. Out.'

Bamdad and I help grandfather to his feet and we shuffle forward. He looks incapable of climbing the steps, bound so tight, but somehow he manages. Screams of fear ring behind me, and I try to block them out.

We step onto the deck into fierce, blinding light and I cannot see and then the colours of the sea and the grain of the ship slide into focus and we are tied off to another boat.

'Not you,' the captain says as we shuffle forward with the slaves.

Sticks crack against slaves' backs and I wince and close my eyes a moment. I cannot bear this, the pain caused and life traded. A woman darts to the edge of the ship, but she does not make it as one of the crew grabs her hair and hauls her back from the edge. Her cries fill the air as he slaps her hard across the face, over and again.

The screams cease.

We watch in silence as eight men with faces masked against the wind board from the other ship. They inspect the slaves and murmur to the captain and one looks to us with black eyes. The captain tells him who my grandfather is, who Bamdad is, I am sure. I bite my lip to stave the tears I know will come. I can be strong, I think, but I cannot. We must escape and I must ensure my grandfather and Bamdad are not sold for a hefty ransom; that my own virtue remains intact.

I look to the sea and escape. The horizon calls and I feel myself answer it.

We wait for what seems like my whole life and a second, whilst the captain talks with the men of the other ship, negotiating I am sure a price for the slaves he carries.

'I would see us free of this,' grandfather says.

'We will be,' Bamdad replies, ever sure.

'Shut your fucking mouths,' our guard sneers, his teeth yellow and his breath rancid and I recoil. 'I will have you,' he says to me. 'We all will have a taste of you before long.'

I maintain a blank expression, the one I imagine Zenobia wore many times.

Grandfather takes my hand. Women sing and the waves lap. The captain's men roam the deck, and our voices are more hushed as they pass.

'What will we do?' I whisper.

'Hold tight, Rubetta,' Bamdad replies.

The door of the captain's cabin swings open and slaves gasp and murmur and strain against heavy bonds. The captain smirks and I suspect he has made a good sale. He speaks with his men and commands are shouted and the slaves are herded like cattle, clubs and sticks wielded.

'Something is not right,' grandfather says.

'What is it?' I say. 'What do you see?'

'I do not know.'

Men stand on the other ship, their faces, too, wrapped black against the salt wind. They do not move but for the wind plucking at cloth. Sailors urge the slaves forward and heat rises in my neck and face as I will whatever happens next not to.

The slaves board, every last one; all screaming, crying, looking at the guardians of death standing over them and I glance at spiked heads along the side of the boat and I am afraid.

The man with black eyes walks back across the plank to our ship and I cannot bear to look but neither can I take my own eyes from him.

'You have them all,' the captain says.

The man nods.

'The gold ...' the captain prompts.

A sword whistles from a scabbard and the captain takes a step back and looks behind him for the support of his crew. It is too late. The masked men have boarded our ship

'What is happening?' the captain asks, nervous and unsure.

The black-eyed man reaches up and pulls down the mask from his face.

'I owe you nothing.'

'Fuck the gods,' Bamdad says. 'Bel's fucking balls. I cannot believe it.'

'*Mehercule!*' grandfather says. 'It is Rostram.'

'We had an agreement!' the captain shouts.

'I do not abide by your laws or your code,' the masked man replies.

The captain spits on the ground and I am confused. I want to ask who Rostram is.

The captain shouts, 'I want my gold or I will have your guts trailing the deck of that ship.' But he can say no more. With one sweep of Rostram's sword, the captain's head is severed from his body and thumps onto the deck.

Dozens of men run forward to meet the crew and their swords are held high and they are screaming a war cry loud and long as they slice at the crew and do not stop.

Rostram comes to us and grins. He is wild with death and hunger and I am uncertain of him, but he bends down and frees my grandfather and Bamdad and they embrace one another as brothers and he places a sword in each of their hands.

'By gods, I did not expect to see you here. It has been a long time,' he says.

'Bel's balls,' Bamdad says again, 'you are right about that.'

Grandfather throws his cloak to the floor and takes the sword hilt in both hands and roars to the sky, crying out, letting the moment consume him, and Bamdad does the same and I know that death will follow.

Shouts and screams and cries of pain reverberate on the waters. Years fade from my grandfather as he moves. He is lithe and he is fast and he kills. He is no philosopher or merchant, he is the man I have always known him to be, a soldier and a general and I see him move as he had been trained to as a boy, the same age as me. Does he owe these men and women, these slaves, something because he was once a slave? I cannot be sure but I see him and watch and whatever other reason he might have, he was born a warrior.

I realise I am alone, the slaves are all aboard the other boat and they are frightened and screaming. I move toward them, skirting the fighting and the killing, cross the plank between the two boats.

'It will be all right,' I say to them, helping remove manacles where I can, each freed man assisting another. I sing sweet lullabies to the small ones in the hope that I can block the sound of killing, because I can hear it, the wails and screams and cries of the dying, the clash of iron and the scrape of bone.

And then the shouting stops and there is no more ringing of swords or jeers, and laughter sounds because the killing has stopped.

'It is over,' grandfather roars, and thrusts his sword toward the god, Helios, blood running down his blade and arm.

I sit staring out at the waters. Bright light flecks the ripples and birds squawk overhead. We are sailing on Rostram's boat, bound for the north coast. Beneath me I know the slaves I had freed of manacles are bound by them once more, treated little better, and for that I could weep.

'It is a pirate ship,' I say to Bamdad.

He sits beside me, a needle and thread in hand, sewing a cut to his leg.

'Well observed, Rubetta,' he says, and I cannot decide if he agrees with the trade or not.

'You know the captain? Rostram,' I say, distaste on my tongue.

I want to leave this ship, to return to land and forget what has happened to us on the river. My eyes are glazed red and I cannot wash it away.

'We have known Rostram many years. Try not to concern yourself. We will not be on the river long.'

'Here,' I say, and take the needle and thread from him and squint at the gash. I pierce skin with needle and pull the wound together. He winces and I grin up at him, relishing causing a little pain.

Grandfather approaches. He has been talking with Rostram and he knows I am unhappy that the slaves are still slaves and that we sit on the same ship as if it has not happened.

'You were a slave yourself once,' I say, 'yet you do nothing.'

'I have spoken with Rostram, the slaves will be seen to land at the next dock.'

I nod, satisfied.

Once finished stitching, I look up at my grandfather. He has washed away the blood from his face and neck and hands and arms. He is what I have always known him to be, a slave turned soldier turned general. He is a great man and a keeper of peace in Palmyra. I love him for that, for his frankness and his honesty and his fearlessness. That he has spent his life putting others before himself, protecting his people and his country, as Zenobia once did.

I want to know more of her, the whole of her, to discover all I can, and I wish then for my grandfather to tell the rest of his tale.

'My apologies,' he says, 'you should not have witnessed the slaughter that took place today.'

I push the blood from my mind, dull the screams and the shouts and try to think once more of the Palmyrene queen.

'Tell me more of Zenobia, of your past.'

'I shall, Samira,' he says. He looks awkward, suddenly, unsure. 'Bamdad, can you leave us a moment?'

Bamdad struggles to his feet and slaps my grandfather on his shoulder and leaves without a word.

Grandfather sits down beside me, uninjured, unharmed.

'I will tell you more of the tale, either written or spoken. I will tell you everything. But you must know, there is a lot more to come, a lot more to Zenobia and the Palmyrene court that I have yet to describe.'

'I know,' I say, because I do. There are years left to tell, and I wish to know all of them. 'Here,' I say, and I pull grandfather's pack from beneath the bench on which we sit and hand him the parchment upon which he has already begun.

CHAPTER 13

Zabdas - 258 AD

'I REMEMBER YOU, REGULUS,' Gallienus said, voice brimming with confidence and authority.

We hung out of sight, unsure if the soldiers who came with a warrant for our arrest had returned, but I heard no one else.

'And I remember you,' Regulus replied. 'I congratulate you on your victory. The city has not stopped talking of it.'

'You are kind, but it is not why I am here. I seek Zenobia and her companion.'

'For what purpose?' Regulus asked.

A long pause. Beside me, Zenobia strained to hear.

'It is imperative I speak with her,' Gallienus resumed. 'She may be in danger. My father has issued a warrant for her arrest and that of her companions. He believes they are here. Soldiers will be on their way. Indeed, they could be here at any moment.'

'You are too late, Gallienus. They have already been here looking for her. They searched my house and found nothing. Is there something else?'

Silence again, long and uncomfortable, as Gallienus appeared unwilling to say more, and Regulus refused to admit our presence.

Zenobia brushed past me.

'Where are you going?' I hissed.

'To speak with Gallienus.'

Gods, I thought, rolling my eyes, and Zabbai and I followed. 'Zenobia!' Gallienus took her hand and smiled.

Zenobia did not exchange pleasantries, but instead said, 'Why has your father issued a warrant for our arrest?'

Gallienus did not appear taken aback, answering without pause. 'He thinks you try to sway me. Which of course, you have.' He grinned. Boyish, I thought, and slightly stupid looking.

'True,' Zenobia said.

'My reason for this visit is merely to warn you,' Gallienus went on, releasing her hand and stepping back to address the room. 'I was too late to stop the order or speak with my father properly. I must do that now.'

Regulus rapped his cane on the tiled floor. 'I cannot believe a warrant has been put out for your arrest! A consul of this very Empire!'

Aurelia put a hand on his shoulder, but his rage did not subside.

'I will contact you as soon as I know more,' Gallienus said. 'I would find you alternative accommodation, but it seems my father's men were satisfied that you are not here.' He kissed Zenobia's hand and offered Aurelia a reassuring smile.

'We do not wish to cause any trouble here,' Zenobia said. 'The east of the Empire is under a great threat. You know that already. I only hope your father will listen to you, for the safety of both Rome and the people of Syria.'

'There are two emperors,' Gallienus replied. 'I will obtain what you seek.'

He inclined his head and departed and the door swung shut behind him.

Regulus gave a long, tired sigh and slumped into a chair.

'Oh Zenobia,' he said, 'if your father saw you now he would be so proud.'

'My father is humbled to call you friend; as am I. You have risked more for us in these weeks than can ever be repaid.'

'I do not deserve such words, Zenobia. There is no doubt

whose daughter you are.' His face seemed to lighten, then his mouth drooped once again as he said, 'I am an old man, but I never thought to see Rome come to this; a squabble between two emperors. Two heads are better than one. Ha! A pox on the man who thought of that.'

'Promise me you will stay safe when we are gone?' Zenobia said.

'Of course I will.'

Before nightfall, we discovered which emperor reigned supreme. We had our verdict.

Gallienus did not return. A messenger arrived with a scrawled note which Zenobia read aloud.

To Zenobia, consul of Palmyra, Syria

From Publius Licinus Egnatius Gallienus, Co-Emperor of Rome

Greetings!

I have spoken with my father. The legions are assembling.

Be ready to leave soon ...

Zenobia broke off. Regulus came to stand beside us. Zenobia passed him the note and his brow creased.

'What is it?' I asked. Why did he not smile or shout with joy? The additional legions were ours. We had what we came for. The east would not fall.

'Ah,' Regulus breathed.

Zabbai took the note, scanned it, then stared absently ahead and continued:

I must return west. My father, Valerian Caesar, will lead the eastern cause.

'Valerian would travel east?' I shouted. 'Why? Why not Gallienus? Valerian is no general! Gods' strength, is there to be no end?'

Zenobia looked at me blankly. 'We have our army. We must be satisfied.'

I took the note for myself and reread the words. *Valerian Caesar will lead the eastern cause.* And below, an addition note, scrawled almost as an afterthought:

It has been my honour to meet with you, Zenobia. If you were a man, you could have been an emperor. May you achieve everything you set your mind to, and I pray we meet again.

'This cannot happen,' Zabbai said. He stood up, paced to the doorway, his back to Regulus, Aurelia and myself. 'Valerian is no general. Gods give me strength.' He gripped his hair with both hands and turned back to us. 'We must write back to Gallienus. Persuade him to come east and lead the armies against the Persians. He is a man of victory, of war. With Valerian I see nothing but failure.'

'You cannot,' Regulus said. 'Long before you came to Rome, Gallienus and his father agreed to divide the Empire in two: Gallienus rules the west whilst Valerian controls the east, and that agreement, it seems, still stands.'

I pondered the capabilities of the older Augustus, and waited for the hour we would set off home. And ached at the thought of never seeing Aurelia again.

Despatches sent, legions woken, orders given, and soldiers ready to march. I cannot describe the strange feeling of excitement and apprehension that gripped me as we readied to leave. Zabbai, fractious about Valerian leading the armies, paced constantly. Zenobia's mood lightened. She had what she came for, and I suspected she longed to return east. Regulus and Aurelia had worn sombre expressions since Gallienus' note had arrived. Regulus because he enjoyed our company, and I hoped, rather than suspected, that Aurelia felt something for me.

I wanted to speak with her, but I did not know what to say, and dwelt ceaselessly on my feelings. She dropped our departure into conversation here and there, yet I had no idea what would come, no way to reassure and no promise I could give. I pushed her comments to the back of my mind and left everything to the gods.

Our bags were packed and transport arranged. We planned to travel the following day and deliver news as fast as possible that Roman forces came to our aid. I sat on my bed, watched the city from my window, breathed in the last of Rome, when a thought came to me. Regulus had always wanted to visit Palmyra. Would he allow Aurelia that rare opportunity, to see something of the world beyond the walls of Rome, outside the politics and bustle of a city as great as this?

Zenobia disturbed my thoughts.

'Are you ready to leave?'

'I am.' Thoughts of Aurelia trailed behind my words.

'I will be downstairs.'

'Zenobia?'

She turned back, expectant.

'What say you to Aurelia coming to court?'

'To Palmyra?'

I nodded.

'If Regulus is happy for her to accompany us, then I see no reason why not.' Her eyes were curious, as if she looked into my mind. Did she judge me then as I judged myself? I knew what Regulus might say, what assumptions he could have.

Aurelia stood in the doorway of my room. Fine silks floated over her body, glimmering in the weak morning light. She wore them well; standing tall and proud and Roman, her slender pale arms chinked with bracelets of gold and silver.

'You are leaving, and it will be as if you never stepped foot in this house,' she said.

She looked hopeful, as if I could say something that might lead to new possibilities, and I realised Regulus had spoken with her.

I smiled.

'I wondered,' she said, 'if it was your idea for me to visit the Palmyrene court?'

I hesitated a moment, not because I did not want to admit that it had been me, but because I feared she did not feel the same, that I might somehow embarrass myself.

'It was.'

I put the clothes I held down on the bed and took her hand, nervous. It was warm, soft, with an underlying strength as she gripped mine in return. I embraced her, and smelled her hair, floral and sweet. I wanted her to convince me that she felt the same. She must, I thought, but I could scarce believe it. We parted. I brushed a golden lock from her face. Stark and honest, her eyes flickered. There was no need to look at her expression to know what she felt then, for I saw it in those windows. Full of sorrow and shame, hurt, longing, pleasure. They were not like Zenobia's; relentless black, filling a man with trepidation at what he might see if they were lit and her thoughts exposed. In Aurelia I saw only warmth; real, open, tangible. I found reciprocation.

'It is time that I wish to spend in your company. I cannot promise how often I might be in the city, but I think you would like Palmyra, and I know there is much to absorb.'

She looked down, nodding, unable to meet my eye.

I kissed her.

When we parted, she smiled. I grinned back despite myself, clutched her face in my hands, not wanting to let go. I could have stood there always.

'And so tomorrow we leave Rome,' she said, and let out a half breath, half laugh.

'I will treasure the moments I spend with you.'

I kissed her again, as I had in the garden. Desperation burned; a feeling so intense I could not master myself. I had watched her, the way she moved and looked at me, glancing then turning away, as if embarrassed to be caught. Every touch between us had been a connection, but I had not quite understood. Not until now.

Timidly, she reached under my tunic, her hands exploring my chest. She pulled the cloth over my head and pale eyes beckoned. I felt her warm skin, sun-kissed earth, as her body pressed against mine. I ran my hands over every curve of her and kissed her more passionately; not wanting to stop, not thinking of stopping, not even knowing how to. She could have been Aphrodite or Venus. She stroked my face, as if wanting to ensure it was I who made love to her. I kissed her hand as I felt my body experience what it was like to be so close to another being; a pure, naked, innocent desire.

I caressed her face and stroked her hair as she wept onto my chest. Then she laughed and sniffed and wiped the tears on me, hot and real. She squeezed me tight, gave a murmur of contentment. And I held her so she could never escape me. I wanted her forever. I wanted this closeness. Whispers of love were not enough, so we said them over and over again, each one with increased sincerity.

The following morning we departed. Standing in the atrium of Regulus' home, we bade him farewell. He hobbled close and handed me a scroll.

'Here,' he said. 'It is a script of Latin. Use it to broaden your knowledge, Zabdas. Julius read it many times whilst in my house. He enjoyed it very much.'

I accepted it, warm in the knowledge that Julius had leafed through the same script.

'Gratitude.'

'It is nothing,' Regulus said, but beamed triumphant as he spoke. He looked to Aurelia and said, 'I have loved you very much, my girl. You have brought much light and warmth to an old man's house. I wish you good fortune, and I am sure I will see you again soon. Take it all in, my child, for when you return from the east I wish to know everything you have seen.'

'I will never forget the kindness you have shown me, Regulus, and the home you have shared,' she replied, kissing him on both cheeks.

'Then this is it, Regulus,' Zenobia said warmly. 'We must leave you. I cannot offer enough thanks for what you have done for us. We owe you a great deal.'

'I bid you a safe journey, Zenobia. My thoughts are with you; you and your father.' He embraced her, as a father would, holding her long and with teary eyes. 'You mean a great deal to me, you always have, even before I met you.'

We left under a cold light and dry sky. I was thankful for that. The Romans claimed Italia to be hot in summer. I could scarce believe the drizzle would stop. With Aurelia in our company and my hunger for home, time raced. We would reach Syria long before the Roman legions. I thought of familiar buildings and people and desert heat and Teymour's unknown fate. I prayed Julius was safe, and guilt clenched my gut for the promises I could not keep.

I pushed our pace hard for home. We travelled in all weathers, willing Palmyra on the horizon. I was not alone; the men anxious to discover the fate of their families, many with wives and children living near the frontier.

Zabbai had been humbled, his lack of faith in Zenobia proved wrong. She had persuaded Gallienus and found success. He was wary but his expression was softer, open to hear her words, listen to advice. She seemed blind to his change, and I could not help thinking of his words to her, and Odenathus' true motives for sending her west. I did not ask her, but I wished I had questioned Zabbai the night we drank much in Regulus' house, to know the truth.

Tides change and they changed for me. With Aurelia I thought less of Julius, less of the need to be in the south. Had she craved, when I first met her, first saw her at the entrance of Regulus' home and looked into those blue eyes, that she wanted to travel to Syria, to be with me? I could not be sure.

Aurelia never participated in our talk of politics. She felt unable to comment, not being of Palmyrene blood. I told her that I myself was not of Syrian ancestry, but it made no difference. She took no notice, claiming she was there because of me. She was genteel and inoffensive. I thought of her life in Rome, and could not convince myself she would do better with me. What had I to offer her? A life on a frontier, no money and no future but an army life. The life her father could have given her had he wanted to? I tried not to think of the general facing the Goths, his reluctance to know his daughter turning my stomach.

We reached the warmth of home, the year almost gone, and breathed the familiar sands, spices, aromas, unable to capture enough. Knowing we were close to my Palmyra, I excited Aurelia with descriptions of the kingdom, remembering the first time I experienced each smell, gazed upon each sight and felt the sand beneath my feet, wanting to savour those sensual pleasures. I was afraid that, when we reached Syria, Aurelia would long for Rome; her home, to return to the city she had been born into and the life Regulus had given her. But in her face I saw astonishment, joy and wonder. Where guilt remained, fear evaporated. A pool in desert heat.

My conscience pulled and I glanced at Zenobia. No trace of her once joyous youth. I missed the Zenobia I knew in Julius' home; laughing and vibrant. Two years and she had grown, her responsibilities and ideals hardening. No mischief and little amusement. She was not the same woman. She had changed, and yet I felt closer. She needed no one, and yet she needed everyone, cultivating relationships with Odenathus, Gallienus, even Zabbai. There would be no man spared.

We passed through ports, all under Roman rule, each one telling of the enormity of the Persian army. They were moving closer. Some said they already breached the walls of our beloved city, others that they reached as far as Carrhae and Edessa. We could not hasten our pace, but it felt as if we did, desperation to reach the east and discover the true extent of invasion.

We made land and the city of Antioch.

Zenobia already felt at home. I saw it the relaxed set of her shoulders and the pleasure on her face. Antioch bore all the marks of the Palmyrene kingdom. It lay to the west of the desert, near the sea. The city walls in sight, we travelled hard; the first night in our home country the driving force behind our haste. Our warrior band breathed a sigh of thanks to the gods. I could only think of Palmyra.

A handful of our company entered the north gate to collect supplies. The remainder set up camp for the evening outside the city walls. We headed for the forum, where wood and pottery balanced on trestles outside shops. Nuts, seeds, fruit and joints of meat outside others. And stalls were hidden behind swathes of fabric.

'We are but a few days from Palmyra,' Zenobia said. 'We will not need much. Enough to see us home.'

Shouts and jeers sounded, but I could not make out the words. Stopped by a crowd massing in the street, I glanced to Zabbai. He shrugged.

'Why do senators always grow fat on our gold?' a man shouted.

I pushed through to the front of the crowd. High sun beat down. Dozens of slaves, naked and dirty, stood upon a wooden stage. Tituli hung around their necks. My skin shrank and my breath grew ragged. I had not seen a slave market in many years. I could not relive again my childhood, stood upon the boards myself, awaiting sale. I tried to pull away, to retreat, but the crowds pushed forward for a view.

'You are filth, Mareades. Filth!' a woman shrieked, fists waving.

Nearby, a boy of four or five whimpered 'father', tears running down grubby cheeks. Next to him his mother stood, her dress clutched in tight fists, tears streaming down dirty cheeks.

I read the Tituli. The slaves came from Iberia, Gallia, the Balkans, Egypt, Africa, Dacia, Parthia, their ailments shown beneath. And then I saw the origin *Syrian* and beneath *Servi poanae*. Criminal.

Zenobia placed a hand on my shoulder, frowning, as if she sensed something wrong.

'What is it?' I asked.

'I have heard the name Mareades before. My father spoke of him. A man of Antioch.'

'What did your father say?'

She peered at the slaves. 'He knew him. He came to Palmyra representing Antioch many times. And later, he traded with him. He claimed him trustworthy.'

'And he has been put to slavery?' Zabbai said.

The noise of the crowd grew louder. Some threw stones. Soldiers moved to stop them but to no avail. This man was not simply a slave, but a hated one. Mareades raised his arms for protection, naked flesh bruised and cut, head shaved.

The mob screamed.

I could not watch and turned my head. Three slaves already sold.

'Purchase them,' I said to Zenobia. 'I beg you.'

'You do not know what he has done,' Zabbai replied. 'What any of them have done, seven criminals amongst them.'

Zenobia said, 'He was once senator of Antioch. I heard he worked tirelessly throughout his career in a bid to secure lucrative, fair trade through this city. That he helped many merchants establish themselves in business.'

Beside us, a man in gaudy green robes, a priest king I suspected, shouted over the din of the crowd, 'You know nothing of dealings in this city, girl!'

'I did not claim to,' Zenobia replied. 'But how does a man renowned for doing good, and with a reputation of honesty, find himself a slave?'

His pinched face and small, greedy eyes narrowed. 'And who are you, to question what this man has done?'

'Zenobia Zabdilas, consul of Palmyra.'

'This man was found guilty of embezzlement.'

Zenobia ignored him. 'I gave you my name, but you have not shown the same courtesy.'

He threw back his shoulders. 'I am a senator of Antioch and a priest of Bel,' he said.

'I know *what* you are, I asked who you are.'

The priest glowered at Zenobia and spat silent words before composing himself. 'My name … is Haddudan.'

The sale stopped, the crowd listening to our exchange.

'Mareades gave my family shelter when our house burnt to the ground last year,' one man shouted.

'And he sent his own doctor to my wife when she was ill,' said another.

Mareades' wife, clutching her son, nodded eager agreement. 'That is right. He did. He is an honest man. He stole nothing. Not from anyone. Please … please …' She cried harder.

'I have the documentation that proves his guilt,' Haddudan spat. 'His punishment is slavery.'

'I will buy the rest,' Zenobia shouted to the Venalitius, who nodded.

'6,000 denarii,' he said.

'Agreed.' To Haddudan she said, 'He is my slave now, and I would like to know what documentation you have?'

'Be careful, Zenobia,' Zabbai murmured.

Haddudan paused and wiped sweat from his temple. 'There are transactions made in his name, in the city and temple ledgers.'

'This man is a trained bookkeeper; one of the best, most experienced that I know,' Zenobia said, turning to me. 'Is it possible transactions in public records could be fraudulent?'

'Of course,' I said. 'His name could quite easily have been put against any number of transactions. Unless you have proof the senator signed for the amounts recorded? That he has the monies under dispute?'

The crowd changed as quickly as the winds change, more and more adding murmurs of agreement, the balance shifting to the probability of innocence.

Haddudan glowed with fury. He gave a sharp look to the hungry spectators and gestured we follow him.

The slaves were lead from the platform. Zenobia tossed a bag of coins to the Venalitius.

'Make sure they are ready to leave the city,' she said to Zabbai.

We wasted time. Part of me wished we had not stopped. We should have headed to Palmyra, informed the king of Rome's decision. I told myself the army was on its way no matter how long we paused. Yet the sight of the men on the platform, stripped naked, their origin and ailments hanging from their necks, sickened me.

I touched the slave mark upon my arm. Knew we did right. That Mareades and the other slaves, guilty or not, criminals or not, were now under Zenobia's protection. But did we need to know if he was guilty? I thought not. I did not matter now, but Zenobia was determined.

She followed the priest purposefully; her stride up the temple steps in time with his. We walked beneath colonnades and entered the cool gloom of the temple. Bel's temple. People wandered the pillared halls, as large as those in Palmyra, ceilings decorated with human forms and geometric patterns.

In his own temple, the priest turned with renewed confidence.

'That man stole from the very gods who protect him.'

'How?' Zenobia asked.

'He had access to the city records, made fraudulent transactions within them. Signed them himself! Once discovered, I looked into those records myself. I can vouch for his guilt.'

Haddudan pursed his lips, drew himself up to his full height.

'As Zabdas can testify, that does not mean to say it was him. How many others have access to the records you keep?'

'Of course it was him!'

'I do not believe you can prove it,' Zenobia said.

'The citizens of Antioch must have their justice. They have been robbed, each and every one of them!'

Zenobia's brow furrowed. 'And yet, the documents you have could be forged?'

'I assure you. I have seen the evidence myself. It was Mareades!'

Another priest approached Haddudan. A few murmured words and Haddudan excused himself, moved aside to talk with his colleague.

'Haddudan covers his own dealings,' she said. 'Of that I am sure.'

'I agree. But what is the point of this? Mareades is under your protection now. Free him.'

'You forget his reputation, Zabdas. Freeing him will not clear his name.' She sighed. 'But we cannot clear his name without proof of the guilty party. All I have done is create doubt in the minds of the people standing in the forum.'

Haddudan returned. Zenobia's face hardened.

I admired what she had done, that she would try to save a man, his life and his reputation, on a whispered breath from me. She did not care what people thought of her, she chose her own path, made her own decisions.

'I am not convinced Mareades was responsible for embezzling public and temple funds. The people outside vouch for his character, and more in Palmyra would do the same.'

Haddudan gave an exasperated huff. 'Then what would you have me do?'

'Clear his name.'

Haddudan's eyes widened, his face grew red, and his mouth fixed in a thin line.

'No,' he said. 'I will not agree to this. The mob will want a man held accountable, and it must be him.'

'Speak with the other senators. Ask their opinion,' I said.

He looked about to argue.

'All right.'

Zenobia and I walked back outside, the sun bright and the crowds dispersed. My first time in Antioch and already I could smell corruption. The lives of men riding on the greed and lies of others.

'I have given them food and drink,' Zabbai said as we approached.

Mareades looked across at us, a broken man, slumped upon a bench, back hunched. The letter F branded upon his cheek.

'Who marked him?' Zenobia asked.

'The Venalitii, before I could stop them. The priest king's orders, that he be branded following sale,' Zabbai said.

The burn wept and I could have wept too. No coin or clearing of name could remove the mark. He could not bind it from sight as I did. He would live with it for the rest of his life.

'Fucking priests,' Zenobia said, and I recoiled at her words, that a curse could leave her lips as easily as it left the lips of soldiers. The injustice of what had happened lacing each letter.

'What did the priest say?' Zabbai asked.

'He speaks with the senators. I had hoped to clear his name, but now …? What would it matter? A cleared name would make no difference. He is branded a criminal.'

Mareades looked up. 'I have told them that I am innocent.' His voice croaked, but his words were proud.

'I know,' I said. 'We are trying to help. You are under our protection now.'

'We are leaving,' Zenobia said. 'You cannot stay here. Do you wish to take your family with you?'

Mareades looked blankly back. Tears welled in his eyes as he shook his head.

We did not wait for Haddudan to speak with the senators. We walked out of Antioch and met with our escort, nine slaves to our number.

A safe distance from the city walls, Zenobia said to Mareades, 'I had no choice but to leave. We could not clear your name, and if we could, what then? You are branded a criminal and a slave. My father once spoke well of you, and Zabdas knows what it is to be wrongly taken a slave. You are a free man now; branded but free. It is all I can do.'

'I cannot go back,' Mareades whimpered again. 'I am a criminal.'

No one replied.

'What am I to do? Antioch was my home. I have lost my family. I can make nothing of myself now.'

Zabbai cast him incredulous look. 'Zenobia can always sell you to another. She bought you after all.'

Mareades did not acknowledge his words. 'Can nothing more be done? Can I not plead my case? Perhaps King Odenathus would speak on my behalf?'

'Are you wishing you had not bothered?' Zabbai hissed to me.

'A little,' I said, a weak grin on my face. 'What now? Zenobia has given him his freedom.'

Zabbai scratched the back of his neck. 'He could come back to Palmyra. Though there is nothing Odenathus could do for him. He will not be welcome amongst the city people. He is marked. The only place for Mareades now is with the nomads.'

Two days later, we parted company. Mareades uttered no word of thanks. Every day his temper grew, until Zabbai suggested he find his own way. The hills called him now. I watched as he walked toward the mountains and wondered if he would live long. I prayed to the gods he would make a new life. Could I have proved him innocent, if I had investigated further, pushed the priest king further? Should Zenobia have left seeing the mark upon his cheek? My slave mark warmed beneath the leather cuff and I was grateful I had survived life as a slave.

Mareades disappeared from sight

'Ungrateful bastard,' Zabbai muttered.

'It matters not,' Zenobia said. 'He might have been innocent.'

'It was not proven,' Zabbai said.

Zenobia made no response.

'I thought the politics of Syria might be simpler than in Rome,' Aurelia said. She linked my arm, watching the former senator grow ever smaller.

'I do not think politics is ever simple,' I said.

Zenobia smiled. She had seen Rome as I had; the pollution of rich men's greed, the lies and corruption, loyalties bought and sold.

I was tired. We were mere days from Palmyra and I was anxious to enter the city walls once more. I pondered on whether Gallienus had been calm, collected and a hero of our cause, or had done us a grave injustice, nominating his father to lead Rome's legions east. Valerian would be gathering and marching thousands of men in our footsteps. It was everything we had been instructed to request, everything we set out to achieve, and yet I felt uneasy. Julius had made the same requests to emperors like Valerian. Where he had found rejection, Zenobia uncovered success. What price would we pay?

On reaching Palmyra I would send word to Julius. Zenobia's strength would be known to him; how she engineered a meeting with the co-emperor and secured his trust and belief in our cause. That she had saved Mareades from slavery, a man Julius himself knew and respected and trusted. And shed her child-hood to become a woman. Julius would be proud, I thought. Of his daughter and everything she achieved. Everything she might yet achieve.

I looked over my shoulder at the places we left behind, never seeing the Roman legions marching, crossing the lands as we did. My heart warmed as the sands became familiar. We crested the same slopes I had crossed more than two years before. Soon we would see the protective walls of Palmyra on the horizon.

Our pace quickened faster still. I described every corner of my home to Aurelia. She hung on every word as I told her of the beauty within, and my excitement rolled with the golden slopes.

Evening, the sun falling behind us, Aurelia joined me on my left and Zenobia fell in to my right as Palmyra emerged from the horizon. She grew, spreading out, dominating the sands. And a red glow lit the sky with vibrant streaks.

Zenobia turned to me and the smile on her face was the very same as that on the first day I met her; full of happiness.

'We are home.'

CHAPTER 14

Zabdas - 258 AD

PALMYRA, THE FINEST OASIS in the east, full of rich desires and antiquities. For everything was the same as before: the stalls, the marble-paved streets, the same variety of people and animals roaming the squares. I inhaled deeply the scent of home and feared leaving again. I feared never returning.

Zenobia gazed at buildings and people, her face relaxed and lips parted in appreciation and renewed awe. Her once braided hair hung loose around her face, the absence of her ladies to dress it the cause. Where I was a fool for familiarity, Zenobia had seen the necessity of leaving. Not once had she complained of going to Italia or spoken of home. I had pined for Palmyra for months, despite my craving to be with Julius, away from the city. After everything we had done, Odenathus might now contemplate allowing me south.

Aurelia admired her surroundings, as I had when I first came to Palmyra. She must desire this place, because I could not bear her leaving, and as I saw her excited face my doubts evaporated.

I wanted to explore Palmyra as if for the first time. To walk each street, wash in the baths, pray in the temples, wield my sword in the training grounds. But there were more pressing matters.

Zenobia, Zabbai, Aurelia and I walked up the steps of the palace. They had not changed either. The evening sun brushed the steps known by thousands of feet.

Worod, the city commander, and not Odenathus, sat in the great hall, his small frame perched in the king's chair. Mina, Odenathus' mother, stood beside him, speaking in hushed tones before noticing our presence.

'Ah, Zabbai, you return from the east and with those favoured by our king!' Worod dipped his head in acknowledgement. Beside him, Mina adopted a stone-face.

'Commander.' Zenobia gave a curt bow. Zabbai and I did the same.

Worod narrowed his eyes, blinked, and smiled. 'A safe journey home, I hope? Your mission, was it successful?'

'We have the reinforcements we require,' Zenobia confirmed.

Worod leaned forward in his seat. 'We do?' his voice tripping with surprise.

'At this moment Valerian Caesar himself marches Roman legions to our aid.' Although level, Zenobia's words echoed triumph. She proved Rome would listen and provide the east with the defence it required to push the Persian forces back, and no one could strip her of that achievement.

'They come?' Worod murmured.

'Indeed, they come,' Zabbai said.

'But, by the gods, this means thousands of men march to aid Syria.' Worod scratched his chin, his face lighting up. 'I must congratulate you all. A task well accomplished.'

'Where is Odenathus?' Zenobia asked.

'My son is at the frontier, with the prince,' Mina said, her eyes narrow and her chin high.

Zenobia responded with a nod. 'Have you word from my father?' she asked the commander.

Worod shifted in his seat and scratched the nape of his neck. 'I have. News arrived a week ago. I do not know what the note contains for I have not seen it myself.'

'Then let me see it.'

Worod hesitated. 'That is not possible.'

'Why is that?' Zenobia's composure began to dissolve and she clutched her fists at her sides.

'Odenathus read the note, but did not speak of it.'

'And the king left no message for you to pass on to me?'

I put a hand on Zenobia's arm. 'Zabbai and I must report to the king. I need to confirm you are safely returned to Palmyra. We can retrieve your father's words.'

Our company rested. We sent word to the frontier that Roman armies were on the move. Five days went by before we set out. Nisibis had not been recovered, and our fears were confirmed.

Both Carrhae and Edessa had been captured, burned and pillaged.

Odenathus and Herodes had made a defence on the road to Carrhae, but were forced back to Zeugma; the only force between the Persians, Asia Minor and the Empire. We were told they could not hold much longer. The aid of the empire must come soon, or the east would crumble.

Zenobia declared she would join us. We had travelled together to Rome. She could match any man in our company as she rode out to meet Gallienus, and so any disagreement I might have had was futile.

Zenobia sent a messenger to Meskenit and Hebony. After months without contact, they hurried to Palmyra to see her before we left for the frontier.

I stood in the palace, not knowing what to say. I did not meet Meskenit's eyes; unable to bear the hurt at her husband returning to war. He fought the Tanukh, Teymour was injured and now Zenobia would travel to another frontier.

Hebony came without her husband. She beamed as she saw me, and I savoured the features so like Julius'. I hugged her, realising as I did so her belly protruded.

'You are with child again?' I said, and could not have been happier. It was all she wanted, her husband and her family, and it grew strong.

'I am.'

'And the first is well?'

'A girl,' she said, smiling.

I embraced her again. 'How is your mother?'

'As well as can be,' she whispered back, 'under the circumstances.' Something in her voice checked me.

'What have you heard? Your father? Teymour?'

She bit her lip. 'The Tanukh have taken a large stretch of the Euphrates and are pushing north. Odenathus sent word because of my father, but requested we tell no one. He wishes to contain the news they are struggling, at least until he knows Rome sends more soldiers. He is fortunate that Teymour holds the far bank of the river well …'

'Teymour is alive?' I said. Relief flooded. How could I have not asked before now? He was alive and Julius well. 'Zenobia, did you hear?'

Zenobia and her mother turned. They looked more alike than ever. Meskenit was the most beautiful of women and I realised with shock that familiarity had masked her daughter's striking features. Zenobia's face melted. She laughed aloud. She laughed and it rang through the palace, injecting every quiet room with noise, every tiny space with hope. She brought light and I began to laugh too, then Hebony, and finally Meskenit.

Meskenit caught my eye, and her face fell, faint lines of age betrayed.

I embraced her, and to my shock she held onto me, for the nephew she had not been able to bear until now, or the husband she missed, I was not sure.

'Tomorrow,' Zenobia said, her eyes sparkling, 'we go to the king.'

I parted company with my beloved city once more. Zabbai had three hundred men at his disposal as we headed for Zeugma to meet the king and wait for Valerian and his legions. It was time to stand against the Persians; to show Shapur the might of Rome!

Aurelia stayed in the palace, away from the frontier and danger, a position secured by Zenobia tutoring the younger household members as she had been tutored by Regulus. She understood, I told myself, my need to go to the frontier, to protect our country, to keep Zenobia safe. I promised I would return with Persian plunder enough to buy her a house greater than those of her home city. And recalled Julius telling me he once said the same to Meskenit.

'Write to Regulus,' I told her. 'Let him know you are here and safe.'

'I shall. Stay safe yourself, Zabdas,' she said, lips lingering on mine.

I pressed my forehead to hers and closed my eyes, summoning the will to turn away and walk to war.

'You must go.'

I sighed and held her face in my hands.

'I will see you soon,' she said, hot tears on my hand.

I nodded. 'And I you.'

I let her go and did not look back.

Zenobia walked at the head of three hundred men; the only woman in our company. We would support the army whilst waiting for the Romans. Hebony had cried as we left and called Zenobia a fool. Her mother had cried too. Hers, I believe, were tears of pride and not sadness.

We travelled as the birds fly, the terrain hard. We would make quicker time than by following the main desert roads, and Zabbai was restless to reach the frontier once more, to see the devastation caused since last we were there. I felt dread. We walked toward our enemy. We walked to war.

I thought our numbers large until we reached Zeugma, where the warriors of the east gathered united against a common threat. Twelve or thirteen thousand or more stood on the banks of the river, the same river upon which Julius and Teymour fought in the south, and as we approached, those thousands of tiny blurred figures came into focus. No man could still fear at the sight of our desert warriors.

The camp roared appreciation as we entered. Up close, I saw each man lightly clad for desert heat. Muscles strong enough to wield a sword single-handed in battle bulged on every arm. They were men who had seen war, some survivors of the skirmish with Herodes, others Odenathus' own men. Zabbai grinned, slapping on the back those he recognised. I was one of the youngest and most inexperienced soldiers, having never known battle or killed a man, and against my height and my youth each of these men was like a giant.

We wove our way through the camp in search of the king.

Zenobia was smaller in height than most of the men, but her posture and fixed expression carried her through the stares. Few women lived within the confines of our marching camp and those who did were whores, unlike like the Persians whose women thronged the ranks. But Zenobia was no whore and no Persian.

Whispers of our presence buzzed like insects on every side until finally we found Odenathus.

He stood on the riverbank, accompanied by his son and stratego, the late afternoon light dancing on the water, licking wet stones and fading on dull sand.

'Odenathus,' Zenobia called as we approached, every eye upon us.

'Zenobia?' Odenathus said, as if questioning it was really her.

They regarded one another, savouring the sight after so long apart. He faltered, as if unsure whether to show personal affection or ignore the niceties of seeing her once more.

Zenobia was unfazed.

'I am told you bring the might of Rome with you?' he said, turning squarely toward her.

Her smile triumphant, she said, 'We persuaded Rome that you needed a few good men, and they obliged.'

'I am grateful. The gods know we are in desperate need. You have done well, Zabbai. As always, my trust in you was not misplaced.'

Zabbai faltered and frowned. 'My Lord, it was ...'

'... difficult,' Zenobia finished. 'We went first to Valerian Caesar without success. It was claimed Rome received reports from their own commanders in Syria stating we were holding and could continue to do so. Valerian would not listen. It was only when we turned to the co-emperor, Gallienus, that we secured support.'

Zabbai continued to frown, eying Zenobia suspiciously. He nodded without further comment.

'We can defeat this enemy,' Odenathus said. He looked much older than when I had seen him last, greying hair and worn face, but his features gradually took on a new strength as he spoke.

Herodes' lip curled. 'When do the Romans arrive?'

'I cannot be sure,' Zabbai said. 'They march in haste. We travelled swiftly and have been in Palmyra a few days.'

'Post fresh lookouts for the night,' Odenathus ordered. When no one answered, he said, 'Herodes, post the lookouts. Stratego, see to your men. Survive tomorrow, and the day after we defeat our enemy!'

The generals nodded consent and left. Herodes scowled at Zenobia and followed. Perhaps he was jealous of his father's affection for her; the daughter of a famous stratego could have been his wife after all. Zabbai had spoken of the king sending Zenobia to Rome to rid the council of her voice, but I could not believe it. Odenathus' infatuation was apparent.

The four of us fell silent. Standing at the water's edge, I saw doubt for the first time in Odenathus' eyes.

'How do I reward you for what you have accomplished?'

'A safe Syria is the only reward required for any of us,' Zenobia replied.

But I seized the opportunity.

'I wish to go south and fight the Tanukh, with Julius. Now reinforcements are imminent, you could spare men to bolster his force. He can only just keep the Tanukh at bay.'

Odenathus' face flooded with confusion.

'How do you know of Julius' situation in the south?'

'I want to join him,' I pressed on.

Beside me, Zenobia said nothing. She could have pleaded with Odenathus, used her position to persuade him, but she did not.

'I cannot allow it,' Odenathus said. 'I will send men to aid Julius, but you are to stay here.'

'Tell me why, my Lord?'

'Do not *dare* question me, boy,' he roared.

Zabbai took my shoulder. 'Come, Zabdas,' he murmured. 'If Odenathus is willing to send reinforcements to the south, you should be content. We all should.'

Odenathus turned away from me. I burned with resentment.

His back to me, voice lower and calm, he said, 'You are too inexperienced to fight with the southern army, lad. Come, I wish to show you something. All of you.'

We walked in silence, following in the footsteps of the great king of the east through foliage, stars clear in the night sky. His voice had been authoritative and we followed him without question or concern. He was not afraid to wager his life to secure his realm. He was under the command of Rome, but he was also a Syrian, and the people of the east looked to him for guidance, law and order, and to provide a defence against the enemies of this land.

'What do you wish to show us?' Zabbai asked.

We crested the hill on the riverbank and looked across to the opposite shore. Thousands of tiny orange dots glowed. I could see nothing else in the grey murk of evening. I looked upriver, then downriver, and saw no end to their existence. They swarmed the far bank, no gaps, just a constant litter of scattered embers.

'Campfires,' Odenathus said.

'How many?' Zabbai asked. He knew that tens of thousands of men sat eating an evening meal around those fires. We all did.

'We are about fifteen thousand,' Odenathus replied. He peered calmly out over the river to the sea of armed men beyond.

'And how many are they?'

'Our spies tell us they number more than one hundred thousand,' he replied evenly.

No one responded, not one hiss of breath could be heard. If Valerian did not come, we would be slaughtered on the banks of this river, cut off by the very empire to which we belonged. Rome used our forces to protect their easternmost boundaries, taxed our merchants and produce travelling through. They demanded Odenathus' loyalty as king. If they would not assist us now ... gods, I could not bear the thought, nor accept that they could turn from us as easily as Gallienus had scrawled his note and slipped it to Zenobia. The thought that it might have been a lie, brief words to cast off an unwanted consul of Palmyra, sickened.

After a while Zenobia said: 'Then I am surprised that you managed to hold them back for as long as you did. You are a great general, Odenathus, do not lose faith in yourself.'

'We do not hold them back now,' Odenathus said irritably.

Zenobia flushed, youth and inexperience flickering upon her oval face for a heartbeat. She remained determined and calm.

'We have lost Edessa and Carrhae. We have not held them.' He clasped his hands behind his back, looked to the ground and began to pace.

'As our king *you* need to stay strong and fill your people with hope and surety,' Zenobia replied with force, her words ringing clear.

Odenathus looked up. For a moment I sensed his urge to

strike her, but then he nodded. If Valerian did not come, the people needed to see their king stand firm in the face of the enemy, no matter how vast; no matter how fearful we all were.

Odenathus retired for the evening, but he would not sleep this night, no one would. He walked to his tent, eyes blank, his fear and worry rippling in his wake. He had fought the Persians for many years and he knew what would happen; he knew the might of Shapur better than any of us, especially Valerian Caesar. He knew their strengths, their weaknesses, how to defeat them. He understood the desert terrain and how to combat their weaponry. The only thing he did not have was an army large enough to match theirs, but with more Roman legions, he would. I had seen Rome, witnessed her supposed wonders. The great capital of the empire had awed me with its vastness.

I looked across at the campfires on the other shore and knew over one hundred thousand Persians waited to plunder every one of our cities.

I returned to the shore alone the following morning. Without campfires, it was difficult to see how far the Persians spread. I spent much of the day there, wondering how we would defeat them, if it was possible and if we would have enough men. Odenathus could have attacked at first light, sent raiding parties further up shore to worry their flank, but Zabbai assured him Valerian would come with the legions promised.

And so we waited, prepared only to fight in defence. We waited the whole day.

And the day after, Valerian came.

I stood beside Zenobia as we watched the first legions arrive. They crossed the plain toward us and I could not help but feel a certain fear as the desert heat reflected from the armour of well-ordered units moving like ants. I had thought they would be Romans, but I had not considered until then that Roman soldiers may not be native to the city of Rome. How foolish. These were men of pale skin and pale hair, much as Aurelia, and black skin and black hair and every shade between.

'Odenathus received the first scouts a few days ago,' Zenobia said. 'These are men from Germania, Noricum, Dacia, Moesia, Spain, Thrace, Bithynia, Isauria, Lycaonia, Galatia, Lycia, Cilicia, Cappodocia, Phrygia, Phoenicia, Mauritania and Osrhoene, and from our neighbours, Mesopotamia, Asiana and Judea.'

Zabbai had found her a small leather breastplate and she now wore it over her robes, her eyes still thick with kohl and her hair loose in a light breeze.

'Gods! They are so many. What did the scouts say?'

She looked at me and smiled.

'Seventy thousand march west to our aid.'

'They fulfil their promise? The gods are watching and would see us win.'

'They would see us amuse them. But Selene is with us.'

'Still, I would not have thought they sent so many. What of their other frontiers; they were hard-pressed, and Valerian himself claimed he could not spare the men?'

'And yet he comes himself. I think we have Gallienus to thank for this. Look at them,' she said of the assembling men, 'they do not match the Persian numbers, but they will be enough for a viable defence.'

'Enough to scourge our lands?' I said.

'Oh, I do hope so, Zabdas.'

On the third day, Valerian himself arrived.

He met with Odenathus, Zenobia, Zabbai, a Palmyrene general named Pouja, and a half-dozen others. I stood at the back of the tent as Odenathus offered Valerian a seat, and sat at the opposite side of a table. I thought of Valerian's house, and the table at which we had sat, when Zabbai had inked our plight upon a map. And of Gallienus' tent, and Zenobia's flirtation with the younger Caesar, and wondered idly how much of our mission Odenathus knew.

Valerian's eyes were ringed with fatigue, four men behind him the same, and yet he sat upright and alert as he accepted a cup of wine and fruit from Odenathus' table.

'You are most welcome, Imperator,' Odenathus said.

Valerian did not respond immediately, but looked around the tent as he chewed on a fig.

'The east concerns Rome greatly,' Valerian replied. 'You have been long without a true commander. It is time Syria and Rome were closer, and not left apart from the rest of the Empire and her policies. I think perhaps you have been given too much say in the east, been too liberal in condoning religion, and bent under Persian determination.'

Anger rippled in Zenobia's face, but she kept her lips tightly closed, her hands clasped firmly behind her back.

'How was your journey?' Odenathus asked.

'Long. I have travelled thousands of miles and brought with me many men, who would be better utilised elsewhere, on the whim of my son. He seems to think our presence here is necessary, despite my reservations, and I have long promised to humour him in his decision-making, for one day he might well become sole emperor when I am gone. I wonder sometimes whether he spends more time thinking of the military or of keeping his bed warm at night.' He glanced to Zenobia but she did not respond.

The words and look were not lost on Odenathus. He peered down at the table, took his cup and sipped.

'I received word that the Persians harry your flank as our forces amass.'

'They do, Imperator.'

'Indeed. Well, we shall have to see what can be done. A third of our army is now here. If the Persians attempt to attack, then we can surely counter. As for your own army, they are under my command now, as are you and all of your generals and commanders. Too long have you had free reign in Syria. From today I will oversee all military activity in the east.'

'My men are not a part of the Roman army,' Odenathus said. 'They are not yours to command.'

Valerian rose from his seat, the meeting at an end.

'Syria belongs to Rome, your men belong to Rome, and you belong to Rome. There is no argument, no debate, it is a simple matter of fact. You would do well to remember who holds the imperium here.'

Valerian rose from his seat and stooped out of the tent.

Odenathus sighed.

'You said he would be a difficult man, Zenobia, and you were right.'

'We must be careful,' Zabbai said. 'You cannot relinquish control of our men to the Romans. A certain amount of control is pertinent. If you lose it now you will not regain it.'

'I agree,' Odenathus said. 'I have no intention of handing the emperor complete control, and I would not think our men amenable to the notion.'

'Let Valerian think he has what he wants for now,' Zenobia said. 'We have his army after all.'

Our men's confidence mounted as thousands of soldiers filled our camp, spreading tents along the western bank like wine on marble.

I had never seen before the amassing of so many men, carrying heavy weapons and heavier armour. We had always had Roman legionaries in the east, but a small contingent, posted as a gesture of Roman power in foreign lands, more brothers than anything else. They were accustomed to desert heat, shedding heavy plate and taking up light leather armour, speaking fluently in our tongue. I was wide-eyed at these new, well-ordered units.

'You would not want to fight them, would you?' Zabbai murmured.

We watched from our favoured spot on the riverbank as the final legions pooled into the camp. Zabbai's position in the army was now equal to that of any general, soldiers posted under his command. I would have been in a higher place, but Odenathus preferred me to stay as part of Zenobia's personal guard, away from the frontier and enemy blades.

'Have you ever fought against Roman soldiers?'

'No,' he said, half laughing, 'only Persian soldiers. I have fought them when they were under the command of Shapur and his predecessor, Ardashir.'

'Ardashir?' I asked, rolling the name in my mouth, unfamiliar with it.

'Shapur's father and a man of great ambition and no mercy. It is said Shapur is even more formidable.'

I thought of the talk amongst our soldiers, the tales they told of flaying and impaling those who fell into Persian hands.

'I heard he kills mercilessly.'

'He does. We have never had a messenger back alive from the Persian camp.'

Time passed quickly as our hopes ran high with the arrival of the Romans. I thought of Aurelia constantly. She kept me warm in the waiting dark as I craved her voice, her touch, the simple fact of her presence. I was alone, I realised; Zenobia too focussed on politics, Odenathus my superior, Zabbai commanding his men, and my fellow soldiers always somewhat distant owing to the time I spent in Zenobia's company. Aurelia wrote, but her words did little to quench my thirst. And as Zenobia's personal guard, her companion, her cousin, I had yet to face real combat.

We were not winning. We were not defeating our enemy.

Two months went by and Zenobia grew pale as our prospects of protecting our people grew faint. We had Roman forces, but Shapur pushed forth his army and we slipped further and further back, losing more and more land.

'Valerian will not listen,' Odenathus said.

We stood beside the ordered Roman legions, waiting for the Persians to advance. Eighty-five thousand against a hundred thousand; not an advantage, but we could still win. We were half-way between Zeugma, which we had lost, and Antioch, the city where Zenobia had purchased the life of the ex-senator, Mareades, and given him his freedom. There was no river and no means to confine and block and outmanoeuvre our enemy. The plain was hot and the sky burning red and I could see the faint glimpse of light reflected in the Roman armour. They stood in formation, infantry to the centre and cavalry and light troops at their wings to protect their flanks. Farther still I could see the Sassanian cavalry and their bows and fair horses. And my gut tightened and lurched as I attempted to stand on that very spot and not show fear.

'You must make him listen,' Zenobia replied.

The emperor, mounted upon his black horse, was but twenty feet from us. He too watched his men facing the enemy.

'I have told him of the Persians' favoured tactics and what he can expect,' Odenathus replied. 'But watch now as he listens not to my advice, but that of his own commanders.'

'He will listen to you,' Zenobia said. 'He will not want to, but he will listen.'

She lied, I could sense it in her gentle tone, so unlike her usual determined voice.

I searched the units for our own men. Beside the Roman cavalry Zabbai led the Palmyrene contingent. I prayed Zenobia was right, that Valerian would indeed listen to the advice given to him by those experienced in Syrian warfare, and our men would not be in danger. Zabbai was a level-headed man, who stood at the fore of the army. If we were to be crushed, he would be the first to fall.

'You should not be here watching this, Zenobia,' Odenathus

said. 'I dare say I fear what your father would say if he knew.'

'Have you word from him?' she asked, ignoring his words.

'Not yet.'

In the distance, enemy drums beat the daunting sound of battle, the thumping rhythm of what was to come. They had raided and raped and burned and pillaged these past two months, and they would continue to do so, and as I looked now at the men before us, their swords and spears in their hands, I prayed to Bel that we would see a certain victory this day.

Behind us, the sound of a galloping horse.

I turned as a rider came to a halt a few paces away.

'What is it?' Odenathus asked.

'Word from the Euphrates, my Lord,' the man said, handing the king a scroll. He turned at speed the way he had come, dust and stones churning behind.

Odenathus loosened the tie about the scroll and unrolled it. I itched to know the words, to know what Julius wrote, whether he was alive or dead.

'What does it say?' Zenobia asked.

Odenathus handed it to her.

'Your father gives his consent and his blessing,' he said.

'For what?' I asked, but as I spoke I realised the meaning of his words.

'Zenobia,' Odenathus said, reaching out his hand, 'your father gives his consent, so will you now consent to become queen of Palmyra and my wife?'

'It would be an honour,' she replied.

Her face was full of hope and a certain satisfaction. She had a place higher than any woman of Syria could dream, and yet we stood in the desert amidst the armies of Syria and the Empire waiting for the shedding of blood that would come.

And me, I could barely control the jealousy which rose in my stomach at the sight of Odenathus taking from his own, smallest finger, an iron ring, and placing it upon Zenobia's own, slim finger in a truly Roman way.

'I cannot wait for an engagement,' he said, 'let this be it.'

She kissed him then, a lingering kiss of promise, as my spite and my hatred boiled.

When they had parted, she scanned the scroll and with a familiarity I had come to know, handed it to me.

I looked at the handwriting I knew well, and cherished reading the words written by Julius. He always drafted his own correspondence:

Forgive my informal address. I write in haste, for although the frontier is stable, and you have no need to worry, I join a raiding party and we are currently on the move.

I must congratulate you on your successes. With the emperor now joining you in the east you must finally find a little rest from the constant exhaustion of Shapur's presence. Or do you? Either way I hope you are accomplishing everything you wish for.

And as for my daughter, it brings me great pleasure to know that you and Zenobia will be bound in Roman matrimony.

There was once a time I feared we would not be reconciled, that the void between us was too great, and I know I am much to blame for the place we found ourselves. I confess I had hoped that Zenobia could bridge that distance, and that our family would be united as was once intended.

Do not wait, Odenathus, for my return. We are pressed hard by the Tanukh and although I would never assume my very presence to be the key to holding the south, I cannot in all conscience risk leaving to join you in what will be a magnificent celebration.

Give Zenobia my love and enjoy your day together. I hope to see you all one day soon.

Your friend and soon to be father-in-law,
Julius~

My heart felt heavy as I read the last lines. I could not speak, nor look at Zenobia and Odenathus, as I found my eyes brimming with tears. I looked out at the men standing on the plain, flags flying crimson red over the Roman columns and in my vision. I did not think of Aurelia. I thought only of Zenobia, the knowledge that she would be irrevocably tied to Odenathus crushing my chest. I tried to breathe, but my breaths came short and shallow and hot. I am her cousin, I told myself, but it was not enough. I knew then my connection to Zenobia was more than that of a relative.

'It will be a fine day if we win this battle,' she said.

'Indeed it shall,' Odenathus replied.

Shouts sounded and the Roman columns, our own men at their centre, moved forward, and the sound of the Persian drums became louder still. Banging and deafening. I tried to break my mind from the brief engagement I had witnessed, but for a moment I could not have cared if we saw victory or if we all fell on these sands. For me we might as well have already lost.

The first clash echoed in the halls of the gods and woke them from their slumber as the Persian cataphract charged the Roman lines and dust billowed into the morning air and the red sun penetrated, casting an eerie glow. Today we would amuse the gods, and give them a battle they would not forget.

Volleys of arrows hissed overhead hitting those behind the front lines.

'Move back,' Odenathus said to Zenobia. 'It is time now, move back out of danger. Zabdas, go with her.'

He motioned us back with his arm as more arrows hissed overhead, striking soldiers just feet away. Screams of agony sounded over the soft thuds and ringing strikes as the tips pierced flesh and iron.

'Come, Zenobia,' I said, remembering the promise Odenathus had asked me to keep the night before. We would be with the army until the last moment, as Zenobia wished, but would retreat when the first charge occurred, back to the safety of our camp a short distance away.

But Zenobia would not be moved. She watched as Odenathus mounted and rode close to Valerian. Whilst the men talked the emperor motioned to messengers and commanders, a pinched look upon his face, a brow creased with worry and the decisions we all knew Valerian incapable of making.

More arrows hissed. The whole Roman army seemed to move back a pace under the weight of the Persian cavalry. Vultures soared overhead, waiting to pick at the flesh of the dead.

'Move now, Zenobia,' I warned, angry with her, for her disobedience and for her engagement to the king and for Julius leaving and Meskenit's disapproval of me and the nights I had spent on the wall and for ever having been a slave. I was angry with it all. Gods, I was angry and I was exhausted and I could have lain down on the sands and let the Persians trample me.

A horn broke through the din.

Zenobia's eyes were wide.

'The Persians sound their retreat?'

'I do not know.'

I looked across to Odenathus to see puzzlement upon his face. And shock.

'They do not retreat,' I heard him shout to the emperor. 'Still your men.'

But the command to pursue to the Persians came, shouted down the columns, repeated by the centurions, and the whole of the Roman army moved forward as one.

Zenobia hung her head.

'What is happening?' I asked.

She did not answer. The Roman lines advanced and we heard screams and shouts and horses screeching an awful, high-pitched mew of death from the Roman front. The Persian cavalry began to divide, half heading toward the right flank where Zenobia and I stood.

The Roman advance came to a halt as Odenathus rode back to us.

'Tribulus,' he said. 'The fucking Persians dropped iron spikes to stop our men pursuing their retreat. You need to get away from here now.'

We three watched as thousands of mounted Persians kicked up the desert, nearing us, riding hard, camels and horses thumping across the dust.

'Go,' Odenathus ordered. 'Ride for Antioch and I will come for you.'

We did not ride to Antioch. We stopped a few hundred paces from the army and watched as the Persian cavalry crashed into the Romans' right flank, causing the Roman cavalry to buckle, horses toppling their riders, spears sticking up from the dead. I looked for Odenathus but I could not see him amidst the horses and men and clashing of iron against iron and the spray of blood and sand. All across the plain Persians and Romans fell to one another's swords and arrows and on the left flank I saw the same, the army pincered between the divided Persian force.

Valerian, his purple pulling in a hot breeze, moved to edge back, a retreat no doubt upon his lips.

I willed the screams of the dying to stop, but they did not. The din continued, neither side willing to succumb to the other, as Zenobia took my hand and stared ahead to where Odenathus fought with his own men, fending off the enemy, doing all he could to save them after Valerian had ordered the pursuit which now saw them caught in the middle of the Persian force.

I thought of Herodes, ordered to another frontier, to Samosata, and realised why his father had sent him there. He could not risk his own death and that of his son in the same battle. And he must have known, too, that the further away from the emperor he was, the safer he would be.

I gripped tight Zenobia's hand, much tighter than I should have, more even than was comfortable, but it was all I could do. I could neither leave her there and join those losing to the enemy, nor force her back to camp or on to Antioch.

The commotion and battle-noise eased as the Roman retreat sounded and the soldiers moved back in formation, keeping their lines together to stave the enemy pursuit. But the enemy did not come. They watched and as our armies pulled back I could see the plain littered with Persian horses, dying on the sands, riders slain. They had suffered loss, but as our lines neared, the gaping holes were evident. The dead and the dying left behind to bury another day strewn across the sands.

Odenathus peeled away from the main force and rode to us.

'Will you ever do as you are asked?'

A bloody splatter covered his breastplate, his face and hair thick with sweat and grime, a new gash livid upon his arm.

'Valerian would not listen to you?' she countered.

He shook his head. 'My men suffered little, I think, but the Romans were hit hard.'

He put an arm about Zenobia's shoulder.

'I pray this day is done.'

We met in Odenathus' low, black tent that night, far from the Persian army, but not far enough to still my fear of a night attack. Zenobia, Zabbai, general Pouja and I sat before the king.

'You speak of the emperor of Rome,' Odenathus reminded everyone, his tone bitter and frustrated. His position as client king tested, and Valerian's words true; Odenathus no longer held the imperium he once had.

'Something must be done,' Pouja said. He was a short, stout man, who refused to speak with Zenobia. I sensed his disapproval of her being there, of her free tongue and command, despite her role in bringing more Roman legions to the country.

'We can do nothing,' Odenathus replied, and his face fell with despair. He always did what he believed right, but now he appeared torn more than ever; torn between the emperor's orders and doing what was best for his realm, his people and Palmyra.

Zenobia sat on the floor in silence, her eyes heavy with fatigue, her face pale and lined in the dim light following the aftermath of defeat. We lost more men in the early morning battle than Odenathus had first realised.

'Then you sacrifice us all for your loyalty,' Zabbai said.

I could scarce believe it. Zabbai's words echoed Julius'. And he was right.

Odenathus looked up, despair replaced with shock. Then his expression turned to anger. None could truly know the situation in which he found himself. We all were our own men, or his men, but we were loyal to our own people. We did not have to show the same allegiance to Rome as Odenathus did, even now, even in the wake of defeat and the loss of so many cities. I always chose Syria and the east, even with thought of Aurelia.

I pleaded in my mind for my friend, my cousin, to talk sense to her husband. She held more weight with him than anyone else, even Julius, and we needed her to make him understand, force him to see reality. To know that action must be taken to ensure Syria's survival.

'He is right, Odenathus,' Zenobia said.

'Do not dare talk to me of loyalty,' Odenathus said, face contorted and voice venomous. 'You cannot even begin to understand the situation in which we find ourselves, the politics between ourselves and Rome. How can you even begin to comprehend the workings of this army, of the Roman army? Caesar himself stands with us.'

Zenobia looked up at Zabbai then rose to her feet.

'I trust you, but you are blinded by your loyalty and your belief in mighty Rome. I tell you this, the senators in Rome bicker and squabble amongst themselves. They lie to their emperor; they care little more than lining their pockets. They are safe, Odenathus, sitting in their senate hall. Valerian can no more lead an army than I can piss like a man. Zabbai is right. They are both right. The Romans are here to aid us in protecting their frontier, not to take command—'

'Sit down,' Odenathus growled, pointing to the ground.

'I suggest we—'

'I said, SIT DOWN.'

Zenobia refused to be seated. She glared at him, unmoving.

Odenathus raised his hand as if to strike.

'Stop this,' I shouted. 'You solve nothing.'

Zenobia flashed Odenathus a look of contempt. 'You would hit your wife, Odenathus? You would hit the woman carrying your child?'

I knew then the reason for her pale features, and was shocked further to recall her standing watching the battle, so close to enemy lines, with a child in her belly.

The king ran both hands through his hair in exasperation.

'I did not mean to,' he mumbled. 'I do not wish to lose another unborn child.'

'My father once said that Syria should not tie itself to Rome, not in this way. He was right. The time has come for us to take charge.'

Her words hung in the air as she stooped out of the tent and into the freezing night. I followed. We walked in silence through the camp until we reached an incline from where I saw the sea on the west coast. We stopped and I watched the lapping waves and moonlight dancing on reflective waters.

Unable to bear the awkwardness any longer, I asked, 'Why did you never say?'

Her chin rose a little higher as she continued to watch the water.

'I lost the first child before I had chance to tell you. Or anyone.'

'You could have told me.'

She shook her head, her face harder than ever as words began tumbling out.

'My body flushed it away, unwanted. But I wanted it. I could not stop the pain and the blood. And then the rest simply followed.' She took a deep breath. This was the first time I had seen her vulnerable. Her eyes had hollowed and her face unmasked, the defeat of the day bearing down on her. 'When I found I had conceived again, I could not tell you. I told no one, afraid that it would not last, that it would be gone before it had chance to breathe.'

'Or of what the king would say?'

Her lack of response told me I had gone too far.

'Why a Roman marriage?' I asked, thinking back on Odenathus' words of engagement and the iron ring. I had assumed Odenathus and Zenobia husband and wife already in the Egyptian way, committed to one another and procreation, no engagement or ceremony to speak of.

'Better a marriage recognised by Rome, if I am to be considered the wife of the king of Syria. Odenathus and I were waiting for my father to return from the south and for his consent before performing the marriage ritual, but with a child making its way into the world, we chose to wait no longer. I would have my child a legitimate heir, and let no man or woman claim otherwise.'

'Why did you agree to become his wife, to bear his children? I never thought you wanted this, to be tied to a man, to be commanded by one.'

'I am not commanded, and I do it because my father wished it,' she said flatly, her moment of weakness gone.

'Julius would never have asked that of you. He cares for you too much to have pushed you into something you did not want.'

'I did want it, Zabdas. And you do not know my father as well as you would like to think. I have always been destined for the Palmyrene throne, only it was Herodes to whom I was tentatively betrothed, no more than a babe in a crib. My father and Odenathus spoke of it, mentioned it and joked on it many times before he left Palmyra. I am unsure if it was forgotten in his years of absence, but I think not. I was to break Syria from Rome, breed the next generation of leader and educate them so that, one day in a distant future, we could sever ourselves from Rome once and for all. And then I met Odenathus, and everything changed. Syria needs me now. My father brought me to Palmyra to infiltrate the aristocracy. It was my purpose to sit on the council on my father's behalf and make a difference. But I have done more than I hoped, more than my father ever dreamed. This is what I was brought up to believe.'

'I do not believe that,' I replied. 'Julius puts his family first. It is the single most important aspect of life to him. He said so himself.'

'It does not matter what you believe. It is true. As your friend and your family, I tell you the truth.'

'I do not understand, Zenobia. Why would you do this? Why go to Rome and plead for troops when you wish to sever yourself?'

'Because my father is right. Syria is nothing more than a client kingdom in a forgotten land, you saw that when Valerian proclaimed himself imperator. Odenathus is on the throne because he swore fealty to Rome. If not him, it would be another; or a Roman senator fallen out of favour at home. They care nothing for us. They themselves are about to fall, so what can they offer us now? What do they have to give? We defend their frontier, pay taxes and do exactly what is asked of us, and in return they allow us a little freedom. But it is not freedom, Zabdas. Valerian marched here under duress then risked the safety of our country. It would be better if he had not come.'

'Then we travelled to Rome for nothing?'

'Perhaps.'

If Julius had behaved as she said, then I did not know him. I clung to him as a father because I lacked one of my own, not because I truly knew him. But she was wrong. He was blinded by his love for this land, as I was, as she was. Surely it only proved his desire for a free Syria if he was willing to sacrifice his daughter's happiness and want this for her. She could have risen no higher, obtained no more power, than she had. Give birth to a boy, and her position was a great one.

'You think I am a fool, Zabdas?' she asked with a wry smile.

'No,' I replied, unsure I believed my answer. I did not believe her foolish, but I could not confess to understanding her.

'You are gullible.' I was about to protest when she said, 'I am sorry. Really I am. You believe in people other than yourself and I love you for that, it is no bad trait.'

I remembered her father saying much the same thing.

The night had turned black, all but for the moonlight lending a little light to the darkness. Peaceful sounds of lapping water and calm breezes swam around me. I studied Zenobia's face. She was illuminated, her features enhanced by the white of the moon and the oils on her skin reflective. One could imagine her immortal.

To me, she was.

Her cloak had slipped from her strong shoulders, but she appeared not to feel the cold.

'You look at me like my father does.'

'How is that?'

'As if I can fix the world with my mother's looks. He fools himself that I am beautiful enough to enchant the entire country, that I can bend men like Odenathus to my will. Here I am, Zabdas. We have been on the frontier for weeks now and seen defeat, and still Odenathus refuses to listen. Instead he sits idly in the emperor's shadow, as he has always done. I think of him as a man of great talent, of leadership skills far exceeding others, but I am disappointed. I am not sorry my father promoted my gaining Odenathus' affections, only that I may fail him.'

'Ridiculous talk,' I said, and smiled.

Zenobia laughed. 'You are right, we should never be maudlin.'

'Julius would be proud of you. I have never known a woman as strong and determined and capable as you. And not many men, either.'

'No, Zabdas, he would be disappointed. He would think that if only he had a son, everything would be different.'

'He has me,' I replied, 'and nothing has changed.'

Zenobia frowned slightly, her eyes moving to look out over the hills, and I sensed there were words she would not speak.

I was young and the world a very old place.

'Do you not wish that you led a simple life and were marrying a merchant as your sister has?' As I spoke I thought of myself, not a merchant, perhaps, but not aristocracy, either.

'Never. It is an honour to follow my father's wishes. We women of the Zabdilas family are descended from Cleopatra the Great. I feel her power and her strength. The royal Egyptian bloodline runs in my veins. I want more than to simply be a wife, more than to sit at court. The gods are with me, Selene shines down, urging me on this path. I am with child, and this child will be the son of a king, and I will unite the blood of Egypt with that of Syria. One day, this child in my womb,' she said, touching her belly, 'will become ruler of our united kingdoms.'

I said nothing. Her ambitious words unnerved me. I worshipped the gods, and I too was descendant of Cleopatra, but I did not feel a special power, or pretend to understand. Perhaps she had become a little mad, I thought, her mind unbalanced by pregnancy. I was unsure what to say, or whether Odenathus truly knew of his future wife's ambitious nature.

Zenobia stayed a while on that spot. I was overwhelmed, uncomfortable, so I walked back to the camp. We had not strayed far and no one came looking for us. Odenathus would still be seething over their quarrel.

We spent two weeks in the area, not far from the battle, and the Persians were more active than ever. Valerian met with Odenathus and his generals every day, though he continued to refuse Syrian suggestions and advice. We rarely saw him. He kept to his tent writing his precious documents: ledgers of the activity, how many soldiers had deserted, how many died and what of, the advances of the enemy, his commands for the day, drills carried out, food consumed and so forth.

Then word spread through the army like fire. Valerian ordered the army to move to the safety of Antioch.

'I am worried,' I said to Zabbai.

'He spoke of it with Odenathus this morning,' he said, his voice tired, drained.

'And Odenathus agrees?'

He shook his head.

'Odenathus wants to sue for peace with the Persians for now; we need to buy time, and peace is less costly than war. He wishes nothing more than to have pleasant relations with our neighbours. No more fighting, no more death, no more threat. But Valerian has been persuaded against such a course for the present. His advisors point out the flaw in this plan: it is the express line of Rome that, if possible, only the sea or an unarmed nation should remain on the borders of the Empire. Persia is neither.'

'You are right, but what now?'

With a grim expression he said, 'The war continues until the Romans or the Persians fall. But for now we head for Antioch, and hope that we are not crushed between two warring empires.'

CHAPTER 15

Samira – 290 AD (Present day)

I SIT IN MY cabin below deck and leaf through papyrus, re-reading the story of Zenobia and wondering at her beauty and the moment she stood and watched the armies of Persia defeat the armies of Rome. I am thinking of my grandfather and what it would have been like to witness a battle upon the sands of my home. Thirty years ago, a long time past, yet he tells the tale as if it were yesterday.

And I smile to myself at the union Zenobia would have with Odenathus, the engagement made with an iron ring moments before battle.

Zenobia. Oh, Zenobia. What do I think of the woman who ventured to Rome, who spoke with not one, but two emperors, to secure the aid she much desired? I have heard of her many times, the tales of her life and the path she took, but through my grandfather I know her more intimately than before. I know of her youth, the words she spoke and the actions she took.

I see upon the pages my grandfather's infatuation with the girl with hair of raven black and eyes thick with kohl, and I imagine that she would do anything to achieve her desires. And I see too my grandfather leaving Aurelia, a pale hint of affection compared to his feelings for Zenobia, and I feel a certain sadness for that girl.

I want to read of Bamdad, and wonder where in this tale he

appears; he is my closest companion now save my grandfather, and I love him dearly. He is my second father now my own is gone.

Tripolis is a distant place I cannot think of now, the beach I ran across and the salt wind in my hair fading from memory. Our home was the sea, and I crave to go back and yet I know it cannot be the same, it will never be as it was, my father and grandfather and me.

I hear footsteps and a moment later grandfather pulls aside the curtain and smiles.

'I thought you would like to see this,' he says.

Above deck I watch as the dockside draws near, the river beneath us calm and the sun breaking the horizon and gulls calling overhead. The dockside is quiet, a few dozen men waiting to tie off our boat and the odd slave about his duties. Today is what I call a yellow day, a day of shining sun and happiness and hope.

Stood beside me and around me, their chatter a sound I will sorely miss, are the slaves my grandfather pleaded with Rostram to set free. They are washed and clean but still wear dirty clothes, for we could find them nothing better on board. But their stomachs are full and they will see land in a few moments.

We tie off and the gangplanks are put in place and the excitement of the slaves is contagious. I am smiling and happy for them and they embrace one another and I feel the tears slide down my cheeks as I watch them step onto land free men and free woman and free children.

My grandfather does not shed tears, but I can see the moment caught in his throat and know that he is thinking back on the day Julius set him free.

The last of the slaves departed, Rostram calls for the boat to be untied, and then he turns to me.

He is of average height with short and soft brown hair. He is much younger than my grandfather, no more than thirty years of age, and despite what I have seen, the lives he has taken and the surety in his posture, he does not appear a cruel man.

'They allow pirates to dock here?' I say, and despite the smile upon my lips, the words ring of accusation.

'A friendly dock,' he says, unsmiling.

'It was good of you to give them their freedom.'

'They have you to thank for that,' he replies, and walks back to the wheel.

I am pondering his words, that I am to thank and their freedom is in some way because of me, when grandfather puts his hand upon my shoulder.

'I have read everything you have written of Zenobia,' I say, looking up at him.

'You must slow down,' he replies, 'I cannot write as fast as you read.'

'I have heard of Zabbai.'

'That is no surprise. In time he became a great general.'

'What was Rome like?' I ask. 'What was it *really* like?'

Grandfather smiles weakly as if I ask a question that requires much effort to answer, and I think it is a question many ask, that all men and women desire to know Rome.

'Dirty,' he replies.

'Dirty?'

'Filthy.'

'And yet it is said to be the greatest city known to man?'

'And thus the scum of the earth gather and breed. Being vast and powerful does not make it more advanced or more beautiful than anywhere else. We mortals have a desire to place our hopes, and Rome is as safe a bet as any. It may seem a city of greatness. It is valued as a centre of administration, of law, order and government, but that does not mean I wanted to be in the centre of it.'

'It is just that people talk of it so often.'

'Perhaps you do not want to believe me?'

'Of course I do!'

'Ah, but you don't *want* to!'

I frown at him for his teasing me.

'Your face will stick like that if the wind changes,' he says, and laughs. 'Besides, you will know what Rome is like soon enough. I dare say it has not changed.'

'I will?' An excitement stirs inside me, of a voyage I dared not think I would ever make.

'I must deliver news of Jadhima's fate,' he says. 'We head now for Rome.'

EPILOGUE

Zabdas – 258 AD

THE LATE AFTERNOON SUN burned orange, the sky fiery hot, casting harsh shadows on the forum. Antioch had changed little in the time since we had saved Mareades. How long he would survive in the mountains only the gods knew. Perhaps he was already dead. But I did not think of him that day, instead I swayed between enjoying a day of celebration, my jealously at Zenobia's marriage, and the knowledge of the politics which lay beneath.

Valerian would not allow Odenathus to leave the army, so it was in late Iunius I stood in the doorway of the government buildings where the officials of Antioch met each day, looking out on a packed forum. Bread was passed amongst the citizens, coins thrown from the steps, and cheers sounded in celebration of the gifts such a day would bring.

Zenobia stood behind me, Meskenit next to her. She adjusted her daughter's white dress and the loose girdle about her waist. She had desperately wanted to witness this day, and Odenathus had sent an escort to bring her to the city, Hebony remaining behind with her family.

'You look beautiful,' I said to Zenobia.

'Your flattery is greatly appreciated,' she replied. She touched my cheek, her hands warm, welcoming.

'If only Julius could be here,' I said.

Zenobia let her hand fall and inclined her head.

'My father is always with me.'

Odenathus joined us, linking an arm about Zenobia's waist, the augur with him.

'I see twelve. Twelve birds circling the forum!' the young augur said, words spoken in haste, mumbled and breathless.

'Romulus saw twelve on the day he chose to build Rome on the Palatine Hill,' Zenobia said.

'It is a good omen,' Odenathus agreed.

We walked inside, into dimly lit chambers, where Odenathus and Zenobia would sign the marriage contract, Meskenit, Zabbai, Pouja, six others and I bearing witness. Herodes was still in the north, and Odenathus' mother in Palmyra, not wanting to travel with the Persians so close. But I thought perhaps she did not wish to see this, the marriage of her son to Zenobia.

'Let today be our turning point,' Odenathus said as he signed his name. 'That we might now see the tides change and the wheel of fortune favour us.'

I nodded my agreement.

Zenobia signed next, the bracelets on her wrists clinking as she did so. Tears threatening in her mother's eyes.

'It is done,' Zenobia said.

'It is done,' Odenathus confirmed.

Our silent party walked outside, stepping from beneath the shade of the colonnade. The crowd fell silent, a dozen birds still circling overhead.

A soldier ascended the steps toward us.

For a heartbeat I could scarce believe it. But true enough, a wide smile upon his face, there was Julius.

I felt the heave of my chest, the welling of tears, the inability to move or to speak. Almost three years and he looked no different, his face had not aged, a slight limp still present in his stride.

'I hope I have not missed the ceremony,' he said as he reached the topmost step.

He embraced first Meskenit, and she returned the gesture,

brief but firm as the first time I had met her. But Julius held onto her longer. She melted into the embrace, and when they parted I witnessed the blush he caused.

Then he held Zenobia, the girl who had taken his dream, who refused to let it die, who would make it true, no matter how long it took, no matter the price that must be paid.

'You make an old man proud,' he said, scarce above a whisper.

She kissed him on his cheek in reply.

Odenathus said, 'I did not think to see you here, Julius. Three years feels a lot like thirty. You are well?'

'As well as can be,' Julius said. 'The Tanukh suffered a defeat three days ago. I believe that has bought me a visit home, although I would not call Antioch home.' He grimaced. 'I hear the Persians are not far from your walls.'

'We expect the attack any day now. I am surprised you reached us,' Odenathus said.

'As am I,' Julius replied, turning lastly to me. 'And you, Zabdas. Gods, you have grown. A man now.'

I did not reply, and I was glad of that, for my throat constricted and I did not believe I could have spoken. A chant had sounded, quiet at first, becoming louder as more people took up the words:

'Zabdilas, Zabdilas, Zabdilas.'

'They remember you,' Odenathus said, grinning.

Meskenit stepped forward and the crowd fell silent. She took the right hands of both Odenathus and Zenobia, and joined them together.

Quiet remained as silent vows were made. A moment later and the citizens and soldiers erupted in shouts and screams and cries of celebration.

That evening as the marriage banquet took place, I stood on the walls of Antioch, looking out at the black desert. The Persians were there, hidden in the dark. We would see them tomorrow, or the day after, or perhaps the day after that, but they would doubtless come.

Julius stood beside me, travelling cloak still about his shoulders.

'It seems the people are enjoying themselves,' Julius said. 'There seem so few days filled with joy of late.'

I wondered if Odenathus and Zenobia found as much enjoyment in the celebrations as the soldiers of Palmyra and the citizens of Antioch.

'Two people joined in matrimony, and yet for two very different reasons,' I mused. 'For Zenobia this Roman ceremony makes her marriage to Odenathus legitimate in the eyes of Rome, for the sons and daughters she might bear, that no man can say different.'

Julius frowned. 'And what of Odenathus?'

'He wanted this for his people. A day of celebration in a time of war.'

'Indeed,' Julius mused, 'I think perhaps you are right. He knows his people well.'

We looked out once more, silent and thoughtful. I thought I saw movement in the darkness, but nothing came. Behind me, I heard the screams and giggles and shouts of drunken celebration.

'I will leave before the sun rises,' Julius said.

My heart sank at his leaving again.

'I trained as you told me to,' I said. 'I have begged Odenathus many times to allow me to come south, to be with you, and each time he has refused me.'

'He has, I know,' Julius replied. 'I asked him not to send you to the frontier, because I could not bear to see harm come to you, not after it took so long to find you.'

His face was half hidden in shadow, yet I saw his grim expression, the pain in his features.

'There was a time when I thought perhaps you were my father.' Whether it was the celebratory wine or the knowledge that he was leaving once more that spurred the words I know not.

Julius' expression faltered, and he smiled warmly.

'Alas, no, you are not my boy. But you are right to be suspicious. You are Meskenit's child.'

I could not speak. No response came. I had never thought, in the years I had known her, the distance she kept, the disapproval I always felt about her, that I could be her child and she my mother. I half laughed at the thought, half sobbed.

'But how? Why? How can that be?'

Julius' smile turned to sorrow.

'Meskenit was raped by Roman soldiers a short while before I met her. She was troubled deeply by what had happened, and so at my suggestion she left you in Egypt with her sister. We could not abandon you of course, I would never have done that, but nor could Meskenit keep you close. I was afraid of what would happen, how her mind would respond if we did. I am truly sorry, Zabdas. We had thought it for the best. We did not know what would become of your new family and the slavery you faced.'

Julius' eyes shone with regret and yet all I could do was smile. His revelation made no difference, for I was still the same boy and Julius still cared.

'Do not apologise,' I said. 'I am more grateful than you know that I am a free man, that I have you and our family. You were right, when you said that Meskenit needed time. I understand that now.'

Time, I thought, for a mother and a son to know one another, a king and his queen to reclaim lost lands, and a country and its people to find freedom.

The story continues in
The Fate of an Emperor, autumn 2014.

HISTORICAL NOTE

Threatened by financial crisis, plague, invasion and rebellion, the 3rd Century AD saw the Roman Empire closer to collapse than ever before. Palmyra – known then as Tadmor – was a vital caravan city on the eastern trade route. It was taken under Roman control in the mid-first century but despite this, its people were of mixed Aramaic and Arabic stock, and the language used a form of Palmyrene: a mixture of Middle Eastern Aramaic and Greek. A recent estimation of the population of the city at that time is around 150,000 to 200,000.

Odenathus was the son of Septimius Hairan, "the Senator and Chief of Tadmor". The year Odenathus acquired senatorial rank is uncertain and could be anywhere between 222 and 254, though his military achievements brought him the title Consularis, and in an inscription dated 258 he was styled "the Illustrious Consul our Lord". It is believed he was self-proclaimed "king".

Zenobia was born with the name Iulia (or Julia) Aurelia Zenobia, although this varies between languages, and on official documents she would use Al-Zabba, meaning "the one with long lovely hair". She claimed to be a descendant of Dido, Queen of Carthage, the King of Emesa Sampsiceramus and the Ptolemaic Greek Queen Cleopatra VII of Egypt. It is suspected she became Odenathus' second wife around 255. Odenathus would have been around 34 and Zenobia is considered to have been approximately 14.

Her father was Zabaii ben Selim or Iulius (Julius) Aurelius Zenobius/Zabdilas; a chieftain/stratego of Palmyra around 229.

In other sources, Zabdilas is also noted as being a merchant.

Although Zabdas features in history, there is no mention of his family tie to the Zabdilas family.

Emperor Valerian did indeed rule alongside his son, Gallienus, splitting the Empire's problems between them; Gallienus taking the west, Valerian the east.

The ex-senator of Antioch, Mareades, was convicted of embezzling public funds, although he is said to have been subsequently banished by the citizens.

Zenobia's going to Rome on behalf of Odenathus, her father's placing her on the Palmyrene council and everything else is either based loosely on mentioned events and people, or purely fictional. As for the characters, those above are recorded in history, as are Hebony, Herodes, Zabbai, Pouja, Shapur I, Worod, and Jadhima, King of the Tanukh.

Thank you for reading a Triskele Book.

Enjoyed *The Rise of Zenobia*? Here's what you can do next.

If you loved the book and would like to help other readers find Triskele Books, please write a short review on the website where you bought the book. Your help in spreading the word is much appreciated and reviews make a huge difference to helping new readers find good books.

More novels from Triskele Books coming soon. You can sign up to be notified of the next release and other news here: **www.triskelebooks.co.uk**

If you are a writer and would like more information on writing and publishing, visit **www.triskelebooks.blogspot.com** and **www.wordswithjam.co.uk**, which are packed with author and industry professional interviews, links to articles on writing, reading, libraries, the publishing industry and indie-publishing.

Connect with us:
Email admin@triskelebooks.co.uk
Twitter @triskelebooks
Facebook www.facebook.com/triskelebooks

Acknowledgements

This book has been a long time in the making. Thanks go to Gilly, Jill, Kat and Liza of Triskele Books for their continuous support and encouragement and honest words, and to Perry for his proof-reading. Thanks also go to all the writers and non-writers who have read and critiqued and offered advice over the years. This book could not have reached publication without you.

This book could have been published, but would have been even more factually incorrect than it probably is (for which I take full responsibility), without the following resources:

Farrokh, Dr Kaveh. *Sassanian Elite Cavalry*. Osprey, 1995.
Fraser, Antionia. *The Warrior Queens*. Phoenix Press, 1993.
Goldsworthy, Adrian. *The Complete Roman Army*. Thames and Hudson, 2003.
Stoneman, Richard. *Palmyra and its Empire*. University of Michagan, 1992.
Watson, Alaric. *Aurelian and the Third Century*. Routledge, 1999.
The massive and incredibly helpful resource that is Wikipedia. And the members of historum.com, which I have only just discovered, but whose members are enormously helpful and knowledgeable.

ALSO FROM TRISKELE BOOKS

The Charter by Gillian Hamer
Closure by Gillian E Hamer
Complicit by Gillian E Hamer
Behind Closed Doors by JJ Marsh
Raw Material by JJ Marsh
Tread Softly by JJ Marsh
Spirit of Lost Angels by Liza Perrat
Wolfsangel by Liza Perrat
Tristan and Iseult by JD Smith
Gift of the Raven by Catriona Troth